Pride Publishing books by Brian Lancaster

Single Books
Companion Required

I0680697

COMPANION REQUIRED

BRIAN LANCASTER

Companion Required
ISBN # 978-1-83943-933-9
©Copyright Brian Lancaster 2020
Cover Art by Louisa Maggio ©Copyright November 2020
Interior text design by Claire Siemaszkiewicz
Pride Publishing

COMPANION REQUIRED

Dedication

Thank you to all my fellow authors and readers at gayauthors.org—and in particular Timothy M—who tirelessly challenged me whenever I posted a new chapter, and helped me to reshape the story every time they thought the plot was becoming predictable.

Thanks to the wonderful team at TEG for taking this rough diamond and helping me shape the story into something more polished, and also for your professionalism, support, helpful assistance and, most of all, for your friendliness.

Thank you also to Osamu Toguchi, bar master of 036 in Naha, Okinawa, not only for the amazing nights we've spent over the years chatting and drinking, but for allowing me to use the name of your bar in this story.

And last, but not least, to my husband, Christopher, and our needy and playful Ragdolls, Branston and Brie, without whom this story would have been completed years ago.

Chapter One

Kennedy
London, England, August 2016

Two triple-shot espressos down and Kennedy Grey massaged his fingers into his temples. Dull throbbing had begun to resemble a migraine. Not because of the coffee—his lifeblood most days—but because the previous candidate had tried his patience to the limit. *'Is the food safe to eat? Isn't Singapore in China? Aren't gays banned in China? And will there be any fringe benefits?'* Questions about food safety he could accept, especially if a candidate had allergies. He could even appreciate them not being familiar with the geography of the travel destination. For that very reason, he had brought along a one-page map of Asia highlighting Singapore. But asking if there would be any fringe benefits had tipped him over the edge. The advert had been straightforward enough on the subject of remuneration.

Not for the first time that afternoon, Kennedy considered throwing in the towel and abandoning the whole precious idea. Maybe this was the year he made a change. After all, the signs of madness were everywhere, what with a game show host being chosen as the official Republican candidate to run for the US presidency and the people of Britain filing for divorce from Europe.

As a penniless young man straight out of university, he would have trampled heads for a heaven-sent dream of a job like this. On the laptop, he scrolled down to the UK Gay Society billboard and reread the contents of the advert.

Gay Holiday Companion Required

Based in or around London. Must have full ten-year passport with at least seven months remaining and be freely available to travel overseas for the whole month of September 2016. Candidate should ideally be between 21 and 25, non-smoking, social drinker, drug free, and must be able to pull off the role of dutiful boyfriend in front of male sponsor's close-knit circle of friends. Acting experience a distinct advantage. Any ethnicity considered.

Successful candidate will receive an all-expenses-paid holiday to Southeast Asia, starting with round-trip flights from London Heathrow to Singapore's Changi Airport, a three-night stay in Singapore, followed by a 14-night gay cruise to Hong Kong. After a two-night stay in Hong Kong, the holiday will culminate in a flight to Bali, Indonesia and eight nights staying at the sponsor's private luxury villa.

Candidate will receive a guaranteed five thousand pounds in cash for services rendered, and a discretionary bonus, should the candidate's performance exceed expectations.

If you are interested, please respond to gayvaccom-@mooddle.com with a recent photo (headshots only, thank you) and CV, to arrange a mutually agreeable time for an interview.

So what if the advert bordered on politically incorrect? Marketing staff at UKGS had assured him that he had breached no advertising codes or legal regulations. Besides, the 'exceed expectations' line had only been tacked on this year, a suggestion from his best friend, Steph—a safe enough addendum, since for the past three years no one ever had.

Moreover, the advertised list of requirements told only half a story. He peered up and scanned the coffee shop. Even a couple of the young men sitting at various tables could have made the grade. In his head, Kennedy had an unspoken list of other requirements, undocumentable, such as the companion being a toned, blond twink, pretty as a royal wedding, but with a relatively low IQ. They should be no more than five feet six, and definitely shorter than his five-ten. Most importantly, they needed to be totally and utterly compliant to Kennedy's whims and wishes. And finally, once they had been paid off and returned to dear old mother England, he never wanted to see or hear from them again.

Since his split with Patrick, his partner of nine years, he'd made a point of continuing to join his friends' annual sojourn to different parts of the globe—his one break each year from the office and the boardroom—but now with a beautiful young acquaintance. Yes, perhaps bringing along a twink companion smacked of vanity, or desperation even, especially for someone in his early forties whose dark hair had begun to display grey streaks at the temples. But the simple truth was that while Kennedy found meeting and conversing with people for business purposes effortless, he found socialising awkward, especially on his own, and had always relied on Patrick to be the catalyst when meeting friends, old and new. Hence, for the past four years, he had paid for a companion to join him.

Palm Springs gay festivals, Hawaiian island hopping, gay tour of Barcelona and Sitges, cruising around the Greek islands with a week in Mykonos.

Pure culture? Maybe not. But a welcome respite from a punishing work life.

Ollie, his first post-Patrick choice, had turned out to be perfect. Previously an intern at Kennedy's corporate security company, the blond Adonis had flirted shamelessly with Kennedy and all other male staff, whether straight or gay. And even though Kennedy had been flattered and tempted, he had never succumbed. After the placement had ended, however, he'd made a point of keeping in touch. Once Patrick had decided to walk, Ollie had been his natural choice as lab rat companion. Perfect, as things had turned out, because Ollie had recently lost his job, so Kennedy had sweetened the deal by offering a sum of money to accompany him. Which was how the arrangement had first begun.

That first year the holiday had gone so well, Kennedy had not only stayed in touch but had invited Ollie along for a second helping. A huge mistake, as things transpired, because Ollie had incorrectly translated the gesture to mean that not only were they equals, but that they were going steady. And Kennedy no longer did 'steady' with anyone.

If his friends suspected anything, they said nothing. Only Steph knew the truth. And he made a point of telling any candidate the arrangement would be strictly nonsexual, unless they wanted more — which was how the idea of the playing card had come into being. But more than anything, he wanted a companion, not an escort. If the rationalisation might have meant anything to any of them, he would have cited Forster's novel *A Room With A View* and the chaperone arrangement between the two main female characters. But after he'd mentioned the reference to Ollie, and had then been lectured about that *'old James Bond movie they keep showing on Netflix'*, he'd stopped bothering to explain altogether.

For the first time since Patrick had walked out, he had been in two minds whether to ditch the charade, to simply bite the bullet and turn up alone. Only five friends had signed up for this year's sojourn — after last year's debacle — and one of those was Leonard Day. Kennedy not only had feelings for him but respected his business acumen. Maybe this year he would finally make his feelings known. If only Leonard didn't come with baggage of his own.

But Kennedy accompanying a plaything had become something of a tradition, a joke among his friends, and he wouldn't want to let them down.

"S'cuse me. You Kennedy Grey?"

Kennedy peered up from his thoughts to find an extremely blond, extremely buff young man standing over him. Steroid buff, Steph would have labelled him.

"I am, yes. And who might you be?"

"Who might I what?"

"Who… What is your name?"

"Francis."

Kennedy glanced down at his notes. Francis Slade, twenty-five years old, three o'clock appointment. Ten minutes ahead of schedule. One point in his favour. Kennedy swore by punctuality.

"Ah yes, Francis. Please sit down. So do you prefer Francis, Frank or Frankie?"

"Francis."

"Great. You've read the advert?"

"Yep."

"Good. So let me go into a bit more detail, give you a few minutes to relax. Then I'll ask you a few questions and finally let you ask any questions you may have. I've got other candidates to see, but I'll let you know whether you've been successful or not by Friday. How does that sound?"

"S'all okay."

Taking the response as his cue, Kennedy went into further detail about the holiday, explaining that in Singapore they would be staying in Kennedy's parents' house. However, the person would be introduced as a friend and would have their own bedroom. Whenever he delved into specifics — especially the rawer aspects — he always studied the candidate's face carefully to see if any of the information caused a reaction. Francis' flat face appeared incapable of showing any kind of emotion.

Whenever Kennedy got onto the subject of the cruise and his friends, he found himself becoming defensive. Yes, they could be a bitchy bunch, and a couple of companions had found them bordering on rude, but they were his long-time friends.

Bali, at the end of the holiday, was not only the cherry on the cake, but the icing, marzipan and ornate decoration. If the companion managed to survive until then, they would be able to enjoy the delights of that magical Indonesian island. By then Kennedy would usually be ready to get back to work, so would spend most of the last week either on his laptop, mobile phone, or writing up proposals.

"So far, so good?"

"Yep," said Francis, yawning and stretching his hands above his head. When his tee pulled tight, Kennedy spotted the outline of nipple rings beneath the material. Tick. Another point in the boy's favour.

"How tall are you?"

"Five-seven."

"Nice," said Kennedy, reaching next to his laptop for the supplementary document. "So here's a list of other requirements. You'll need to take a medical examination before you travel."

"Why?"

"A precaution. To make sure you're in good shape, physically."

"I'm negative, if that's what you're asking."

"That's not…" Kennedy huffed out a sigh. "Look, the year before last, my travel companion came down with acute appendicitis three days into the trip. And due to severe rupturing—which was touch and go for a while—he had to spend six days in a private hospital in Florida after which, quite naturally, he wanted to fly straight home to be with his family. If he had taken a medical examination before the trip, it's likely the appendicitis would have been diagnosed early, avoiding his suffering and my equally ruptured bank account."

"Ain't got an appendix. Got it removed when I was eleven."

"That's not the point—" Kennedy ran a hand through his hair. "I need to make sure the person accompanying me is fit and healthy in all respects. And that condition is non-negotiable. So if it's a problem for you, then you need to let me know right away."

Francis stared down at the paper for so long that for a moment Kennedy thought he'd changed his mind.

"You'll pay?"

"Sorry?"

"For the medical?"

"Of course."

"'S'okay, then."

"Great. Any other questions for me?"

"How old are you?"

"Forty-two."

Francis grinned then. At least, that was what it appeared to be to Kennedy. Either that or the lad had wind.

"You like 'em young, then?"

Kennedy had to stop himself from answering that more than anything, he liked them compliant. And most younger guys tended to be less free-willed, more willing to please, mainly because they needed the money.

"Is that a problem?"

"Nope. I'm into Daddies."

Oh, heck, thought Kennedy, *Steph is going to have a field day if Francis becomes this year's chosen one.*

"So I've got your number. I'll be in touch Friday."

When Francis stood, whether purposely or not, he yawned again and stretched his arms above his head so that the bottom of his tee rode up slightly to reveal a ripped stomach and a dark-blond trail of curly hair running down and disappearing beneath the waistband.

Kennedy almost handed him the job right there and then.

Chapter Two

Kieran

Four o'clock in the afternoon and Kieran West was tapping out a rhythm on a textbook with the rubber end of his pencil, trying to distract himself from the whiny voice across the room. If he didn't get his postgrad social science essay on perestroika and glasnost in by Friday, there was no way the lecturer, who had already been more than lenient, would give him another stay of execution.

Thursday afternoons in Sam's Coffee House was his haven, his little slice of peace and quiet away from university, where he could concentrate in peace.

Not today, though.

Despite efforts to tune them out, he found distracting snippets of the interview being held by the smart-looking businessman across the room far more interesting than the transcript of Gorbachev's 1986 speech at the 27th Congress of the Communist Party. However, the inane responses for some kind of personal assistant role, by either effeminate or muscled — but all essentially clueless — men, had begun to irritate.

Four candidates later and Kieran had managed to surmise that the man needed an assistant to join him on a business trip to Southeast Asia. Phrases like 'all expenses paid' and 'five thousand pounds cash in hand' had really piqued his interest. What with his recent redundancy from the estate agents', and still trying to support his own as well as his brother's studies, and funds were running desperately low. Across the coffee shop, the loud whiny voice once again rose above everything.

"I don't know, do I?"

"Do you at least have an up-to-date passport? With seven months outstanding."

The question seemed reasonable enough, but the girlishly pretty blond appeared to have an issue with this. Sharp nose and lips constantly pouting, his dyed hair had been styled almost Mohican fashion, with both sides rising into an untidy ridge in the middle from front to back, leaving him looking like a fair-haired chicken.

"Seven months what outstanding?"

"Before expiration."

"What?"

"When's the expiry date? The date the passport runs out?"

"How should I know?"

"In order to travel, you need to have at least six months remaining on your passport, plus an extra month to cover the four weeks away. I explained all of this in the advert. Did you bring your passport with you as I asked?"

"No."

"Why not?"

"'Cos I bought a photocopy, didn't I?" said the skinny blond, getting hostile. By now, Kieran would have told the little shit to take a hike. The older man appeared to have the patience of a nursery school teacher.

"Can I take a look?"

Almost reluctantly, the blond pulled a piece of paper out from his trouser pocket and tossed the crumpled mess across the table. Calmly, the man unravelled the sheet and peered at the information. Satisfied, he nodded once and jotted something down in his notepad.

"Do you get seasick?"

"How should I know?"

This time the man squeezed his eyes shut, pinched the bridge of his nose, paused and inhaled deeply before continuing.

"If you're going to be on a cruise ship for fourteen days, you really ought to consider getting seasickness medication, just in case. There's nothing worse than having motion sickness on a rocking ship with nowhere to hide."

"Can't I skip the boat part? Just meet you in Bali."

"The job is for a holiday companion, for the whole duration. Either all the way, or none. Are you in, or are you out?"

"In, I suppose."

As soon as the interview ended and the candidate sashayed out of the coffee shop, Kieran decided to make his move. Dumping himself into the recently vacated seat gave the man—who had been on his phone—a start, although, credit where it was due, he recovered quickly. After ending the call, he stared quizzically at Kieran, who began talking before the man had a chance to speak.

"My name's Kieran. Kieran West. I know this might sound a little unorthodox — or maybe even a little presumptuous — but I couldn't help but overhear you interviewing for a personal assistant. I just wondered if I might be considered. I have a ten-year passport which has nine years outstanding and I can travel at any time." That wasn't strictly true. He would need to check with his tutor, to defer the next module of his master's, as well as with his brother and mother to make sure they could do without him for four weeks. But he tucked those thoughts away and continued to smile. "And I have never suffered from seasickness."

While the man began to process Kieran's words, his face went through a series of expressions, starting with incredulity, to irritation, and ending with what Kieran assumed to be humour.

"Do you know what I'm advertising for?"

"I think so. A personal assistant, isn't it?"

"Yes. But a very specific kind of personal assistant. More of a specialised travelling companion."

"I'm not sure I understand."

"Maybe if I ask you a few questions first, to determine your suitability?"

"Fire away," said Kieran, grinning and leaning back in his seat, arms folded.

"Smoker or non-smoker?"

"Non-smoker."

"Good. Do you drink? Alcohol?"

"Occasionally, but not to excess."

"Excellent. How old are you?"

"Twenty-nine."

"Hmm, I see. How tall are you?"

"Six-one."

"Okay. And how long have you been out of the closet?"

"I—I'm sorry?" stuttered Kieran.

"How long have you known you were gay?"

"I'm not gay," said Kieran, quietly.

Folding his arms, the man let out a sigh and leaned back. At first he appeared to be waiting for Kieran to clarify, until something across Kieran's shoulder caught his attention.

"I believe my four o'clock has just arrived," he said, pulling a document from a file. "I'll tell you what. Why don't you take this printed copy of the advertisement and this list of other requirements. I'm sure you'll find it helps clarify certain *critical* elements of the role."

While Kieran stood, the man beckoned the new arrival over. A buff, good-looking candidate came to a halt next to him and gave him a coolly assessing once-over. This one had curly golden hair—clearly dyed—and looked to be a biracial mix of Caucasian and West Indian. Kieran moved back to his seat across the shop and began to skim the details, starting with the advertisement.

Even before the end of the first paragraph, he let out a huff, knowing he didn't fit the bill—not even close. The problem was, once Kieran West made up his mind to go for something, nothing short of an alien invasion could stop him. Besides, his funds had all but dried up. Five thousand pounds would keep the wolves from the door for a good while. He might even, finally, be able to offer his sister something for allowing him to doss down on her couch for the past three weeks. It was far from perfect, but better that than being on the streets.

His girlfriend, Jennifer, had kicked him out of her apartment because he would not — could not — commit to anything more serious. 'Ring or road' had been her mantra. Wisely or not, he had chosen the road.

As he scanned the last page — details of the cruise and places they'd be visiting along the way — the cold trickle of premonition stopped him. The ship would be stopping at the island of Koh Samui in Thailand. Although he would never tell another living soul about the experience, would never admit to being intrigued by something so fanciful, when he was twelve his group of four friends had taken turns to see the fortune teller at a school fete. Even now he remembered the old woman's crinkled face. She had been the grandmother of one of the friends, wearing a red silk scarf around her head, silver hoops like curtain rings in her ears, and using an upturned fishbowl as a crystal ball. He remembered sitting patiently opposite as she spouted a lot of vague nonsense until she stopped and took a sharp, surprised breath before looking up, deep into his eyes.

'I know this may sound strange and might not make sense right now, but there is something you must always remember. It doesn't happen often, but I have just glimpsed an image of you from the future. You are on an island in Asia standing beneath a giant Buddha. You are waiting to meet your destiny.'

One way or another, he had to get this job.

Chapter Three

Kennedy

When the final candidate left at four-thirty —
bisexual Leon, who had been drawn to the idea of a
cruise but had not realised the holiday entailed long-
haul flights and had admitted to suffering from an
acute fear of flying — Kennedy sat back and mulled over
who he should select. As shortlists went, this one could
easily be labelled concise. Two choices actually,
between the twenty-three-year-old, quiet but good-
looking and gym-fit blond, Francis, who spoke very
little but looked cute and would fit the bill fine, and the
twenty-one-year-old ginger Ed Sheeran lookalike
called Steven — *'call me Ven'*. Unlike Ed, he came across
as talentless, camp and over-groomed, but could chat
incessantly about media fluff and other mindless trivia,
and had an infectious if slightly immature sense of
humour. So the choice fell to two very different twinks,
one of whom would fill the quiet moments with

mindless banter, or the other who would say little, but look good by his side.

Kennedy pushed his laptop lid down, to find the guy from across the coffee shop—Keegan?—sitting in the chair opposite him, his jacket and bag hung over the back, which did not bode well. If Kennedy was going to be brutally honest, this older man—yes, he was definitely a man compared to the non-shavers he'd interviewed so far—was easy on the eye. With palpable discomfort, the poor guy squirmed in his seat, wearing an earnest, if anxious, expression.

"I'm in," he said decisively, tossing the single sheet of paper containing the advert onto the top of the laptop, the document landing face down. Kennedy noticed that, on the back, he had written out a number of answers to questions in neat handwriting.

"You're in...what?"

"I'd like to apply for the role."

"You're..." Kennedy reached down, flipped the paper over and spun the advert around on the table. "Can you read the headline back to me?"

"Gay holiday companion required."

"Gay holiday companion. *Gay*. We've already established you don't qualify."

"Not necessarily. I read that as Gay Holiday." For effect, the guy produced air quotes around the two words then paused. "Companion Required. What I mean is, it's not clear whether you're asking for a companion, someone to accompany you on a gay holiday, in which case surely I'm still eligible, or whether you're asking for a gay companion to go on holiday with you."

Actually, the guy had a point. Had he shown them, Kennedy's marketing and legal managers would have had a field day with the wording.

"I told you already. The person needs to be gay."

"You do realise that's discrimination."

"What?"

"Just because I'm not gay doesn't mean I can't do the job." What was with this man? No fear, no hesitation. Assertive and straight to the point. Kennedy liked those traits in work colleagues. Just not in his fake beaus. "Anyway, just how gay would you want this person to be? My uni friend is gay and he's neither blond nor muscular."

"Get him to apply then."

"He has a boyfriend. And anyway, he doesn't need the job. I do."

"Look, Keegan…"

"Kieran."

"Kieran, then. I'm sure there are other jobs out there for you—"

"There aren't. And I don't care, anyway. I want this one."

"*Look*—"

"No, *you* look. I'm reasonably good-looking. I am sociable with all kinds of people in all sorts of situations. I am not homophobic—far from it. Yes, I might be older than your stated requirement—which is a bit ageist, by the way—but if you want someone to pass as a legitimate companion, then I am a way better choice than that queue of blond Justins you've just seen. How old are you, anyway?"

"I'm forty-two."

"As far as contemporary age gaps are concerned, twenty-nine and forty-two could be deemed acceptable. Anything under twenty-four could be seen as questionable. Does the contract include these guys having to have sex with you?"

Kennedy paused for a second. Was this guy trying to catch him out?

"Of course not. Sex would be by mutual consent only."

"Excellent. So instead of worrying about whether this companion is going to put out or not, hire me and you can be sure right off the bat that I won't."

"And how exactly do you intend to convince my friends you're gay?"

"I'm not. I'm guessing they know you wouldn't bring along a straight guy. So if you're asking whether I'll adopt any mannerisms, or rethink my dress sense, then apart from accusing you of stereotyping — or worse still, internalised homophobia — I'd say you're clearly out of sync with the new generation of gay men. Anderson Cooper, Tom Daley or Keegan Hirst, for example."

Not many people had Kennedy Grey at a loss for words, but this young man certainly had a way about him. Trouble defined him. Kennedy gave him his usual professional smile and decided to run with the path of least resistance.

"Leave me your number and I'll get back to you by the end of the week."

"You won't though, will you?" said Kieran, folding his arms.

"Not if you don't give me your number," said Kennedy, slapping a pen on top of the advert before fishing for his wallet in his jacket pocket. "Here's my business card. If I haven't called you by Friday at four o'clock, feel free to ring my direct line."

Kieran scrawled his number on the sheet, then leaned back and studied the business card.

"Kennedy Grey, CEO. Grey Havens Security Systems? *The* Kennedy Grey? Get out of here! You run the family business that installs digitalised commercial security systems? We covered your company in our master's programme, successful family businesses of the new millennium. In the recent edition of *Business Week* your operations guy — Sloan something — didn't rule out the possibility of you going public next year. You've pretty much got that niche area of the market sewn up."

The first thought that crossed Kennedy's mind was why he hadn't been told about the article in *Business Week*. Had his chief operating officer, Sloan Williamson, pulled another fast one behind his back? Not that he would be surprised, given the man's ruthless ambition — one of the reasons Kennedy had hired him. But even so, Kennedy's marketing team would normally have sanctioned the interview with him. And Sloan should not be speculating publicly about plans for a stock market launch. The second thing that struck him was that this man, Kieran, was clearly both informed and intelligent. And as far as travelling companions were concerned, that would never do.

"One and the same," said Kennedy, then sat back wide-eyed as an impressively sized Kieran rose and leaned across the table.

"An absolute pleasure to meet you, Mr Grey," he said, holding a large hand out. "And can I say, you are much better looking in the flesh."

Still seated, Kennedy leaned forward awkwardly and shook the offered hand. Kieran gripped a little too long, squeezing a couple of times, while maintaining almost uncomfortably consistent eye contact.

"Gay enough for you?"

Kennedy smirked then and rolled his eyes. Yes, this one would certainly cause a stir.

"Thanks for your time, Kieran. I'll be in touch."

"And I'll very much look forward to hearing from you," said Kieran, grinning, before collecting his jacket and satchel from the chair and heading for the door.

Kennedy put his hands behind his head and stared at the long, lean legs of the confident figure striding out of the cafe. On the plus side, this guy was definitely attractive, with his shaggy brown mop, sad eyes and beautiful full lips. And as Kennedy had stated in his very specific demands, he expected companionship, but not sex. Besides, if he did pick straight Kieran, he could legitimately slip away for some anonymous sex on the gay cruise without upsetting anyone, something generally acknowledged as being as available as the twenty-four-hour sushi bar—not that Kennedy had ever partaken of either.

Moreover, for the three days in Singapore, his father might actually be able to tolerate this one. He would certainly enjoy being challenged on his political ideology, something Kennedy had never found of any interest. And the gay cruise? Kieran would have to fend for himself, but he didn't seem the faint-of-heart type, more like the sort of man who could brave any storm — metaphorically speaking. And as he'd said himself, he really needed the job.

Stop, Kennedy told himself, shaking his head. *What the hell am I thinking?*

Chapter Four

Kieran

On Friday, opening the front door to his home — his temporary home — Kieran looked around the shoebox one-bedroom apartment. Out of respect for Jules and Terry, his sister and her boyfriend, he always rose early from his bed on the two-seater sofa, tidied away his bed covers, put fresh coffee on, showered and left the apartment before either of them had awoken. Usually he would breakfast at the corner cafe and return around ten, once they had both left for work. As much as he could, he minimised the evidence of him being there, of him relying on their goodwill.

Having previously resided with his ex-girlfriend Jennifer, his life right now felt more like a scraped existence, lonely, desperate, barely surviving. Although he knew his sister wouldn't throw him out, he wanted to make sure neither of them had any reason to even consider the idea. Signs of their morning ritual remained — cereal bowls and mugs left unwashed on the sideboard, the coffee pot almost empty, clothes dotted around the room. Jules knew he would clear up after them, would even make their bed without her asking, basically because not only did he dislike any kind of mess, but because he felt indebted to them both.

After putting his laptop on the table, he hung his bag on a coat hook before setting about tidying up. With only one bedroom, the apartment didn't take long to clean. After he had finished, he put a fresh load of laundry in the washing machine, which included some of his own clothes. A drawback to staying with them and having no bedroom of his own was that he had nowhere to store his clothes. Jules had emptied out one of the drawers in the living room cabinet, beneath the television. She had also allowed him to hang his interview suit and a couple of pairs of trousers in their small wardrobe.

However unlikely, he desperately needed this one-off job with Kennedy Grey, which would mean he could give them back their apartment for the whole of September. And if he could land a permanent job — the job centre had gone quiet again — he might be able to use part of the money to put a deposit down on an apartment of his own. One thing was for sure — he couldn't keep living like this. Unemployment benefits barely covered the cost of bills and food. What he needed right now was a healthy dose of luck.

Sitting at the small table, he opened a browser on his laptop and Googled Kennedy Grey. Maybe he shouldn't have been surprised, but Kennedy had a Wikipedia page dedicated to him — not with a photo or much information, barely two paragraphs, but still. From the small amount online, Kieran read that Kennedy had salvaged the company originally run by his uncle—his mother's brother—Ashwood Havens. Clinging to old VHS technology and unable or unwilling to embrace the digital age, Havens had pretty much run the company into the ground before Grey came on board and started turning things around. Success began shortly afterwards. Grey Havens had introduced the first fully-integrated digital surveillance system subsequently adopted by major hotel chains around the world. Never one to rest on his laurels, Kennedy had made sure they refined and upgraded their offerings, as well as expanding into other commercial areas—shopping malls, airports, exhibition halls. On a number of other searches Kieran found photographs of Kennedy, usually speaking at conferences or in business conversations, rarely at anything social. One photograph at a social event had him standing beside another man—dark-haired, handsome, but unsmiling, both of them looking dapper.

Before his next search, he took a few deep breaths. Even with nobody else in the apartment, he still looked around before typing the words 'gay sex' then hitting the search button. Maybe he should not have been surprised by the number of sites that popped up, but some of the descriptions had him mystified. What the heck were BBC, slurping, rimming and edging? Selecting one site, he searched a couple of video clips until he found two reasonably good-looking guys around his age. Clicking on the clip, he waited to see how much he could stand to watch. At first they just spoke to the camera. After a while, however, they began to make out. Two men kissing didn't faze Kieran at all. Having said that, neither did the sight push any buttons. But when they started to get naked, and one went down on the other, going to town with a blow job, he noticed his heart began to beat faster. As though someone had flicked a switch inside him, his breath quickened and his cock became swollen. *Shit*, he thought, *what does that mean?* As he was about to slam the lid of the laptop closed, a pop-up message appeared on his screen telling him his friend Coleridge was online. Fumbling the touchpad, as though he had just been caught doing something illicit, he shut the browsers down and cleared the history.

Coleridge — Cole — had taken a couple of the classes Kieran attended for his master's. More importantly, Cole was gay. After taking a few steadying breaths, he clicked onto the pop-up and asked if they could talk. Within seconds Cole's grinning face popped into view.

"K, my man. How's it hanging?"

"Not bad. I'll be pleased to get this assignment out the way. Listen, do you mind if I run something by you?"

"As long it's got nothing to do with Russian bloody communism. I can't get my head around it."

"No, this is — uh — a gay thing."

"Gay thing, eh? Then you've arrived at your destination, buddy. Fire away."

Kieran told the story about meeting Kennedy in the coffee shop, about the man searching for a companion for his holiday. While chatting, he emailed Cole a copy of the holiday requirements attachment Kennedy had provided, to get his friend's thoughts. Somewhat out of character, Cole listened without once interrupting.

"So what do you think?"

"What do I think? I think you're pig-shit crazy to even be considering the idea. You know what my people call this kind of thing?"

"No."

"Gay-for-pay. Straight guys who do all kinds of things with gay guys for money. Jerk off on camera, play around with sex toys — some even have sex with men. They either get addicted to the money, or the drugs the money buys. And one cute tattoo turns into a whole body covered in ink, because they can't bear to look at themselves. Most of them eventually fuck up their lives."

"This is nothing like that."

"This is *exactly* like that. Shit, man, how does Jennifer feel about this?"

"Jennifer and I are done. Or at least having a cooling-off period. I'm staying with my sister right now."

"She kicked you out?"

"No, she — well, yeah."

"She kicked you out, man? After you'd lost your job? After you'd spent those weekends decorating her place from top to bottom? She fucking kicked you out?"

"She wanted more, Cole. And I wasn't ready to — "

"Of course you weren't ready! What a prize fucking bitch! Good riddance. Who in their right mind would want to dive into that kind of commitment without a stable job with prospects in their pocket? Or at least with your master's under your belt... Woah! Did you read this bit on the travel requirements page?"

"Which bit?"

"Page five. There's a whole list of stuff you need for the holiday."

Page five had a long inventory of all the items of clothing Kieran would need to bring, including a tuxedo. His heart sank. All he had was the one work suit which — if he was going to be perfectly honest — had seen better days. Kennedy wouldn't even need to tell him he hadn't got the job, because he couldn't afford to take it anyway.

"Ah well. That solves that little quandary."

"Trust me, K, you're much better off."

Just then his phone rang with an unknown number.

"Another call coming through. Talk to you later, Cole. Thanks for the advice."

"Any time," said Cole, before dropping the link.

"Hello?"

"Can I speak to Kieran West?"

Kieran recognised the voice instantly.

Kennedy Grey.

Chapter Five

Kennedy

Nothing seemed to be going right that day.

In Kennedy's absence, COO Sloan Williamson had rescheduled an important meeting without consulting him, one that now sat slap bang in the middle of his planned holiday. On the other hand, Sloan had been the one to orchestrate the whole merger with Cold Steel Security, something that made total sense on paper. Cold Steel remained one of the top five brand leaders in home security in the States and Canada, and had begun to branch out into the UK.

"Who asked for the change?"

"Giorgio Milletto," said Erin, his marketing director.

So the CEO of CSS himself had requested the change. Interesting that he hadn't contacted Kennedy directly. But if the merger went ahead—more of an acquisition for Grey Havens really—his company would consolidate their position as number one global security provider, even though CSS' main focus was home security and they had only recently stepped into the corporate arena.

"I see."

"We can't ask them to reschedule again."

"I know that, Erin. And we're not going to."

"Are you going to cancel your holiday?"

Many of his top managers continued to voice their concerns about him being away from the business for a whole month, even though he'd done so for the past seven or eight years. With Grey Havens being a family business, Kennedy worked tirelessly, early mornings and late nights, seven days a week, including public holidays. Sleeping three or four hours a night, he was essentially on-call twenty-four-seven. If he could not leave the company safely in the hands of his professional, well-paid, highly skilled and respected managers for a month, what the hell was the point in having them? In truth, he knew he'd created the problem himself, due to his tendency to micromanage his staff, adopting an outdated, paternalistic style of management. Of course they would always be nervous without him around, but then, wasn't that how people grew? And if push came to shove, he was always at the end of a telephone line or an online conferencing system.

"No."

"So will you dial in? From wherever you are? Surely they'll have Wi-Fi?"

Of all his staff, Erin probably clung to him the most.

"You know that's not an option. With something this important, I like to watch the faces of the people on the other side of the table, see the whites of their eyes, especially those who aren't speaking. That is so important when we're negotiating."

"Skype?"

"Not the same."

"Then what, boss?"

As though prompted, Sloan Williamson chose that moment to stride into the room. Kennedy had chosen him well. Charismatic in a movie star kind of way, he oozed confidence and sex appeal and had the staff at Grey Havens eating out of his hands. Singularly straight, at only forty, he was already working on marrying for a third time. Sometimes his good looks fooled those he did business with, beguiled them into believing that he had no business acumen. Not a mistake they ever made twice. If someone took the time to analyse his history, really scrutinised — and Kennedy had — they would discover a trail of broken businessmen along the way who had made the fateful error of underestimating him. Publicly, Kennedy's management team presented a united front. Privately, Kennedy had a suspicion that Sloan wanted his job.

"Ah, Mr Chief Operating Officer. Your ears must be burning."

Without missing a beat, the man propped his backside on the end of Kennedy's desk and undid a button on his Armani suit jacket. Even though Kennedy could not deny the man's attraction, his brand of slick handsomeness did absolutely nothing for him. Erin had a different reaction — she rose from her chair and beamed, her cheeks flushed, and gazed in awe as she clutched her folder against her bosom.

"My ears burn all the time. What have I done this time?"

"This meeting with CSS."

"Ah yeah, sorry about that," said Sloan, pushing a lock of blond hair back over one ear. "Milletto asked for the change."

"So Erin said. Reason?"

"Didn't say." Sloan's stare didn't waver as he responded to Kennedy.

"Do I need to change my plans?"

"Up to you," said Sloan with a shrug.

"Or can I rely on you to deliver the goods?"

"You already know the answer to that. The merger's already in the bag. It's just the minutiae that need hammering out, something me, Karl and Erin here can deal with."

"Good, that's what I want to hear. And you know if you need me urgently, I'll have my phone on day and night."

Both of his staff members remained unmoving in his office.

"Anything else?" he asked, spreading his hands out, palms upward. "Otherwise this is the part where you both get back to work."

"No, boss," said Erin.

She gathered her papers then hurried out of the room. Sloan hesitated a moment before going over and closing the door, but remaining in the room.

"Why do you think so highly of Karl?" asked Sloan, his back to the door.

Kennedy had personally headhunted Karl McDonagh, his head of legal, because the man could smell a bad deal a mile away. Beside the fact that the man had a wealth of experience in both finance and law, he was loyal to a fault. Of all Kennedy's senior staff, only Karl stood up to Sloan. Kennedy enjoyed watching the pair of them try to outplay each other.

Where Sloan used his charisma and opportunism to climb the ladder, Karl relied on watertight facts and figures. Even though they disliked each other, they made for a damn good management team.

"You know why. He's solid and dependable. He's our goalkeeper."

"He's a pen-pusher. Without an original idea in his brain."

"That's not what I employ him for—that's why I employ you. He's there to keep the company on track, to make sure everything we do is above board."

"By holding us back."

"By ensuring we don't make rash decisions."

"I don't need him there at the CSS meeting. Erin and I can deal with Milletto."

"Sorry, Sloan. Either Karl's there, or the meeting doesn't go ahead. That is not up for negotiation. Are we clear?"

Sloan's poker face remained unchanged. He nodded once and left the room. As soon as the door closed behind him, Kennedy buzzed his secretary and told her to hold his calls and appointments for the next hour. He knew instinctively that Sloan had his own agenda, but as with all things in business, Kennedy had to be patient until the man showed his hand.

On his laptop, he opened his personal email and scrolled down to a message he had received earlier in the day, from red-headed Ven telling him he needed to pull out of the companion role for 'personal reasons'. Not a huge loss, because Kennedy had decided to go with Francis. Checking the contacts in his mobile phone, Kennedy thumbed the number. After several rings, Francis answered—on a high street somewhere, by the sound of traffic noises in the background. Never one to mince words, Kennedy announced the good news and waited for Francis to speak.

"Can't go."

"What do you mean, you can't go?"

"I can't go, can I?" came the affronted voice.

"Why not?"

"Ollie won't let me."

"Ollie? Who the hell's Ollie?"

"He's my boyfriend, isn't he? Changed his mind. Won't let me go on me own."

Kennedy pinched the bridge of his nose.

"Why on earth did you apply for this position as companion if you already had a partner?"

"We both thought of it as a part-time job. Saw no harm in trying. But Ollie changed his mind. Gets a bit jealous. He's like that sometimes. Unless you'd consider paying for both of us to come?"

"Goodbye, Francis."

Kennedy scratched the back of his head and looked down at his 'possible' list. Two of them would drive him crazy before they even joined the cruise. For some reason, his eye kept getting drawn back to the straight guy, Kieran. Things would be different with him. There would be no pretence at anything sexual between them.

What the hell, he thought. *At least this one didn't have a whole list of demands and, more importantly, needed the job.*

Before he second-guessed himself, he picked up the phone and called the number.

"I want to offer you the job, but clearly with certain conditions. You'll still need to play the part of companion, but I wouldn't expect anything else from you."

"Sex, you mean?"

"No, I mean *any* public displays of affection. Sex was never a part of the deal. So are you interested?"

Only soft breathing came from the other end of the phone. Irritation started to rise in Kennedy again, but just as he started to speak, Kieran cut in.

"Look, Mr Grey, I truly am interested. I was just—I was going through your clothing requirements and, well, I don't have half of the items listed there. And rather than waste your time, I was going to call to say I'm afraid that financially I'm not exactly in a position—"

Kennedy had already begun to chuckle, which brought Kieran to a halt.

"What?"

"Don't you have a module on law in your management programme?"

"Yes, of course."

"Then maybe you should read the fine print. The first two lines on the beginning of page six."

Kennedy could hear the faint sound of a mouse clicking a couple of times before the line became quiet.

"You'll provide the clothes for me?" came the confused voice. "Why would you do that?"

"Think of these items as your uniforms. I can hardly expect an employee to pay for clothes which, let's face it, might not be to his taste, and some he's unlikely to wear again. That would hardly be fair. Which is why, if you look further down, you'll see that I need your key measurements, to make sure we get you the right size. Or if you'd prefer, we can go shopping together on a day you have free. Maybe the same day you get your health check done."

"Our health checks," said Kieran firmly. "If I'm to suffer the indignity of getting tested, then so are you."

Kennedy inhaled deeply. This companion would be a challenge, but what choice did he have?

"Our checks, then. And once the holiday is over, you get to keep whatever clothes you want or give them away. You decide. So I guess the only question that remains is — are you in or not?"

"Yes. Yes, I'm in. Thank you very much for the opportunity, Mr Grey."

"Oh, and Kieran. That's the last time you call me Mr Grey. It's Kennedy from now on. Are we clear?"

Kieran chuckled.

"Crystal clear. Although, can't I call you Ned? I had a hamster called Ned when I was a kid. Loved him to bits."

Kennedy found himself enjoying the banter and struck back immediately.

"If you're going to reduce Kennedy to Ned, then I'm sure you won't mind if I refer to you, Kieran, as Key. Can't wait to see my friends' faces when I introduce them to Key West."

The burst of laughter coming down the phone was unexpected, and made Kennedy smile.

"I think that's your way of telling me no, so let's keep to our original names."

"Smart boy."

"And that, Kennedy Grey, is the last time you get to call me a boy. Deal?"

The comment caught Kennedy off guard and he laughed aloud.

"Touché."

Before signing off, they agreed to meet on a Saturday for tests and shopping. Tossing his phone onto his desk, Kennedy stared down at the blank display, shaking his head and grinning to himself.

Kieran West was going to be an interesting handful.

Chapter Six

Kieran

Kieran skipped his lectures on the Friday of their flight to Singapore, his whole body buzzing with a combination of excitement and trepidation. He had arranged to shower at Cole's place after finishing packing away the last of his own personal things in the large case—wash bag, beach towel, swimwear, sunblock, a huge bottle of aftersun and a couple of different factor suntan lotions. Except that, while packing, something unfamiliar inside the case caught his eye.

"What the hell's this?" he asked, holding up a small zipped-up pouch.

"A holiday gift. From me to you. Emergency first aid, of sorts," said Cole, leaning against the doorjamb and grinning mischievously.

Despite Cole's earlier warning, Kieran's gay-for-pay temp job had been an endless source of amusement, and he had become Kieran's co-conspirator and confidant. On Cole's advice, he had told Jules the absolute minimum, told her he would be an assistant to a CEO, travelling abroad, nothing more. Even storing the huge new suitcase full of holiday items at Cole's place had been his friend's brainwave. Had he brought the colossal thing back to his sister's apartment, she would probably have sneaked a peek inside when he wasn't around.

Kieran unzipped Cole's gift and pulled out two packs of condoms and a tube of lubricant. Tilting his head to one side, he raised both eyebrows at Cole.

"Seriously? I hope you kept the receipt. You're more likely to use these than me," said Kieran, zipping the bag closed. "In fact, why don't you keep them?"

"Do your Uncle Cole a favour and take them. You never know, you might get lucky."

Once he had dried his curly locks and dressed in the new black tracksuit and trainers Kennedy had provided — something casual for the long-haul flight — he collected his luggage from Cole's bedroom. In his life, he had flown less than a handful of times, and only within Europe, but he remembered how cramped the seats could be, especially with his long legs, his knees usually getting wedged against the seat in front.

Apart from the tracksuit, the other clothes he and Kennedy had shopped for two weeks ago already sat packed inside the case. Far too many, really, but Kennedy had insisted, telling him they would be away for twenty-eight nights and he didn't want to rely on the cruise ship laundry service. Kieran had washed and ironed the items at Cole's, and packed them away immediately despite Cole urging him to give a couple of the CK tees or Armani shirts a test run. The only item of clothing he had baulked at was the black dress suit ensemble, which included a wing-tip shirt, bow tie, burgundy cummerbund and shiny patent leather shoes. Still unsure about wearing anything so formal, he had tried none of those items on in the hope that he wouldn't actually need to showcase them. But Kennedy had insisted on the last-minute purchase. Every cruise offered a formal evening at the captain's pleasure, he had told him, and no companion of his would look out of place. He had even thrown in the huge new designer suitcase on wheels to pack everything in.

After getting a text message from Kennedy, he gave Cole a hug and peck on the cheek before heading out to the road. On the pavement outside the tenement block opposite Wandsworth Common, he stood waiting, more than a little anxious, wondering if he had done the right thing.

But the Saturday they had spent together had been surprisingly pleasant. At one point, laden down with shopping bags, Kennedy had asked him if he was enjoying his *Pretty Woman* experience. When Kieran had looked blank, Kennedy had rolled his eyes and told him he really needed to brush up on gay trivia if he hoped to survive a gay cruise. That had prompted a diversion — a trip to the movie section of one of the few surviving HMV stores and the purchase of a dozen or so DVDs which Kennedy had labelled 'homework'.

Kieran half suspected that Kennedy had road-tested the day to see if they would be able to get along, whether they could spend time together without getting on each other's nerves. He had booked their medical tests at a private clinic on Carnaby Street first thing so they could shop throughout the morning, then have lunch in a humble Italian restaurant at the back of Piccadilly before finishing off shopping and heading back for their test results. Both of them had a clean bill of health, and Kennedy had dropped him off by taxi on his way home later that afternoon. Since then they had barely been in contact.

Ten minutes later than their agreed meeting time, he began to get concerned, wondering if he had misunderstood any of the instructions. That was until Kennedy sent him a message saying he was on his way. Twenty minutes later, distracted by other messages on his phone, he barely noticed as a black Bentley pulled up at the sidewalk and a driver, complete with black uniform and chauffeur's cap, stepped out.

"Mr West? Let me take your bags for you, sir," said the tall man, opening the back door and gesturing inside. "Mr Grey's waiting for you."

Unsure how to respond, and looking around quickly to check whether anyone had seen the spectacle, Kieran slipped into the back seat. Kennedy sat there in his business suit, phone clamped to his ear. Almost dismissively, he turned and nodded to Kieran while continuing to talk to someone. As they drove off, Kieran listened in on some of the conversation.

"If you could be in Okinawa on the twenty-first? We dock there overnight in Naha. Perfect. Let me know where? I'd suggest one of those small bars tucked away down the back streets. Anonymous and quiet enough to chat. Bring along whatever you have ready. Also, find out everything you can about Giorgio Milletto of Cold Steel Security, doesn't matter how personal or insignificant. Send everything to my private account, yes? And what's the name of that talented techie guy who works for you? Hiro, yes. Bring him with you to Okinawa. Take business class, if you have to, and bill me privately. Okay, Tim. See you soon."

Once he had ended the call and slipped the device away, he turned to Kieran.

"We're running late. Been trying to clear up a few issues before the flight."

"Is this an Uber?"

"Hardly," snorted Kennedy.

Without clarifying more, Kennedy pressed a button on the centre console and a disconnected voice sounded.

"Yes, Mr Grey?"

"Just a guesstimate will do, but how long to Heathrow?"

"I'm checking the traffic cams and RouteMaster. Rough estimate, an hour and ten."

"Thanks."

Without another word, Kennedy thumbed through his phone and dialled a number.

"Gina? Hello, this is Kennedy Grey from Grey — yes, the same. Look, I wonder if you might be able to help. We're on our way to the airport, flying to Singapore tonight at eight-fifty, but we're running late and the traffic is, well, you know what Friday night traffic is like. According to the driver, we'll probably be at the terminal around eight. Anyway, I wondered if there was anything you could do to help get us through? Sorry, say that again. Yes, we both have luggage, but I've already checked us in online. It's really just bag drop and security. Two persons. Yes, of course. I see. Excellent. That would be perfect, thank you so much for your help."

Once again, Kennedy pressed the comms button on the console.

"Ben, when you reach terminal two, look out for someone who'll be waiting with an airport buggy."

"Roger that, Mr Grey."

Smooth. Efficient. Polite. No fuss. Not afraid to call in a favour. Kennedy Grey, the businessman. Kieran smirked out of the tinted window, wondering if this man could even request the plane to be delayed.

They arrived at Heathrow airport with scant minutes to spare. Outside the departure terminal, the driver — Ben — found the small enclosed airport buggy and loaded their bags. After a few private words with Kennedy, Ben the chauffeur headed off. When the buggy driver began to take them into the underbelly of the terminal, Kieran realised the route must be there for dignitaries or celebrities. Apart from both of them being scanned at an internal security post, they did not step off the buggy until the boarding gate.

By the time they reached the impossibly large plane — via a stairway to the upper deck — all other passengers had already boarded. Once again, Kennedy led the way and Kieran hurried to keep up. He marvelled at the sheer size of the double-decker aircraft. His flying experience had been limited to small jet planes travelling to destinations within Europe. As they stood at the cabin door, Kieran once again witnessed the Grey charm, as he smiled professionally, flashed their tickets and chatted with the cabin attendant. When she personally accompanied them to their places, turning left towards the front of the plane, Kieran did his best not to gasp when they stopped at two huge, luxurious chairs.

"Business class?" he asked as Kennedy settled next to his.

"Naturally. What? You think I'd ever fly economy long haul?"

"Not you, no, but I thought maybe — "

"You thought I'd stick *you* in the back? No, not my style. And we've got background work to do before we reach Singapore. Get you up to speed not only about my family, but also about my friends."

Kieran had just placed his bag in the overhead compartment and taken the huge comfortable seat, when a male voice sounded from the aisle beside him.

"Something to drink, Mr West, Mr Grey? Champagne?"

With a friendly smile, the handsome cabin attendant indicated the tray of assorted drinks he held. Kieran reached for the pocket of his tracksuit pants and pulled out his wallet, ready to hand over money. Kennedy placed a hand on his wrist to stop him.

"We'll take two champagnes, please," said Kennedy. "One each."

After placing the flutes with coasters down in front of them, the attendant picked up something else from his tray.

"And here are your landing cards and menus," he said, placing them next to the drinks before straightening up. "My name's Eric, by the way, and if there's anything you need throughout the flight, just call me."

When Kieran peered up, he noticed the steward had singled Kennedy out with his dazzling smile. Kennedy simply nodded back, completely at ease with his surroundings. Feeling out of his depth, Kieran remained quiet, his head down studying the menu.

"I'm not sure what type of airlines you're used to," said Kennedy. He had waited until Eric had moved down the cabin before leaning a fraction across the divider, and speaking in a lowered voice. "But on this one, food and drink are included in the ticket price.

And up here, the food's generally above average. So relax and enjoy yourself, and more importantly, order anything you want. After we've finished our work, you might want to check out the entertainment system. Or if you're feeling tired, you could ask them to help make up your bed."

"Bed?"

"Your chair doubles as a flat bed. The controls are on the arm of your chair."

The heat in Kieran's cheeks intensified. Less than five minutes on the plane and already he felt out of his depth.

"Don't worry, Kieran," said Kennedy, his head in the menu. "There's a first time for everything."

Chapter Seven

Kennedy

As the plane taxied out to the runway, Kennedy switched his phone off, sat back and indulged in the simple pleasure of flying undisturbed by clients or employees. Quiet moments focusing on the business came along so rarely, and flights gave him precious time to think ahead and strategize. Without question, Sloan had moved his first pawn — or at least that wa's what Kennedy's intuition told him. But then, he enjoyed these games and challenges. They kept him alert, focused and grounded. No CEO in their right mind would ever have allowed their senior managers to hold a potential merger meeting without being present themselves. Kennedy was no exception.

What none of them realised was that he would still be present, if not in person, and he would be able to see and hear them, even interject if the necessity arose. He had not only survived but thrived for over eighteen years in a tough business environment dealing with cutting-edge security systems and had not done so without picking up a trick or two along the way. A piece of advice came back to him from his late uncle. *'Be generous with the rope you hand out to those ambitious souls who surround you. Just make sure to keep a firm grip on one end.'*

Not long after take-off, wanting to get the chore out of the way as soon as possible, Kennedy began to give Kieran the low-down on his family and friends.

"If he bothers to talk to you at all, my father will probably ask you to call him Jeff. He's a pompous, miserable old bastard by nature and rarely smiles, so don't take his rudeness personally. He's spent practically his whole life in Singapore. Our grandfather worked for the British Government before Singapore gained independence, and continued to do so afterwards. My father only left the country once for any extended period of time and that was to go to university in Cardiff, Wales. He hated being wet and cold, and couldn't wait to get back to the humidity and sunshine that is Singapore. Following in Grandfather's shoes, he also worked for the consulate as assistant high commissioner until the day he retired. Personality-wise, he's a snob, still acts as though Singapore is a colony, and thinks he should be treated like royalty. Although he's never said as much, his disdain for me is, I think, because his only son is gay. Thinks he's been robbed of the chance of another Grey male heir to carry forward the family name. Once you've finally met the rest of the Grey clan, you'll understand what a blessing that is for the world."

"Surely he's impressed with what you've achieved?"

"As far as I'm aware, he either doesn't know or doesn't care."

"How about your mother?"

"Claire Hamilton Grey nee Havens. Unless there's been an article about me in *Cosmopolitan* that I don't know about—which seems to be more and more likely these days—she doesn't keep tabs on my career. Ridiculous, really, because I took the family business over from her late brother, my uncle. These days she's a typical ex-pat trophy wife. Bridge club and coffee mornings. Although, according to my sister, she's now more partial to jugs of afternoon cocktails with the rest of the ex-pat wives. Can't say I blame her. Having to live with that old sod every day of her life, who wouldn't choose insobriety? She deserves an OBE."

"Brutal. Your father doesn't drink?"

"Of course he does. Cliché to a fault, he's a cognac and cigar man, the latter of which my mother hates."

"Will she like me?"

"They'll both be polite. Dad will probably ignore you most of the time. Mum's fine. She's a fan of royal family trivia, if you know any."

"Hmm. Not really my thing. Is that it?"

"There's my sister, Reagan."

"Named after King Lear's daughter?"

"Guess again. But if it helps, my father's full name is Jefferson, and he named his kids Kennedy and Reagan."

"American presidents?"

"Correct. One of his interests is global political history."

"Do they have a bulldog called Bush?"

"Not yet," said Kennedy, smirking. "But I'll mention the idea to Mum."

"So what's your sister like?"

"We get on okay. She's three years younger. Graduated in textile design and could have done really well in fashion, but she married an Australian guy called Bernie and decided to spend her time bringing up babies. They've got three boys — Adam, Glenn and Dennis. Can't remember their ages. My secretary diaries their birthdays, so they get a card and a handout from their uncle each birthday and Christmas. They split their time between Singapore and Melbourne, so no doubt you'll get to meet them."

"Is Bernie a fan of cricket?"

Kennedy peered quizzically at Kieran.

"Funny you should ask — he is, actually. Huge. Works as a freelance writer for a couple of sports magazines. Why *did* you ask that? Because he's an Aussie?"

"No, because their kids have the names of famous Aussie cricketers — Adam Gilchrist, Glenn McGrath and Dennis Lillee."

Once again Kennedy grinned. He'd never made the connection. Not that the given names of his nephews were in any way unusual, but he had always assumed they'd been picked at random. Which once again confirmed the sharp intelligence of this year's companion.

"You'll have to ask him, if he's around. Apparently he's often travelling. Okay, so onto my friends on the cruise. Easy enough, because there are only five coming this year. Steph and Laurie are a couple I've known since uni. Well, Steph, anyway. They have their own little shop down in Sussex which specialises in antique furniture renovations and doubles as a hairdresser's. Yes, I know, an odd combination, but you'll get along fine with both of them. Then there's Pete and Eric, who are permanent fixtures. Eric's retired and Pete is — actually, I have no idea what Pete does for a living. But he's the one who brings us all together, so do your best to endure his irritating and persistent sense of humour. And finally, there's Leonard."

Kennedy went quiet for a second, remembering Leonard's kind words when he and Patrick had parted ways.

"Go on," prompted Kieran.

"The last time we talked, Len had a number of companies — early on, he developed a knack for juggling a lot of online businesses — and does really well. Specialist real estate, holiday rental properties, vintage cars, among other things. Of all my friends, he's the entrepreneur, the smart, successful businessman."

"Wow, is that faint praise I hear? So he's single, too?"

"Yes, but unlike me, his partner died. Don't think he ever really recovered, so he threw himself into his work."

"You had a partner, too?"

"Patrick, yes."

"And what happened to him?"

"He left me. But fortunately, he's not going to be there, so you don't need to know anything about him."

Thankfully, Kieran had the sense not to push the subject. Kennedy did not want to talk about Patrick, did not want to open that can of worms.

"So why only five this year?"

"Because the others tend to side with my ex. So if he doesn't come, neither do they."

"Wow, sounds really grown-up. Okay, is that everyone?"

"That's everyone," said Kennedy, before turning to Kieran. "Now how about you? I suppose I ought to know something about your family. In case anyone asks."

For a moment Kieran appeared a little uncomfortable, shifting in his seat. After taking a sip of his champagne, he sighed deeply and started speaking.

"Not much to tell. Got a younger brother and an older sister. Julie's thirty-one. Sean is twenty-two. On the day Mum announced to us all that she was expecting Sean, our father checked out. Disappeared off the face of the planet. Although we suspect he went back to Argentina. He has family there. Mum was left to bring up a newborn and two young kids. Jules and I had to step up, but thank goodness we also had Mum's parents to help. Couldn't afford to send Julie to university, but I went and Sean's there now, finishing up his degree in Leeds. I help with his fees where I can."

"That's got to have been tough."

"We survived. I had a couple of jobs since leaving full time education. The last one in real estate started out good—lasted four years—but when times are tough nobody wants to buy or sell. I was let go three months ago. Not long after, I split with my girlfriend, who also kicked me out. Since then I've been sleeping on my sister's couch. Which is why I desperately needed this sick and depraved job. Am I allowed to say that, now we've reached cruising altitude?"

"What? About this sick and depraved job that has you sitting in business class sipping vintage champagne?"

"Okay, point taken. There is that."

"Now, before I let you watch movies or sleep or whatever, I have a couple of small items for you."

Kieran appeared a little uncomfortable.

"Honestly, you don't need to —"

"Hear me out. These are things I've given to all my travelling companions at the outset of a holiday."

Kennedy took out a small brown envelope from his pocket.

"Inside here, there's a nominal sum of different currencies for all our Asian destinations. Yes, I know this may feel as though I'm giving you pocket money, but it's mainly because I want you to have funds in case of emergencies. If you need a taxi, something to eat or drink, or see anything you want to buy. I don't want you to feel as though you need to rely on me to pay for everything."

"I do have some money of my own that I can change up."

"Of course you do, but I thought this might be more convenient."

Although he didn't appear entirely happy, Kieran placed the small envelope into his tracksuit pants pocket.

"Thank you."

"Everything on the cruise is either included, or can be signed to the cabin. Understood?"

"Okay."

Finally, Kennedy took a playing card out of his shirt pocket and handed the item over. After hesitating for a moment, and with one eyebrow raised, Kieran took the card.

"I don't understand. What am I supposed to do with this?"

"What card is it?"

"Jack of spades."

"Otherwise known as a Black Jack. Yes?"

"Yes. But why do I need it?"

"Usually I hand these out for a very different reason. But for you, let's say that if things are getting a bit too much and you need time out, or help — or as a last resort, to quit and come home, or…whatever. Just hand me the card and I will sort things out."

"Like a 'get out of jail free' card."

"If you like," said Kennedy, before staring pointedly at Kieran, concern in his eyes. "But please tell me you'll do your best to stay away from foreign prisons."

After that they barely spoke. From time to time, Kennedy noticed Kieran marvelling at the delights of business class. An hour into the flight, on hearing whirring sounds, he turned to see Kieran discovering the functions of his business class seat by pushing buttons to make the chair contort into a variety of positions. At other times, he smiled to himself at Kieran's enjoyment, such as when he bolted upright, eyes wide, as the pick of four choices of main course rolled up on a trolley, or when he lounged back with the large headphones perched on his head, laughing a little too loudly at a movie on the entertainment system. When the cabin lights finally dimmed, Kennedy switched on his reading light to continue scanning the financial reports Karl had provided. Every now and again, in between research, he peered over at Kieran, who lay curled on his side in the bed, sleeping soundly. A tiny smile tugged at Kennedy''s mouth. Going back to his reports, he shook his head and swatted away the tiny bud of affection forming there.

This holiday partnership would be strictly business, Kennedy reminded himself.

Strictly business.

Chapter Eight

Kieran

Kieran could not believe the experience of flying business. After completing his landing card, he'd managed to sleep for a full seven hours of the thirteen-hour flight, woken only three short times — once by rough turbulence, another to use the restroom and the last to collect and stow his duty-free purchase. After weeks on his sister's soft couch, the bed's firm comfort came as a welcome relief. And he woke now to coffee aromas floating out from the galley. Next to him, Kennedy, still in an upright seated position, had a folder open on his chest, but his sleeping head lolled to one side. Somewhat endearingly, he appeared vulnerable in sleep, his face unlined and at peace, not the tough persona he gave off when awake. Kieran liked him, didn't feel threatened by him at all, but needed to keep in mind that at the end of the day, this was simply a job, a means to an end. Theirs was never going to be a lasting friendship.

After unclipping his seat belt and resetting his seat into a sitting position, Kieran crept to the toilet to freshen up. Even there, he laughed to himself at the opulence, spraying an Evian mist into his face, followed by one of the array of citrus colognes. Yes, he could certainly get used to this. But was he ready to meet the Kennedy clan, he asked his reflection? And what would they make of him? From what Kennedy said, he'd never brought any of those vacuous Ken doll kids with him. But surely his ex-partner had visited? So should he just be himself, or melt into the background, make himself scarce. No, he thought, standing tall in front of the mirror. 'Kennedy's family would meet his true self, and whether they liked him or not was their choice.

When he finally returned, Kennedy had awoken.

"Morning, sleepyhead," said Kieran.

"What time is it?"

While sitting back down in his seat, he checked his wristwatch.

"Eight in the morning."

"In London, maybe. What's that in Singapore time?"

"No idea. Shall I call one of the cabin —"

"No need. It's on the monitor. Almost three in the afternoon. Two hours until we land. Singapore's seven hours ahead, in case you want to reset your watch."

Afternoon, mused Kieran, refastening his seat belt. Cole had warned him about jet lag, about getting used to different time zones. Jules had told him that if he could sleep on the long haul flight, he could work through the change and not experience jet lag at all. Time would tell. Right then, however, he felt fresh and awake. More importantly, the cabin crew had begun to set up his table for breakfast.

"Breakfast at three o'clock in the afternoon. Haven't done that since uni."

"Don't think about it. Might take a couple of days to get acclimatised, but my advice is don't fight tiredness. If you find yourself needing an afternoon nap, just go for it."

"I feel fantastic."

"You do now. But jet lag has a way of creeping up on you."

"Ah, but you see, I have youth on my side."

Kieran didn't miss Kennedy's raised eyebrow and smirk. But to be honest, right then, with his stomach full of fresh fruit, omelette and coffee, he felt ready to conquer the world.

Landing and disembarking happened so leisurely — memories of fighting to get his luggage from the overhead, and being crushed and jostled off a low-cost carrier flight in Ibiza, still haunted him — that they were in the carpeted bowels of Singapore's trendy Changi airport within minutes. Immigration passed in a well-organised blur until they reached the luggage claim, their bags having already arrived. Even in that short time, Kieran sensed Kennedy getting tense, noticed him peering at his phone then looking around outside the big glass wall separating luggage claim from airport arrivals. Eventually he understood why.

"Is someone picking us up?"

"My father. Grab your bags and let's go. Let's not piss him off before we've even said hello. He hates to be kept waiting."

Unsurprisingly, Jefferson Grey turned out to be an older, shorter but broader version of Kennedy. Dressed casually, as though he had been interrupted from a game of golf, he wore a grey polo shirt, grey tartan trousers, white belt and white sports shoes. Unsmiling, he gave his son a handshake followed by a perfunctory hug, the words 'son' and 'dad' being the only endearments passing from one to the other. Kieran almost smirked at the formality. After a few further banal pleasantries, Kennedy turned to introduce Kieran. When Jefferson's face registered a flicker of distaste followed by an ensuing visual inspection, Kieran decided to go into action.

"Good afternoon, sir," he said boldly, stepping forward and holding out a hand. After a moment's hesitation, Jefferson took his hand and Kieran provided a firm handshake. "Can I say what a pleasure it is to be here and how grateful I am to you and your wife for allowing me to stay with you. Kennedy has told me so much about Singapore, and I'm absolutely delighted to have the opportunity to visit the republic first-hand."

Perhaps he had laid the greeting on a bit thick and, peripherally, he noticed Kennedy turn to stare at him. The effect on Grey senior was instantaneous. The older man's eyes widened and he nodded.

"Uh, you're more than welcome. Any friend of my son's, as they say."

While Kennedy's father flustered a reply, Kieran reached into his small backpack.

"And I've bought you a gift of thanks, a bottle of cognac." Kieran handed over the duty-free bag to Jeff, once again to Kennedy's astonishment. "Kennedy told me you enjoyed a tipple every now and then. Hope you like Hennessy XO, sir?"

"Um, yes, I do indeed. Very much so. That's very kind of you. And please call me Jeff."

Jeff began to lead them off towards the external doors.

"Jeff it is. So, Jeff, is the weather always this hot in Singapore? Or do you have distinct seasons?"

"Well, we're almost right on the equator, so it's pretty hot all the year round. Ask most Singaporeans and they'll tell you we only have two seasons — hot and wet. Come Christmas, there's not a snowflake in sight, except polystyrene ones in the shopping malls. Follow me now. I've parked up in the short stay. How was the flight?"

Kieran nodded to Kennedy then, allowed him to take over the small talk. As they passed through the automatic doors of the air-conditioned arrivals hall out into the day, the humidity hit him like stepping into a steam room. Kieran had experienced nothing like the wall of damp heat that enveloped him. Together, they trailed their luggage into the nondescript inside of the car park until Jeff reached a white Toyota Camry.

Comfortable again in the air-conditioned car, Kieran relaxed on the back seat behind Kennedy, peering out of the window to a sun-bleached afternoon. Singapore appeared more like home than anywhere he had seen in Europe. Clear road signage in English, vehicles driving on the left side of well-maintained roads or three-lane expressways, all bordered by lush green vegetation, exotic-looking but equally well maintained. Before long, simple high-rise apartment blocks appeared on their right, Jeff explaining that on their left they were tracing the coastline. Fifteen minutes later they crested a hill, with Jeff pointing out a handful of the landmarks — Marina Bay Sands hotel resort and casino with what looked like a barge balanced on top of three giant blocks, the futuristic Gardens by the Bay with Martian-like tree structures, the Singapore Flyer, similar to, but bigger than, the London Eye. Kennedy's father appeared to enjoy being the tour guide, and probably did so only for Kieran's benefit, because Kennedy must have seen the sights before.

Eventually, they turned into a more residential neighbourhood — exclusive, by the number of landed houses — until they came to a black iron gate. Jeff picked up and pressed a small device on the dashboard, causing the large gateway to swing inwards, allowing them to drive up a short lane. Before them, the two-story house lay in its own grounds, surrounded on all sides by metal fences and tall trees.

"In Singapore, we call these kind of houses 'black-and-whites' because of their distinctive Tudor style. My father bought this one back in the sixties and we've had her updated a lot since them. Kennedy, you have your old bedroom and I've put Kieran in the room at the back, above the pool."

Impressive did not even begin to describe the house. Set amid perfectly trimmed lawns, the front of the house jutted out on columns so that the open space below fell in shade. At one time, this must have been where vehicles drove up to the house. Now the space beneath had been fitted with striped blinds which lent themselves perfectly to the colonial feel of the structure.

"You have your own swimming pool?"

"We do. A fifty-foot lap pool. A blessing if, like me, you favour an early morning swim."

Kieran leant forward and spoke into the back of Kennedy's head.

"Kennedy, you never told me you were descended from royalty."

Although Kennedy didn't say a thing, next to him, Jeff chuckled.

"Hardly royalty, son. But I have mixed with some famous people over the years. Come along, let's park up, get you settled, showered and changed. Then you can come and meet the rest of the family."

They parked around the back of the house under a long canopy next to a large black four-wheel drive. An older man and a young boy—Indonesian perhaps, and maybe household staff—came out of a two-story building at one side of the grounds and headed towards their car.

"Reagan's here?" asked Kennedy.

"It's the only time she had free. As you've only deigned to stay for three nights."

"We're on a tight schedule—"

"Which is clearly more important than family."

Kennedy didn't reply, but sat stiffly in his seat. And right there, Kieran sampled the initial signs of familial frostiness.

Shit, he thought to himself, *if they were going to survive the next few days intact, the time had come to ramp up the old West family charm.*

Let the show begin.

Chapter Nine

Kennedy

Climbing the slow rise of oak stairs to his room, Kennedy remembered the sounds and smells of the old house with mixed feelings. Even though he had only lived there until the age of ten — after that, he had been packed off to boarding school in England — he recalled the pungent smell of pine floor polish and camphor, shuttered windows diffusing the fierce daylight, the constant thrum of ceiling fans running throughout the house, now replaced by almost silent air conditioners, the unique heat of each day except when the respite of cooling monsoon rains hit, and the sound of geckos chit-chatting and toads croaking throughout the night. As memories went, they were not bad ones. But this was no longer his world and never really had been.

Matius, the Indonesian housekeeper, walked ahead of him, insisting on carrying his bags. Before his death, Matius' father, Agus, had run the household. Matius would have been only twenty-five when Kennedy was bundled off to England. Now married with his own son and daughter in their twenties, he and his wife, Maya, continued to work for the family.

Live-in domestic help had been a way of life in Singapore — in many Asian countries — for many years with the huge disparity in wealth between the rich and poor, and high unemployment forcing people to seek overseas jobs simply to survive. Although many of Matius' relatives still lived in Bandung — south of Jakarta — for over two generations, his family had resided in the two-bedroom apartment above the kitchen in the outbuilding at the side of the house. Many houses and apartments in the region came with a wet and a dry kitchen. Usually the wet room stood unenclosed by walls, open to the elements, where wok cooking happened, allowing the potent Asian spices to dissipate into the air. Dry kitchens were used primarily to prepare food for cooking and, in the case of the Kennedys, to house a large oven, fridge and other electrical appliances.

"My wife, Maya, cook for you tonight, sir," said Matius — Matty — turning in to Kennedy's room and dropping the bags at the foot of the bed. Apart from the squeals of Kennedy's nephews playing in the swimming pool coming through the half-open bedroom window, Kennedy could already smell the delicious aroma of cooking from somewhere outside. Matty had his trademark cheeky smile on his face as he spoke. "As you know, she is very good cook — only reason why I marry her. She cook your favourites. Satay chicken, chilli crab, tiger prawn, beef rendang, gado-gado. She even has cendol for dessert. Hope your friend will like, too. Or is he like your other guest?"

Kennedy couldn't help smiling. During the two times Patrick had visited, he'd been singularly unadventurous with food, often requesting a simple omelette or sandwich for dinner. Local food had been a staple of Kennedy's childhood, and chilled cendol—green rice flour jelly, red beans, coconut milk and palm sugar syrup—had been a true luxury after a sweltering cycle ride home from school.

"I'm sure my friend will be fine, thanks, Matty," said Kennedy, holding out a hand. Polite as ever, Matty shook his hand and bowed a couple of times. Years ago, Kennedy had given up asking Matty to call him by his given name. Being called 'sir' made Kennedy feel like his father, or an employer—when Matty was more like a friend. But Matty had once confided how his father had drilled in him to address male adult guests as "sir" and female adult guests as "mam", and how this had proven much easier than trying to remember names. "By the way, I'm sorry I couldn't get back for your father's funeral."

"That's okay, sir. I know you are busy man."

"It's not really okay. Your father was very special, a kind and caring man. Especially to me. I'm honoured to have known him."

The sort of man a father ought to be, thought Kennedy.

Agus had been his go-to whenever his own father had ridiculed or scolded him. After dinner, on the night Jeff had casually thrown into the conversation that Kennedy would be going to boarding school in England that autumn term, ten-year-old Kennedy had listened without speaking or reacting—a rule of the house for children at the dinner table—but as soon as they had been excused, he had gone straight to Agus and cried. Kennedy remembered his words well, about being strong and the importance of honouring a father's wishes, but he'd known Agus was just as upset, could not understand why a father would want to send his only son away. Kennedy missed his simple kindness.

"Thank you, sir. He was very happy here."

Once Matty had left, Kennedy sat on the edge of the bed and looked around his old room. Nothing remained of his childhood except for the view from the window, showcasing the old mango tree. Many years ago, Agus had hung a swing from a lower bough for him, his sister and Matty—until a few weeks later, Kennedy's father had demanded he take the eyesore down. Now his room stood unrecognizable, completely redecorated since his last visit, a guest room with the addition of a double bed and stylish antique furniture. But then Kennedy spotted a painting of his on the wall, a watercolour of his old dog Chester, a black Labrador they'd had as children. He'd been eight when he'd painted the picture, something Agus had helped frame and hang on his bedroom wall. His mother must have decided to keep that particular memory.

Showered and changed, he stood outside Kieran's room at the far end of the corridor, at the back of the house overlooking the pool, and knocked lightly on the door.

"Come on in."

Kennedy turned the handle and stood just inside the doorway, his hand still on the doorknob.

"Are you decent?"

"Never have been, not going to start now," quipped Kieran, coming out of the bathroom smiling, wearing a white cotton shirt and khaki chino shorts. As looks went, this one suited Kieran well.

"Best behaviour," said Kennedy, suppressing a smile.

"Yes, sergeant major. I can't believe your family house. Not only do I have my own bedroom, but it comes with an en suite bathroom and a huge bed. Hey, I've got my swimmers on under my shorts. Do you think your dad'll let me have a dip a bit later on?"

"After dinner, maybe. By the way, are you okay with Indonesian food?"

"I—uh—I don't think I've ever eaten it before. But if that's what I can smell cooking, then count me in."

They found his mother, father and sister sitting at the back of the house, next to the swimming pool, in a horseshoe arrangement of comfortable sofas around a Thai-style coffee table. His nephews played happily in the shallows. Beneath the back porch, Kennedy spotted the large dining table that had already been set up. Kieran wisely stood behind Kennedy, while he got his hugs and hellos out of the way with his sister and already squiffy mother. After that, Kennedy introduced Kieran, who charmed them both the way he had done with his father. Once seated, they shared a few pleasantries about various general subjects—the flight over, Reagan's boys, life of retirement in Singapore—until the inevitable fun and games began.

"When's the last time you were home, darling?" asked Claire, pouring them both a long, tall glass of something opaque. When Kennedy held the glass away from him quizzically, Reagan mouthed the word 'mojito'.

"That would have been the day before yesterday. The day before I flew here."

"Don't be smart with your mother," said Claire, curtly, over the rim of her glass. "You know what I mean."

"Five years ago," said Reagan. "The same year misery left him."

Kennedy flashed her a warning glare. None of his family had warmed to Patrick. Even though his parents had said nothing, Reagan had labelled him precious and standoffish. But he didn't want the conversation to focus on his ex.

"Where's Bernie?" he asked.

"Working, of course," she said, irritation clear in her tone. "In Cape Town right now, covering some rugby tournament or another. So what do you do for a living, Kieran?"

"Right now, nothing. I worked for an estate agent in London, but times got tough and half of us were let go. I'm punting around for work, but I'm also finishing up my master's."

"Master's?" said Reagan, surprise clear on her face, before throwing a glance at Kennedy. "With a focus on which particular area?"

"International business management. I've got two modules to go, then I'm going to be following through for my MBA. Another six modules."

"What would be your ideal job, Kieran?" asked his father. Kennedy was mystified by how quickly he had taken to Kieran. Both times Patrick had come to stay, the two had barely spoken.

"That's a good question, Jeff. Something I love about the master's is that you get a chance to dip into all areas of business management. And even though I take to the finance subjects like a duck to water, the area that really floats my boat is marketing, especially e-commerce."

"Smart choice," said Jeff.

"Our group used Kennedy's company, Grey Havens, among others, for our group assignment in marketing. An example of a well-managed, innovative family business. Quite an inspiration for would-be entrepreneurs. Best of all, we got a high distinction, and a special mention from the tutor."

"Are you serious?" asked Reagan, grinning at her brother.

"Absolutely," said Kieran. "Your brother here's the Richard Branson of commercial security systems."

Reagan laughed aloud, and even his mother couldn't help grinning.

"Hardly," said Kennedy, trying to downplay the compliment.

He felt his face getting warm, something that never happened these days. If Kieran had been sitting closer, he might have tapped his ankle with his foot, but perhaps the awkward silence would do the trick, help change the subject.

"So how did you two meet?" Reagan asked Kieran, mischief lighting her eyes. She appeared to have taken to Kieran, but Kennedy stalled for a moment. They hadn't discussed how they would handle that particular question. While he was considering how to answer, Kieran had already begun speaking.

"We met in a coffee shop, of all things. I was trying to finish off an assignment on Russian history while Kennedy was knocking back espressos and taking phone calls, as always. We got talking and, well, just instantly connected."

Brilliant, thought Kennedy. *Stick with the truth – or as close as possible – and you can't go far wrong.*

"Is that right?" said Jeff, a little suspiciously. "When was this?"

"A month or so ago," continued Kieran.

"That's not very long, is it?"

"The thing is, Jeff, when you know, you know," said Kieran with a shrug, before turning to Kennedy, winking and flashing him a warm smile. Kennedy found himself smiling back. When he looked across, he noticed Reagan smiling too.

Interrupting them all, Maya came to the head of the group and quietly informed Claire that food was ready to be served. Immediately, Reagan leapt up and started yelling at her brood to get out of the pool and get dressed for dinner.

Kennedy missed eating outdoors, something that rarely happened in England. In his childhood in Singapore, beneath the porch, they would even sit al fresco when torrential rains hit—as long as no strong winds accompanied the downpour—pulling down the blinds to stop errant raindrops hitting them. Kennedy had enjoyed those times, the cooling shower bringing down the temperature, the clatter of raindrops filling the silences at the dinner table.

After the excellent meal provided by Maya—something Kieran enthused about after having seconds of each of the dishes—Kennedy relaxed back on the sofa while Kieran swam and played in the pool with Reagan's boys. His sister appeared distracted about something, becoming a little distant every now and then—very unlike her—but when pressed, she laughed off his concern. That particular trick she had learned from their mother. Most importantly, though, they liked Kieran, so that was one battle he would not have to fight. By ten o'clock, Reagan had decided to drive the boys home to bed, prompting everyone else to turn in. After wishing his parents and Matty goodnight, Kennedy strolled up to the top floor with Kieran, each of them carrying a large glass bottle of drinking water.

"You did well today," he said, trying not to sound too condescending. "My family aren't the easiest people in the world to get along with, but they seem to like you."

"I like them, too. They're easy company. Even your dad."

"You've been here half a day. Don't judge too quickly. Now, if you find yourself awake in the middle of the night, the remote for the television is in your bedside cabinet. Top drawer. Just keep the volume down."

"Don't worry about me," said Kieran. "I'm so tired, I'm going to sleep like a demon tonight."

Chapter Ten

Kieran
3:10 a.m.

Kieran sat up in bed, wide awake, hands clasped behind his neck, listening to the gentle hum of the air conditioner and the distant but constant night-time sizzle of cicadas from outside. Just as he'd predicted, he had plunged into a deep sleep the moment his head hit the pillow, but found himself waking fresh as a snowflake a few hours later. He'd already checked his phone, read and answered his messages and emails, had even tried Kennedy's suggestion and watched television, but nothing really caught his attention.

Of course, he had texted Cole and Jules about the past twenty-four hours. The flight—he had kept the menu as a souvenir—the amazing house Kennedy's parents lived in with five bedrooms with its own private swimming pool, and the amazing banquet they'd served up to welcome them. Even though they seemed formal with each other, the family had been friendly and civil to him. So much so that Kennedy's earlier belittling of his parents felt brutal and unwarranted. But then, what did he know? Maybe they were putting on a show for his sake.

Eventually he got up, went to the window and pulled aside one of the heavy blinds. Below, lights illuminated the pool. Would he disturb anyone if he got up and had a swim? Kennedy's parents' bedroom stood at the far end of the house, while Kennedy's own bedroom was next to them.

What the hell, he thought. *Who would even know?*

In the bathroom, he squeezed back into his damp swimming shorts and grabbed one of the plump white bath towels. With the addition of a plain white tee and flip-flops, he collected his laptop and headphones on the way out and made his way quietly back to the pool.

For half an hour, he swam freestyle up and down without stopping, enjoying the freedom, the release of energy and the water cooling and caressing his skin. When he finally stopped, panting heavily, he hauled his dripping body out, ready to dry himself and relax alone at the small table where he'd left his things.

Except someone else was sitting there, puffing blue smoke into the night air.

"When I mentioned an early morning swim," said Jefferson Grey, with good humour, "I was thinking more along the lines of six or seven in the morning. Couldn't sleep, young man?"

"What can I say?" said Kieran, towelling his hair. "Turns out jet lag is a real thing. So I thought I'd use the time to exercise. What's kept you awake?"

"Insomnia. Comes with old age, I'm afraid. And I heard someone swimming. Either my son or you, I figured. So here I am." Jeff blew a cloud of smoke into the air and wiggled his cigar. "Which also gives me the opportunity to smoke one of these babies without being badgered. Do you smoke?"

"I don't," said Kieran, taking a seat at the table. "Well, actually I did once—cigarettes—but label myself a non-smoker now. Sometimes I have the occasional puff—if I'm stressed. Not very often. Don't say anything to Kennedy. He thinks I've never smoked."

"You've only just met. I'm sure there's a lot you don't know about each other."

"I know he can be very particular."

"Just like his mother," said Jeff, nodding and flicking ash into a plastic saucer. "You know, you're a lot different from Patrick."

Kieran sat back then, wanting to take advantage of the opportunity.

"Kennedy doesn't talk about him. What was he like?"

Jeff sat quietly for a moment. He appeared to be considering Kieran's question.

"Did Kennedy tell you what I used to do for a living?"

"You worked for the British High Commission."

"For over forty years. And, let me tell you, in all that time thousands of souls passed through our offices. Not only did we have dignitaries, but also people from all walks of life, and from all nations. Something my wife will tell you about me—one of the nicer things—is my ability to sum up a person's character. Within a short space of time, I can tell whether someone is open, honest and trustworthy. She calls it intuition, but I think it's more a skill one builds over the years working as a public servant. Patrick was—he came across as—sullen and distant. Both times he stayed here, he barely left his room. If we managed to get a 'good morning' out of him over breakfast, it became a cause for celebration. Not once did he thank us for our hospitality, the way you did when I met you at the airport yesterday. But they lived together, had known each other for nine years, so we assumed they were content. Their last time here, he and Kennedy argued constantly. Maybe the writing was on the wall. What I'm trying to say is, when they were here I sensed no happiness between them. I'm sure Kennedy told you we weren't exactly thrilled with our son's lifestyle choice, but parents still want to see their children end up happy. Five years ago, just after they broke up, Kennedy came here alone. He never told us exactly what happened between them, but I could tell that my son was changed, had put up a wall around himself. I can only assume the break-up did that to him. The whole week he was here, I don't remember seeing him smile once, let alone laugh."

"He laughs now. Usually at me. He has a pretty cool sense of humour." *Key West, indeed*, thought Kieran, remembering and smirking.

"He's different with you."

"Is he?" Why did that observation send a small thrill through Kieran? "How do you mean?"

"Calmer. As though he has less to prove. As though he can trust you, I suppose."

Kieran deflated. Of course Kennedy would be calmer, Kieran was being paid to be there, a little snippet he would definitely *not* share with Jefferson.

"And I get the impression you like him, too," added Jeff.

"I admire him."

"Admire? For what?"

Kieran sighed, grabbed his laptop and flipped the top open. Within seconds he had opened a browser and brought up a number of windows showcasing Kennedy's achievements. He'd already saved many to his personal favourites. When Jeff explained that he couldn't make out the text in the articles without his glasses, Kieran obliged by reading them out loud to him. Twenty minutes later, Jeff sat in quiet contemplation.

"You know, when people ask me about my son, I have no idea what to tell them, because he's never let me into his life. I know I was a strict father—like my father was with me—but I was equally strict with Reagan, and she never shut me out. Thank you for showing me this. We knew he ran the business capably, but had no idea he'd been this successful. And he did all this without my help, financially or otherwise."

"Hope you don't mind me saying this, Jeff, having only just met you. But I sense that all he ever wanted from you was your approval."

"Sounds to me as though he doesn't need it, or that it'd be too late, anyway."

Kieran tilted his head back and stared into the night sky.

"I had this English Lit teacher at school, tough as nails and as straight as they came, teaching my least favourite topic. But I needed to get a good grade to get into my university of choice. For me, Shakespeare was like trying to understand a foreign language, and kept dragging my overall grade in the subject down. I could never get past a B minus. Didn't help that I thought she didn't like me, but at least she was consistent, because everyone else in my class thought she hated them, too. So I threw myself at the main problem—*Hamlet*, of all bloody plays—read everything I could get my hands on, studied weekends, evenings, saw multiple remakes of the film and even sat through a couple of performances at the Old Vic. Kind of got to love the story in the end, got to see so many human flaws in Hamlet, the man, and so many subtle themes running through the play. And when she read out the class results of the mock exam, announced that not only had I got an A, but that my essay was something everyone in the class should aspire to, I almost burst with pride. Managed to get A-stars in four other subjects, but that was the one I was most proud of. What I'm trying to say is, it's the people we least expect to hear praise from whose praise we value the most. Does that make sense?"

Jeff stared at Kieran for a moment before his gaze dropped to Kieran's shoulder and became unfocused.

"For someone so young, you are wise beyond your years. Yes, what you say makes perfect sense. My father preferred to point out our shortcomings and ignore our successes—said that's what makes a man—and I suppose I adopted the same method with my children. Looking back now, I almost feel as though they've both succeeded in their own way in spite of me, not because of anything I said or did."

"You're proud of them both?"

"Of course I am."

"So I guess the only question you need to ask yourself is, do they know?"

After one final puff, Jeff stubbed his cigar out repeatedly, his gaze trained on the saucer. Even though he said nothing, Kieran could tell he'd processed the question. Maybe Kieran had gone too far.

"On that note, young man, I'm heading back to bed. See if I can grab a couple more hours before breakfast. I suggest you do the same."

"I will. After I've dried off a little."

Jeff stood and went to leave, but then hesitated and turned back.

"I never asked about your own father. What does he do?"

"No idea. He walked out on us when I was seven, just before my brother was born."

Jeff said nothing then, but gazed up at the stars, gently shaking his head. "What kind of man would do that to his children?"

"You see, Jeff? You're already better than you think in the fatherhood stakes."

Jeff sighed deeply and began to walk away, but faltered once again.

"Kieran?"

"Jeff?"

"I'm glad you're here. Good see my boy finally finding someone sociable and genuine. And I get the feeling he needs that right now. To bring a little sunshine back into his life. Good night, son."

"'Night, Jeff."

After Jeff departed, Kieran sat staring at the ash-filled saucer, feeling like a total fraud.

Chapter Eleven

Kennedy

Kennedy stood hidden from view inside the shade of the open-air kitchen, a mug of fresh coffee held against his chest, watching in wonderment as his family and Kieran chatted amiably around the breakfast table.

Over the past few days, Reagan had rearranged her plans. Sunday, she had booked them all into the St Regis for a champagne brunch — much to his mother's delight. On Monday, a public holiday, she had taken Kieran and her kids to Universal Studios, while his mother and father had gone off to play golf. Kennedy had declined the theme park, needing time to catch up on work and make some urgent calls.

Just as well, too, because he'd heard from Karl how, just that morning, Milletto had once again requested a change of dates for the meeting, now in the middle of the last week of Kennedy's holiday, when he would be in Bali. More worryingly, Karl had an urgent meeting with their financial auditors that particular day, one he could not shrug off. At ten in the morning GMT, Kennedy had arranged a team conference call to find out more, and ended by telling them he would most likely be dialling in for the meeting and to please use their main conference room. He had his reasons. But he also wanted to know what Sloan's next move would be. When he put the phone down, he checked his private email to see if Tim had sent him anything, but nothing had yet arrived. Determined not to let this development spoil his holiday, he finished his work and went for a punishing swim.

Now, Tuesday, their last morning together, Reagan had turned up alone for breakfast to see them off, having dropped the boys off at school. Four days into the holiday and Kieran had already proven his worth. Kennedy watched Kieran talking animatedly, envied his easy nature, the way he comfortably chatted to anyone. Reagan's kids, who rarely engaged Kennedy, already referred to him as Uncle Kieran. What the hell was he supposed to do with that when all this was over?

Something in Kennedy had changed, too. He could feel as much deep down. Rarely had he enjoyed visiting his parents. Most other times he would have ended up arguing with his father about one thing or another—or with Patrick—and usually couldn't wait to get the fuck out. Maybe they had all mellowed with age, but seeing his sister laughing now reminded him how much he loved and missed her.

"Your friend. He very nice man," came Matty's voice beside him. When Kennedy turned, Matty was holding a tray with toast, butter and assorted pots of Maya's homemade fruit jam. "He come this morning to thank me and my wife for everything, said she is very, very good wife and cook — and probably much too good for me."

Matty's laughter had Kennedy grinning, too. Yes, that sounded like Kieran.

"I tell him, sorry, she not understand English."

Kennedy laughed along with Matty, which had Kieran and his sister looking over and smiling at them. Today they embarked on the next part of their journey, and he wondered how Kieran would fare with his friends.

"Here, let me take that," said Kennedy, putting his mug on a countertop and taking the tray. "I need to be the good son and join them. I'll come and say goodbye before we leave."

As he approached the table, his mother singled him out.

"Your father's offered to drive you to the port."

Kennedy placed the tray in the middle of the table and gave his sister a quizzical look. All of them knew only too well not to arrange things for his father on Tuesdays, when he attended his old boys' club — held sacrosanct in his retirement, the one day of the week he spent with his ex-consulate and other male buddies.

"There's no need. We can call a taxi."

"I'll take you. No point wasting money," said his father, turning a page of his newspaper.

"What about club day?"

"There'll be plenty more of those. Family comes first."

Kennedy sat down heavily. Had he shifted into another dimension overnight? When he looked at Reagan she shrugged, also looking bewildered.

"In which case," said Reagan, standing, "I need to go home, tidy up and do some urgent chores."

She came around the table, giving each of her parents a hug, before stopping at Kieran. He stood up from his seat and hugged her. Kennedy had no idea what she said, but she whispered something in his ear that had him grinning broadly and nodding. When she reached Kennedy, she grabbed his arm and pulled him up.

"Come on. You can walk me to the car."

In comfortable silence, arms linked, they strolled towards the car canopy and stopped to face each other at the front grille of her black SUV.

"It was great to see you and the boys, Reagan. Send my love to Bernie when he gets back. Tell him I'm sorry we missed him."

When they hugged, she clung on tightly and when she did let go, an odd expression transformed her face, part affection, part sadness. Maybe she had enjoyed having him back in her part of the world, but there seemed something more.

"What's going on?"

She looked away for a moment, appearing to collect herself, then met his gaze with a more stoic expression.

"Bernie's having an affair."

"What? Are you sure?"

Finally, the undercurrent of sadness he had observed in her made sense.

"The night before he left for Cape Town, while he was in the shower, a couple of pretty explicit text messages popped up on his phone. From someone called Shirl. I think it's his secretary in Melbourne, Shirlene."

"Did you confront him?"

"Honestly, I was too stunned at the time. Didn't know what to say."

"Shit, Reagan. Why didn't you call me? What are you going to do?"

At that, a small, sad smile crept onto her face.

"I know I'm a Bennett now — by marriage — but I'm also still a Grey at heart. And we don't take things lying down. So I'm not going to ignore this. But I also have the boys to think about. Fortunately, I had the sense to snap a photo of the display on my phone, in case he tries to deny anything. He's due back on Friday, so I've asked Mum to take the boys that night so Bernie and I can go out for dinner together. Haven't told her anything else. But anyway, I'll confront him then."

"If there's anything you need from me, I mean *anything*, let me know."

"I don't like to worry you—"

"But you *must*, Reagan. Something that's hit home for me this visit is that I've been absent from your lives for too long. And that's not healthy for any of us. Of course, I can't be physically here to babysit the boys for you or hold your hand, but I can offer both emotional and financial support, if that's what you need. I'm your brother. I promise I'll be there for you, okay?"

"Okay, thank you," she said, grinning broadly. "Hey, Kieran's a catch. You fell on your feet with that one. Do you think you've finally found a keeper?"

"We'll see," said Kennedy, thrown off guard by the change of subject, and he looked away.

"Come on, Kennedy, he's nice," she said, before tugging on his sleeve and getting his full attention. "What's wrong with him?"

Kennedy sighed and shook his head. How the hell did he explain to his sister that Kieran was nothing more than paid help—*straight* help, come to that?

"Nothing's wrong with him, I just—"

"You think you're not good enough, think he'll leave you, too, don't you?"

"Eventually."

"That bastard ex well and truly messed you up, didn't he? If I ever run into him, so help me, I'll—"

Kennedy started laughing then, stopping his sister in her tracks.

"What?"

"You remember what Dad always told us? One battle at a time. Take on too many, you dilute your attention and are more likely to lose them all. Sort your own shit out first."

They laughed together then, his sister pulling him into a farewell hug.

"Talking of which, are you going to say anything to them, Mum and Dad?" he asked.

"Let's see what happens first. I'll keep you posted, too. Enjoy the rest of your holiday. I know you don't do social media, but email or text me some photos."

"Will do."

After she had driven away, he and Kieran spent the rest of their morning packing and readying themselves for the next leg of the trip. Bang on ten, Matty arrived at his bedroom door, insisting once again on taking his bags down to the car. After his mother bade them both a teary farewell, they drove out to the port, where the Diamond Princess towered over every other vessel.

Impressive did not even begin to describe the sheer size and structure of the cruise liner. Seven stories of cabin balconies sat between other floors of restaurants or cafes or gyms — they were difficult to discern from the exterior. Kennedy had almost become immune to the sight, having taken cruises so many times, but in the rear-view mirror he could see Kieran sitting open-mouthed and enchanted.

"Good heavens," said Jeff, pulling up at the drop-off point. "Looks like a floating city."

"She pretty much is," said Kennedy. "Built to accommodate up to around four thousand passengers, not including crew."

"And they're all — you know — like you? The passengers?"

"More or less, yes," said Kennedy. He decided not to try to explain that the organisers aimed the cruise at the full range of the LGBTQ+ community, as well as welcoming older guests, thin or more full-bodied, and all races, which made for a far more friendly crowd. One of the other cruise lines his friends had researched had been more exclusive, just for men, but if a person wasn't ripped, in their twenties, and hot as hell, they were essentially invisible.

Without too much ceremony, Jeff helped them get their bags out of the trunk. This time around, however, instead of the formal handshake, he pulled Kieran into a hug and, just like his sister had, said something to him that Kennedy couldn't hear. Finally he turned his attention to Kennedy.

"Come and see us again soon, son. Your mother and I aren't getting any younger."

"You know, you can always jump on a plane and come see me."

"With your work schedule? Would we ever get to see you?"

"Fair point. But I'd make the time."

"Let me talk to your mother. You know how she feels about travelling and especially about cold weather. But it might be nice to spend Christmas in England."

Kennedy fully expected his father to shake his hand in farewell, and was surprised when he almost pulled him off his feet into a fierce hug.

"Look, son," he said, still holding tight, "I know we don't always see eye to eye, but I want you to know how immensely proud I am of you, of everything you've accomplished. I see now that you've done everything single-handedly, which can be very hard on a person. So take time out for yourself every now and then. And take care of that lovely boy. He's...he's very special. I'd be honoured to have him as a part of our family."

When his father finally let them go, turning and quickly getting in the car so Kennedy could not see his face, he realised his own eyes had misted over. Something that hadn't happened for years.

Yes, he thought, *things had definitely changed.*

Chapter Twelve

Kieran

Inside the bowels of the Diamond Princess, despite the spotlessness and attempt at wood-panelling-and-plush-carpet opulence, the corridors felt oppressive. Kieran kept having flashbacks to the scenes in the movie *Titanic* where Kate and Leo tried desperately to escape the sinking through one identical corridor after another. Kennedy walked in front, trailing behind the white-suited Asian steward who had insisted on carrying his bags. Kieran had been left to bring his own. Stopping outside a large white double-door, the steward brought out a small cardboard pocket containing key cards. Before he had a chance to step inside, Kennedy put a hand on the man's shoulder to get his attention. Taking the cards with one hand, he stuffed a banknote in the steward's top pocket with the other.

"Thanks, Simeon. We can take it from here. I've stayed in this room before. I know my way around."

"As you wish, Mr Grey," he said, his smile beaming. "Everything is arranged for tonight as requested. They'll come by at five-thirty to set up. But if there's anything you need, sir. And I mean *anything*, day *or* night, just call. I'll be your personal attendant for the whole journey. Have a wonderful voyage with us."

His gaze barely skimmed Kieran as he backed away from them. When Kennedy returned his attention to the open door, Kieran felt sure he rolled his eyes. Without a second thought, he followed Kennedy's footsteps across the cabin threshold and moved inside, but then immediately stopped, a gasp escaping him.

"Yeah, nice, isn't it? One of the ship's six loft suites. Had to book this baby up early," said Kennedy, dropping his bag at the door and critically assessing the space.

Opening into a two-level space, the cabin had stately hardwood panels lining three of the interior walls with floor-to-ceiling windows running along the ocean side. On the mezzanine level, a bedroom with a huge, super king-sized bed — the loft, Kieran supposed — sat overlooking the spacious living area. Standing in the middle of the room, he did a quick three-sixty. Wall-to-wall bookcases, three double settees, a fully stocked bar in walnut, an eight-seater dining table and —

"No fucking way. A baby grand? Are you yanking my chain?"

"Comes with the cabin. And tonight, we're having a cocktail party. Complete with drinks waiter and piano player. Friends only."

Kieran didn't want to think how much this lot had set Kennedy back.

"Am I going to have to put out for all of this?"

Kennedy laughed aloud, a sound Kieran was really starting to enjoy. The man didn't laugh nearly enough, according to his father and sister. He still found it funny how both had whispered parting words with almost the same intent, to come back soon with Kennedy, because he brought out the best in him.

"Nope," came Kennedy's voice, bringing him back to the scene. "A deal's a deal. And although I may be a ruthless bastard when it comes to business, I am an honest one. But there is one drawback. Only one bedroom and only one bed," said Kennedy, turning and scrutinizing Kieran. "Now, I'm happy to get the settee here made up for you each night, but upstairs will be a lot more comfortable and I promise to be a complete gentleman. And apart from me sleeping in sweatpants and a tee, that mattress is huge, so there'll be no accidental rolling over and brushing up against each other in the night. So I suggest we give it a try and, if you're not happy, you can have the couch. Unless, of course, I get lucky, in which case those curtains will be nailed shut and you'll be on the couch anyway."

Kieran peered up at the loft. A waist-height glass balcony and heavy white curtain — currently opened — partitioned the bedroom from the living room. If Kennedy brought someone back, Kieran would be able to hear everything.

"For all your bravado, you are quite gullible at times," laughed Kennedy, heading towards the window. "Relax, I'm only kidding. The last time I got lucky, Tony Blair was still Prime Minister."

Not for the first time, Kieran took in the man and had a hard time believing he'd have difficulty getting laid. Classically handsome, and someone who clearly looked after his body, he screamed sophistication and style, from his designer jeans to his perfectly fitted white flannel jacket.

"Okay. Now it's just you and me, I need to ask you something," said Kennedy, turning to the window and thrusting his hands into his jeans pockets. "What did you say to my father?"

Kieran made a point of avoiding Kennedy's gaze.

"About?"

"You tell me."

"I'm not sure what you want me to say. We chatted about a whole heap of things."

Kennedy waited for him to make eye contact, but didn't seem angry. After a moment of silence between them, he grinned.

"Well, whatever you said, the father I just said goodbye to is not the same one I remember as a kid. And if that's because of something you said, I need to thank you. But I also need you to know I didn't hire you to fight my battles. So please, on the cruise, be yourself, enjoy yourself. I have nothing to prove in front of my friends. Agreed?"

"Agreed."

"Now, a few house rules," began Kennedy, leaning his back against the window.

Kieran perched on a stool by the bar.

"Each day we're onboard, we'll have breakfast brought to the room. Part of the deal. After that, I'm not expecting you to be glued to me all day—you can go and get up to whatever you want until dinner time. But we'll always dine together. Is that understood?"

"Of course."

"And if there are any special events going on— costume party, captain's pleasure dinner, even other guests' private parties—then you'll accompany me as my plus one. We'll decide on the port stops whether either or both of us want to join the excursions ashore, as and when they happen. Maybe my friends will chat more about that later. But when we're together, I'm not expecting any touching or other public displays of affection, but I do expect you to remain by my side and not flirt with any other guests. And I include the female ones in that. Are we clear so far?"

"Crystal."

"Any questions?"

"What the hell am I supposed to do between breakfast and dinner?"

"Seriously? This is a gigantic floating holiday resort. And there'll be a lot of people your age. Okay, admittedly most of them will be gay and trying to get into your pants, so maybe use the opportunity to brush up on your conversation skills," said Kennedy, before pointing to the bar counter. "Right next to you, on the bar top, there's a guide with a rundown of the whole fourteen days, including a list of excursions if we're docked in port, or other activities. Things like gyms, fitness classes, cinemas, casino, swimming pools, live bands. Or you can always chill and sunbathe up on deck."

Kieran peered down at the itinerary, where the first port of call after Singapore jumped out at him—Koh Samui. Not only that, but a trip was offered for passengers to visit the Big Buddha Temple.

"What will you be doing?" he heard himself say.

"Most of the time? Probably working some, but I'll also hang out with my friends."

"Leonard?"

Why had the name of that particular friend started to grate?

"And others."

"What if I want to be glued to you? Do you have any objection if I tag along?"

"Of course not. I—I just thought you'd want the freedom to explore. On your own."

"And during the fourteen days, I probably might, from time to time. But—and you may want to sit down to hear this—I enjoy your company, Kennedy. And I have a feeling I'll like your friends, too."

Kennedy responded with a smile that seemed almost shy and gave Kieran an odd twinge of pleasure. Without replying, Kennedy turned and reached for a spot at the window, before sliding open a glass panel and letting the floor-to-ceiling lace curtains billow into the room.

"Come look at this."

Only then did Kieran realise he still had hold of his luggage handle. After propping the case against a chair, he followed Kennedy. When Kieran stepped out onto the deck, once again his breath was taken away. Another eight-seater table, wooden-topped this time, had matching chairs. Stunning views of the Port of Singapore met his gaze, with a backdrop of the city centre's high-rise buildings.

"Okay. This is too much," muttered Kieran, moving to the railing and shaking his head.

"You know what? I get one holiday a year. One. The rest of the time I spend working my arse off. So if I do splash out while I'm away, if I do enjoy a little bit of luxury, it's nobody's damn business but my own."

"I wasn't criticising," said Kieran softly, his gaze trailing out to sea. "I'm dazzled, that's all. Never in my life did I think I'd see something as incredible as this, let alone experience it. Things like this don't happen to me."

After a few moments of quiet contemplation, he sensed Kennedy joining him at the sea rail. When he glanced sidelong, he saw Kennedy grinning fondly at him.

"Welcome to the ball, Cinderella."

Chapter Thirteen

Kennedy

By the time they had unpacked, showered and dressed, with Kieran getting Kennedy's opinion on a stylish ensemble of a floral shirt comprising faded pinks, oranges and blues, together with white chino pants and tan deck shoes — a look Kieran totally rocked — the cruise staff had already arrived to set up for the drinks party.

Kennedy wore a simple linen combination, a comfortable fit of white shirt untucked over fawn-coloured pants and open-toed brown leather sandals. His friends would expect no less. When he descended the circular stairs to the main floor, he noticed Kieran helping the two staff lay out finger foods and arrange glasses.

"Kieran, you're on holiday. Leave the professionals to do their job."

"I want to be useful."

And just then, Kennedy realised the truth. Kieran felt nervous about meeting his friends, wanting to impress them and make sure everything went well. Once again, an overwhelming affection hit Kennedy, that Kieran was trying because of him, something none of his other companions had done. Before he could say anything, there came a knock at the door. Being the nearest, Kennedy went to answer.

"Are we too early?" asked Steph, her head poking through the open door.

"Aren't you always?" said Kennedy, pulling her into the room and into a hug. "I bet you could hear the Cosmopolitan shaker all the way from your cabin, couldn't you? Come on in."

If Steph appeared a little tired, Laurie looked positively haggard. Not that he would tell her as much. Plus-sized and proud, they rarely dressed down, and while blonde Steph wore a deep scarlet pantsuit and gold accessories, auburn-haired Laurie had black jeans and a black silk blouse decorated with tiny red and gold koi carp.

"Before you say anything, we may not be looking our best right now — despite half an hour of emergency makeup. We flew in last night, so we're both more than a little pooped. Might not last the whole night."

"Jet lag's real, isn't it?" added Kieran, coming to Kennedy's side. "I found that out the hard way. Loving that fishy blouse, by the way."

"And who might you be?" said Steph, casting an approving glance at Kennedy before returning her full attention to Kieran.

"I'm Kieran," he replied, throwing an arm around Kennedy's shoulders. Kennedy grinned and looked away, not wanting them to see how much he liked the gesture.

"So you're this year's plus one, huh?"

"I am indeed," said Kieran, detaching himself from Kennedy. "And more importantly, you're without a drink. What can I get you?"

"Okay," said Laurie, stepping into the cabin. "So you're now officially my new best friend. Steph'll have a long, tall vodka tonic with fresh lime. I'll have soda water with ice and lemon."

"Soda water?" said Kennedy as Kieran headed off. "Since when?"

"Since ten weeks ago," said Steph, grinning sheepishly at Kennedy.

"Oh my God, are you—?" asked Kennedy, turning to Laurie and waiting for her to reply.

"I sure am," said Laurie. "Ten weeks on Jenny Craig and already twenty pounds lighter."

"What he was going to ask, darling," said Steph, rolling her eyes, "was if we're pregnant."

"I was not—" lied Kennedy.

"Oh, pur-lease," said Laurie, flicking her hair. "One miracle at a time, darling man."

When Kieran came back with drinks for the girls, he joined in the conversation and seemed to enjoy their banter. Listening out for the door, Kennedy almost missed Steph's comment.

"You should be honoured. You're not his usual type. Most of the others looked like sticks of candy floss. With the kind of sparkling conversation you'd expect from sickly fairground confectionary."

"Steph!" said Laurie, aghast but laughing.

"What? It's true."

"I *am* standing right here, ladies," added Kennedy, even though he was used to ribbing from his friends. When another knock came at the door, Kennedy went to answer. To Kennedy's surprise, not only had the piano player arrived with an armful of sheet music, but Pete and Eric were accompanied by Leonard. The whole gang had arrived.

"Permission to come aboard, sir?" asked Leonard, grinning, after Pete and Eric had moved inside.

Leonard had always possessed an appealing smile. He looked good today, too, in jeans and a striped yellow and maroon rugby shirt, his greying goatee highlighting familiar dimples as he smiled.

"Always more than welcome," said Kennedy. While he studied Leonard, he noticed the man's eyes drawn to someone across the room.

"And who might that young specimen be?"

"Roll your tongue in, Len," said Kennedy. "That's Kieran. First of all, he's far too young for you. And secondly, he's with me."

"With you, or *with* you?" asked Leonard, arching an eyebrow.

When Kennedy followed his scrutiny, appraising Kieran from a distance, he felt a sudden pang of protectiveness. Kieran—already cornered by Pete—looked perfect in the casual clothes Kennedy had chosen for him. Caught laughing at something Pete had said, Kieran clutched a hand over his mouth as though to hold in his amusement. On one hand, Kennedy wanted his friends to get along with Kieran, but he didn't want them to make him feel uncomfortable by flirting with him. Heaven knew, he'd had his fill of that on the last cruise.

"Lay off, Len. He's a really nice guy and new to all this. Looks as though Pete already has his fangs into him. Go say hello to the girls, while I try to rescue him."

As he approached them, he heard Kieran monopolising the talk, firing question after question at Pete.

"What about him, the nice old guy, Eric?" Kieran asked. "What do you call him?"

"Him I call Dad."

"Huh? Why Dad?"

"Because he's my father."

"Your father's gay?" said Kieran, his mouth dropping open.

"Not in the slightest. But he's been joining us ever since Mum died. And because we sometimes share these cruises with the bottle blue brigade — senior citizens — he normally gets more action than the lot of us put together. Oh shite, is he starting on the red wine already? Here, hold this a moment."

Kieran took hold of Pete's champagne glass and turned to smile at Kennedy.

"How are you doing?"

"Learning a lot about your friends. Hope you don't mind, but I've asked the pianist to play some golden oldies — Katy Perry, Snow Patrol, Coldplay, that kind of thing."

Golden oldies, thought Kennedy, *then what the hell does that make me?* Only then did he realise the pianist was playing a gentle jazz rendition of 'I Kissed A Girl'.'

"Pete's quite the character, isn't he?" continued Kieran, either missing or ignoring Kennedy's expression. "He has names for everyone. Steph and Laurie are the 'Weather Girls', Leonard he calls Doris because, apparently, Leonard's last name is Day. He used to call him 'Any Day', but I haven't quite figured out why—"

Kennedy knew why, but wasn't about to let on. He'd once joined a conversation where Pete was explaining that 'any day is better than Lenny Day', and had then gone on to detail Leonard's many moments of moroseness. Only rarely did Kennedy lose his temper, but he had torn a strip off Pete in front of everyone. Many years ago, Leonard had lost someone he really loved. If he wasn't always sunshine and roses, then he had a damn good reason why.

"What does he call me?"

"Do you really want to know?"

"Go on. I can handle it."

"He calls you Mr Happy, because he says you rarely are," said Kieran. "And in your defence—yes, I know I'm not fighting any more battles for you—I said he might need to re-evaluate the name by the end of the holiday."

"By the end of which, no doubt, he'll have christened you, too."

"Oh, he already has. I'm to be known as Queer One instead of Kieran. Ouch. So my cover should be good for a few more weeks."

Kennedy's good humour stalled. Being among so many gay people with their unfiltered banter might well prove to be uncomfortable for Kieran, and he didn't deserve that.

"Look, Kieran, if you get hassled or find you can't take the smack talk—"

"Hey, Kennedy, I'm good. Okay? And honestly, I have a really good feeling about this cruise. Please don't ruin it for yourself by worrying about me. Believe me when I say, I can hold my own."

Kennedy maintained his gaze, then started to smile and say something inappropriate, but Kieran folded his arms across his chest and tilted his head.

"Really? Don't even, Ned. You *know* what I mean."

Once they'd settled in, after Kennedy made sure everyone had drinks, he got them all to sit together on the sofa arrangement.

"Okay, people," he announced, after asking the piano player to stop his rendition of Coldplay's 'Yellow'. "First order of business. Rule number one. No repeats of last year."

"That's an easy one," said Pete. "Without Paddy and his posse."

"We need to talk about who's doing which of the trips. Usual score."

"Is anyone else doing Japan?" asked Pete.

"Steph?" asked Kennedy, stepping away from the front. "Can you take over?"

Over the next twenty minutes, Steph patiently took votes on who would be attending which shore excursion. Kieran seemed really keen to go to the Buddhist temple in Samui, something that held no interest for Kennedy. Fortunately, Steph, Laurie and Leonard would accompany him.

Partway through the evening — they had only meant to have pre-dinner drinks and snacks before the welcome dinner, but his friends got along so well together — Kennedy stood back and observed them with a mix of happiness and pride. Kieran stood laughing with Pete, the toughest nut to crack in their group of friends. A wave of fondness overcame him, having all of his friends together, getting along. Not that he didn't value the visit to his family, but friends were different. These particular friends had no hidden agendas or expectations, were not only loyal but were along for the simple pleasures of fun and enjoyment.

While Kennedy chatted with Pete and Leonard—his eyes constantly drawn to Kieran, who was working the room like a professional—he noticed Kieran detach himself and head to the cabin door.

"Who is it?" called Kennedy, laughing over Pete's shoulder to where Kieran stood at the open door. Something about his change of composure and the ashen expression stopped his laughter. "What is it? Who's there, Kieran?"

"It's me, Kennedy," came a loud voice from outside the door, one he knew only too well. "Is this pet monkey of yours going to let us in or not?"

Patrick.

Chapter Fourteen

Kieran

Kieran recognised Patrick immediately from the online photograph he'd seen of Kennedy and another man at a social function. Both dark-haired, Kennedy always appeared well turned out, with wisps of grey at the temples of his well-groomed hair, his chiselled features, and those stunning deep Atlantic blue eyes. Patrick's hair sat in tight curls on his head like a helmet, and his almost black eyes burned into Kieran like accusations. Three other men stood with him, a younger one who appeared a little uncomfortable and two others standing unsmiling behind Patrick like personal bodyguards. Perhaps they were. But what the hell was Patrick doing on the cruise? And more importantly, why would he want to gate-crash this party? Unless he had been invited or was here to make trouble? Kieran felt instantly uncomfortable. How was he supposed to deal with this?

"It's okay," came Kennedy's voice, as he approached the door, stopped next to him and placed a hand on his shoulder. "Let them in. They're friends too, and — even if unexpected — more than welcome."

Kieran could hear an immediate change in the tone of Kennedy's voice, a cold, business-like formality. That alone irked Kieran, who had noticed that before this intrusion Kennedy — the real Kennedy — had finally surfaced, had started to relax, laugh and enjoy himself.

Patrick and Kennedy shook hands like heads of state, the stern gaze between them unfathomable. Kieran wanted to intervene, to say something, but no words came.

"You know Richmond and Mike," said Patrick, indicating the henchmen dwarfing him, then turned to the nice-looking guy a few years younger than Kieran. Something in his discomfort told Kieran he'd also been an unwitting bystander in the decision to invade the party. "This is Joey. He's accompanying me this year."

"And this is Kieran, my plus one," said Kennedy. "Everyone else here you know. Come in and make yourselves at home."

Kieran's twinge of pleasure at the label 'plus one' was short-lived. On their way in, only Joey made an effort to smile and shake hands with him. The other three ignored him, and one of them actually brushed into him without a word of apology. Kennedy escorted the four new guests over to the bar, leaving Kieran standing alone. He looked around for Steph and Laurie, but they were nowhere to be seen.

Finally, Pete came to his rescue and dragged him over to where his rosy-cheeked father was sipping on a large glass of wine. Considering they were father and son, they could not have looked more different —

chubby Pete with his wild chestnut hair exploding from his pear-shaped head, and Eric, carefully groomed with a full head of straight white hair and matching handlebar moustache. The perfect double act.

"Don't worry, Kieran. None of this has anything to do with you. I asked Patrick if he wanted to join us this year, wanted me to book him a cabin, and he categorically declined, after what happened last year. As did Richmond and Mike, which was no biggie. They're like the Three Musketeers, joined at the codpiece. And now they even have a fourth, their very own d'Artagnan, the young, handsome hero. Although I've no idea who he's supposed to be here with."

"Patrick. Accompanying him."

"Whatever *that* means. You know, even after they split, both Kennedy and Patrick used to come on the cruises—separately, of course. Until last year. Did Kennedy tell you what happened?"

"No, he didn't mention anything."

"So, a word of warning. Don't get sucked into being sweet-talked by Richmond and Mike—I call them Rich and Poor, by the way, because Mike's last name is Porter—unless you want Kennedy to throw a wobbly. Last year, they had a three-way with Kennedy's then boyfriend, Ewan. Caused one hell of a stink, I can tell you. Honestly, I still believe Patrick put them up to it, to get back at Kennedy. So, you know, just watch yourself around them."

"Trust me, Pete, that's not going to be a problem."

"Yeah," said Pete, assessing Kieran. "I believe you. Can't quite make you out yet. You are not like the usual vacuous twink he brings along. Is our man over there finally growing up and moving on?"

When he followed Pete's gaze, to where Kennedy stood at the bar, Kieran's heart wrenched a little to observe Kennedy's discomfort, even though he appeared to be putting on a brave face. Leonard must have sensed the tension too, because he immediately stepped in to join Kennedy in support. At almost the same time, they noticed Steph and Laurie descending the staircase from the bedroom mezzanine level. They'd clearly been having a sneak peek around the cabin. Steph's face was a picture when she noticed the group at the bar. Frozen mid-staircase, with Laurie almost bumping into her back, her mouth dropped open. Looking over at Pete, she mouthed the words 'what the fuck', which even had Kieran grinning. But troopers to the last, they descended and went straight over to the new guests, liberally providing theatrical hellos, hugs and kisses.

"Why doesn't Leonard bring anyone on these cruises?" Kieran asked Pete, absently. When Leonard laughed, his eyes sparkled and the goatee revealed deep dimples in his cheeks.

"Good-looking bloke, isn't he?"

"Had he been here, my friend Cole would have been all over him."

"How old is he? Your friend?"

"In his early twenties, I think, but very good-looking."

"Not Leonard's type, dear. Leonard's into Daddies."

"He's — what?"

"Yes, I know. The man's forty-four. But his late partner was twenty years older. Passed away years ago. We all just assumed it was one of those things — they met young, connected, stayed together. Until the first time I brought Dad along on the cruise four years ago, and Leonard tried to jump his bones."

"No!" said Kieran, stifling a laugh.

"Flattered," slurred Eric. "But I'm afraid I'm a bouncy boobies ladies' man."

"Christ, Dad!" chastised Pete. "Gross, or what?"

After Pete offered to refill his drink, Kieran made a point of circumventing Patrick and his minders, and escaped to the safety of the outside balcony. Only then, as he stood there, did he sense the motion of the ship, and realise the vessel had left the port and was heading out to the open seas. After ten minutes standing at the sea rail, he sensed someone come and join him, and turned to see Joey standing there. More than likely, he too wanted to get away from the tension in the room. After nodding a welcome, they swapped stories about each other. Interestingly, they both lived south of the Thames river in different towns in London. Joey worked for the NHS, doing his foundation training on the way to becoming a doctor. Kieran found him entirely genuine and explained candidly about his own work-study situation before asking how Joey knew Patrick.

"We met a couple of months back, at a bar round the back of Charing Cross. This holiday is totally last-minute. Richmond and Mike booked a two-bedroom suite and friends of theirs dropped out. Sorry about coming along today, but they insisted. How long have you known Kennedy?"

"About the same time."

"He seems okay. But from the way Richmond describes him, you'd think he was a mass murderer."

Interesting, thought Kieran. *Richmond, not Patrick, is bad-mouthing Kennedy.*

"You know Patrick and Kennedy used to be an item?" said Kieran.

"Every bloody day we're together. Feels like I'm competing with the ghost of Kennedy Grey. And I can't compete, of course. I'm two years into my postgraduate training and scraping by. But I really like Patrick. I just can't give him the material things Kennedy could. Not right now, anyway. And on top of that, Patrick has a lot of baggage."

"How do you mean?"

Before Joey answered, he turned and gave Kieran his full attention.

"Tell me about you and Kennedy, first of all. What is it you like about him?"

"A lot of things. He's smart, works bloody hard, treats people he loves really well and, if you want my honest opinion, deep down he has a good heart."

"You really like him?"

Kieran stared out to sea and mulled over the question, but the answer came instantly.

"Someone else recently asked me the same question. And I'll tell you the same thing I said to him. I admire Kennedy. I think he's an inspiration."

"Wow, man. You've got it almost as bad as me," said Joey, smiling and following Kieran's gaze out to sea. "Patrick had issues with Kennedy and his family. Said they all looked down on him. Made him sleep in a separate bedroom in their house when he visited. Complained that Kennedy cared more about his work than being in a relationship."

"Kennedy certainly works hard, that much I know. You don't become successful in this day and age without putting the hours in. I'm sure you know all about that if you're working on becoming a doctor."

Peripherally, Kieran noticed Joey nodding.

"Did they make you sleep in a different bedroom? His parents?"

"Yeah, they did. Loved it. My own en suite bathroom and a huge bed."

"But you're sleeping together here?"

Kieran paused for a moment, wondering how to answer the question.

"Yep. You win some, you lose some."

Joey laughed at that, before asking, "Which estate agency did you work for?"

"Landreal Properties, based in Croydon."

"Shut the fuck up!" said Joey, aghast. "Then you must know my sister. She's still the Surrey regional manager. Chloe Drinkwater?"

Kieran froze. He knew Chloe well—she had been the one pushing to keep him when voices from the top began to let a whole raft of salespeople go. The trouble was, Chloe also knew his ex-girlfriend Jennifer, and got on really well with her. Chloe and her husband had been out for drinks and dinner with Kieran and Jennifer three or four times. For a second, he faltered, wondering how much to tell Joey.

Right then, the balcony door slid open. Laurie poked her head out and rolled her eyes.

"Sorry to interrupt, but we've all been summoned. Patrick has something he wants to say to us all."

Back inside, everyone either sat on sofas or stood awkwardly, looking towards the bar, where a slightly uncomfortable Patrick stood at the bar counter, about to give a speech, obsessively rubbing his left forearm.

"Look, we didn't want to hijack your welcome celebration. But sometimes one needs to take the bull by the horns. So I just have a few words I want to say then we'll bugger off to dinner and leave you alone. We're here on the cruise last minute, so I'm sorry you weren't forewarned. I'm also truly sorry last year's holiday didn't end well, and I'm not about to start laying the blame at anyone's feet. What happened, happened. But the fact is we're all here, and this is a huge boat, with a hell of a lot of people, so we can easily lose ourselves among the crowds. At the end of the day, old friends can withstand a few knocks, don't you think?"

Kieran thought the words sounded heartfelt, but when he peered at Kennedy, he noticed him glowering at the floor. A couple of people around the room murmured their agreement, while others simply nodded.

"And if anyone's interested, we're having our own afternoon drinks party. On the eighth day at sea, after Vietnam. A small gathering before the captain's table banquet in the evening. Our cabin's a little cosier than this one, but you're all very welcome to join."

"A toast," said Pete, who had stood the whole time with his arms crossed, but now raised his flute of champagne. "Here's to having fun and adventures on the high seas."

"Hear, hear," said Eric, topping up his glass with red wine and taking a gulp.

Maybe Kieran imagined the reaction, but everyone appeared to join in half-heartedly. Straight afterwards, Patrick and his friends filed out of the cabin, Joey smiling a farewell at Kieran. Hopefully he had forgotten his earlier question. Almost as soon as the door closed, the room breathed a collective sigh of relief.

"What the fuck just happened?" said Pete, almost the same time as Steph took over.

"Oh my God, Kennedy," she said, turning on Kennedy. "I totally forgot to mention. There's a ballroom dance competition the night of the captain's table. I've already entered us."

Kieran noticed that Kennedy's mind had been elsewhere, but she now had his full attention.

"Shiply Ballroom. And people, me and sex god Kennedy here are going to wow everyone with our signature tango to the Latin version of Roxanne — El Tango de Roxanne. Not exactly the same dance, but the same song as the *Moulin Rouge* movie version. So we'll need you there to support."

"Yeah, I don't think so," said Kennedy.

"You dance?" asked Kieran, incredulous.

"Darling," said Pete. "These two have moves you would not believe. They've been dancing since university days. Kennedy, you have to say yes. Just to fuck Patrick off."

"You do," said Laurie, who had initially appeared unsure, but was now nodding. "That bastard needs to be shown that you're still fun to be around."

Kieran could not imagine Kennedy dancing to anything, let alone ballroom. But maybe the man he had come to like had hidden depths.

"Let's at least have a practice run," said Steph. "Find an empty space and go through the dance steps. See what we can remember. What do you say?"

* * * *

Once the party finished, their group headed to the restaurant, and although Kieran ate his fill of the buffet food, Kennedy's appetite appeared to have evaporated. Steph's suggestion that they end the evening with a couple of potent cocktails at the bar on deck had worked to soften everyone's mood before they headed back to their respective cabins.

That night, after Kennedy had finished in the bathroom, Kieran took his turn to get ready to sleep. If he'd felt any apprehension about sharing the huge bed with Kennedy, everything melted away when he saw Kennedy sitting up, arms folded, glaring into space.

"Look at us," Kieran said, as he slipped beneath the covers, trying to make light of the situation. "In bed together with absolutely no intention of having sex. We ought to be married."

Kennedy had no reaction, still lost in thought staring at the foot of the bed.

"Sorry, I'm talking nonsense. Nervous, I guess. It's the first time I've shared a bed with a guy."

In response, Kennedy snorted softly.

"I told you I'd be a gentleman."

"I know, I know. Sorry. Are you okay?"

Kennedy turned his head to Kieran and attempted a smile.

"Go to sleep, Kieran."

Kieran snuggled beneath the quilt, his head sinking into the pillow, staring at the ceiling. Kennedy had been right—he barely noticed him moving on his side of the bed when he readied himself to sleep.

"So—err—what happened? With you and Patrick?"

"We're not going there."

"Okay then, but tell me if I'm fucking up here? Give me something I can work with."

Kennedy sighed loudly.

"You're not doing anything wrong. In fact, I'm really glad you're here. There are just things between Patrick and me that are unresolved. And I think I'm going to have to grow a pair and put that right. Something I'm not looking forward to."

"I see," said Kieran, even though he didn't. "You want to know something I'm looking forward to?"

"What's that?" asked Kennedy, sounding a little guarded.

"Seeing your moves on the dance floor."

Finally, Kennedy chuckled next to him.

"Goodnight, Kieran."

"Night, Ned."

Chapter Fifteen

Kennedy

Kennedy woke late the next morning to an empty bed. After using the bathroom, he descended the stairs into the main living area. Only then did he notice the curtain billowing softly into the room. Out on the sun-drenched terrace, Kieran sat at a beautifully arranged breakfast table complete with pristine white tablecloth and laden with a mouth-watering assortment of breakfast victuals — a basket of Danish pastries and croissants, a jug of fresh orange juice, a fruit bowl, a rack of golden toast and two plates covered by silver domes. In sunglasses and white bathrobe, his feet crossed at the ankles up on the chair seat, a knee on either armrest, Kieran sat texting on his smartphone.

"Morning, dear," he said, looking up and grinning. "You looked so peaceful, I didn't have the heart to wake you. Hope you don't mind I've started breakfast without you. Simeon brought you a double espresso —

just now, so it's still hot—said to ring if you needed anything else. And I mean, anything Mr Grey needs."

As he moved around the table to take a seat opposite, Kennedy tried hard not to smile at Kieran's impression of Simeon.

"What's my laptop doing here?" he asked, noticing his computer sitting on his placemat.

"I put it there," said Kieran. "Is that okay? I noticed how you always checked emails first thing in the morning at breakfast at your parents' place. So I saved you the effort of fetching it."

"Thank you, but you didn't need to."

Kieran shrugged nonchalantly before reaching for his coffee cup. To be honest, Kennedy appreciated the gesture, liking the fact that Kieran had noticed his habit of keeping abreast of news and work first thing in the morning.

"Steph's managed to blag a member of the cruise staff to let you two use one of the nightclubs this afternoon to practice your routine. Between two and three. They don't open to the rest of the passengers until four-thirty, so they can let you use the space for an hour. Shall I tell her yay or nay?"

"You're texting Steph?"

"We set up a chat group last night. Pete, Steph, Laurie and me. Shall I add you?"

"No, thank you."

"And how about this afternoon?"

Kennedy's mood hadn't improved overnight, but he needed to lighten up around his friends, otherwise he was going to bring them all down.

"What the hell. Tell her yes."

"Excellent. This I cannot wait to see."

"You're not going to be there."

"The hell I'm not. I want to see everything you've got, Kennedy Grey."

"We're sharing a bed now. I'd be careful how you phrase things like that around me."

This time Kieran tilted his head back and laughed into the morning. Kennedy chuckled along with him. Pouring coffee for himself, he realised how lucky he was to have chosen Kieran. His mood had already improved.

"Can I say," said Kieran, grinning playfully, "and please don't take this the wrong way — but, at a stretch, I could imagine you having interests outside work. Squash, chess, tennis, swimming, art collecting — big game hunting, even. But ballroom dancing?"

Once again, Kennedy found himself smiling. Kieran had correctly nailed him as being someone who enjoyed individual as opposed to team sports. Steph, who had also grown to love ballroom dancing as a kid, had been astonished to find out he could dance when they'd first met up at university.

"Mum and Dad. Every Saturday morning for two years, my sister and I were dragged off to dance lessons. I think he thought I'd follow in his footsteps later in life, you know, diplomacy. And because he — they — had to attend a number of formal occasions and social functions throughout the year, being able to do the basics, like the waltz, quickstep, foxtrot and tango, went with the territory. At first I hated it — I'd have been eight at the time, stuck in a hall with a bunch of prissy girls — but there's a discipline to dancing, a strategy to the moves, and even within that strict control, there's a feeling of freedom, of letting go."

Kennedy had been staring out to sea, the rim of the coffee cup held against his lip. When he turned his head, Kieran had an odd look on his face, something Kennedy hadn't seen before.

"Hidden depths?" asked Kieran.

"Hey, I'm not saying I'm any good. But Steph and I usually move well together, and if things go wrong, we're pretty good at faking it."

"'Shit," said Kieran, his face dropping. "Talking of faking it, I need to confess to something. Yesterday, when I spoke to Joey, Patrick's boyfriend, I was probably a little more candid about myself than I ought to have been. And you know the old expression 'small world'? Turns out it is. I know his sister, who also knows Jennifer, my ex-girlfriend."

"I don't see the problem."

"If he talks to her about me, he'll find out I'm not really gay."

"Are you and Jennifer still together?"

"Of course not. Not for three months. I told you already."

"Then what you are now is anything you want to be. And, more importantly, it's nobody's business but your own." Letting Kieran mull over his words, he pulled the silver dome off the plate to reveal scrambled eggs and smoked salmon on toasted muffins. After taking a spoonful, he flipped up the top of his laptop and booted up the machine. "What are you planning to do today?"

"I thought I'd explore. Steph and Laurie are swinging by at ten. How about you?"

Kennedy peered down at his desktop and noticed a few emails had arrived in his private account. When he opened to his inbox, he noticed one from Tim with a couple of attachments.

"Working. Just this morning. How about I meet you guys for lunch?"

"Sounds like a plan. And then we can all head straight to your rehearsal."

* * * *

Despite Steph's form — since he'd first met her, she'd always hovered around size twenty-six and been proud of the fact — she was amazingly light on her feet. Truth be told, she was the better dancer. Their routine included both of them wearing dinner suits, Steph in white, Kennedy in black. Steph would take the lead, traditionally the man's role. Typical of her, since the last time they'd danced this particular tango she'd changed a couple of the moves, to keep things fresh.

Over the following hour, they began by walking through the steps, practicing and re-practicing the new ones until Kennedy felt comfortable. Of course, their first full run through with the music was a train wreck. Every now and again, he glanced over to where Kieran and Laurie sat at a lounge table, observing them and chatting together. Kieran had agreed to sit in on their rehearsal and record their session on his phone. That way, they could watch together later on and decide what worked and what did not.

When they managed to run through three times in succession without stopping or making a mistake, they agreed to call it a day and went over to join Laurie and Kieran. As they approached, the pair burst into applause, Kieran grinning broadly at Kennedy.

"Are you full of surprises or what, Kennedy Grey? That was frigging awesome."

When Kennedy threw himself down, Kieran put his arm around Kennedy's shoulders, pulled his head towards him and kissed him on the top. Not only did

Kennedy feel a warm twinge of pleasure at the praise and the contact, but his cock also began to sit up and take notice. And he had a fair idea why.

That morning, as they'd both taken turns to use the bathroom, Kieran had left the door open, and Kennedy had glimpsed his naked figure getting into the shower cubicle. Like a good gentleman, at first he had turned away, but then had not been able to help stealing a peek at Kieran's body. Beautiful, long, lean but not skinny, he had pale, hairless skin except for the dark patch of pubic hair around a generously sized cock.

All morning, with Kieran gone, the image had kept floating into his head and interrupting his work. Only the message from Tim, and another from Karl, had managed to keep him focused.

Karl had written that the meeting date was still the same, but that they would need to use a local hotel, because their conference room had suffered water damage from the offices above. Kennedy smiled to himself. Sloan either knew or suspected that Kennedy had installed his own security devices around the room, knew his boss would be able to watch and hear everything going on.

Tim had managed to find reams of information on Milletto, and had included something he liked to call an 'FYEO' file—For Your Eyes Only—which always drew Kennedy's attention, and where the crucial information would sit. Milletto's file had nothing much he didn't already know, except that, at fifty-eight, Milletto was essentially in his prime as a businessman, had pretty much done the same for Cold Steel as Kennedy had for Grey Havens. Why, then, would he want to sell? Even though he would remain in an advisory capacity—part of the deal—he would essentially hold no power, have no share of the pie. Of course, Tim must have known Kennedy would look at the attachments in sequence, because as soon as he typed in his private password to open the FYEO file, the truth jumped out at him.

Very clever, Sloan.

Very clever.

Chapter Sixteen

Kieran

On the third day at sea, with not a cloud tainting the morning sky, the cruise ship anchored at Koh Samui in Thailand for the first of their excursions.

Even without the rainbow flags and pink feather boas streaming out of a couple of the coach windows, nobody on the street could have been in any doubt as to the orientation of the passengers inside — well, the majority of them. Kieran had never seen so much colourful spandex or leather harness, so much glitter and makeup and so many tight vests, shorts and half-naked muscled bodies in one place.

Whether the local coach driver had been warned or not, Kieran had no idea, but the man grinned broadly each time the holidaymakers boarded and re-boarded the bus. Two minutes away from the previous stop, and the crowd — most a little the worse for wear after discovering a gay-friendly bar selling cheap Singha beer — began a rousing chorus of Abba's '*Mamma Mia*'.

Three of them, dressed in boas and wigs as Meryl, Christine and Julie, provided a coordinated dance show down the narrow aisle between the seats. Kieran enjoyed the coach entertainment almost as much as the trip itself.

Almost, but not quite.

Sitting next to Leonard in the luxury air-conditioned coach, Kieran's forehead rested against the cool window, as he observed the stunning coastline of calm, aquamarine sea, and the almost white sands bordered by lush green vegetation lining their route. The next and final stop on their island tour would be the Big Buddha, viewed at sunset. Butterflies had set up shop in his stomach. If he was going to be honest with himself, he wished Kennedy had joined them, missed having him there to share the experience. Twice in the past few days, he'd noticed Kennedy ogling him naked in the shower. Not that he minded. To be perfectly honest, he left the door to the bathroom open on purpose now, found the attention strangely flattering.

But as usual, Kennedy had work to finish, and had wanted to give Kieran time on his own. In the seat behind him, Steph snuggled up to Laurie, and opposite them, Pete sat with his dad. Leonard had insisted Kieran keep him company, and had even given him the window seat. From a couple of their conversations he learned that Leonard had no interest in meeting anyone on the cruise, and, like Kennedy, had taken time out from his busy schedule to relax with friends. Kieran had grown to like Leonard on the short excursion — had even been invited to call him Len — and was glad he'd spent time getting to know him. He sat there right now, occasionally making approving noises at views Kieran pointed out, but mainly frowning down at his tablet computer.

"You like this place, don't you?" came Len's voice.

"It's stunning. I could happily retire here."

"Got a few good years before that happens, buddy."

Next to him, Len snorted, before cursing softly under his breath. Kieran turned and noticed him repeatedly brushing his finger across the display of the tablet computer. He'd been playing with the device, and intermittently huffing, ever since they'd boarded the bus from the Thai silk market.

"You okay there?" Kieran asked.

"I'm trying to get to the next page of this bloody site, but the damned thing keeps freezing. It's driving me nuts."

"Can I take a look?"

"Be my guest," said Len, thrusting the device at Kieran.

Kieran already knew Leonard had no problem accessing the Internet, because they shared the same Wi-Fi dongle. But the site on the display—for what appeared to be antique furniture—had frozen. Kieran copied the URL, closed the browser down and tried again. This time the page opened to the main page of the site, and Kieran selected the one Leonard had been trying to reach. After a minute, he handed the device back.

"Not your fault, Len. Looks to me as though that site was cobbled together in the nineties. I realise they're selling antiques, but the home page shouldn't have to work like one. Heavens, a twelve-year-old could build something better these days. Surprised they manage to sell anything at all."

When he turned to Len, the man had a grim smile on his face.

"We don't. At least not much."

"Oh, shit," said Kieran, placing his fingers over his lips. "Foot meet mouth. A bad habit of mine. I'm so sorry."

"No, no," said Len. "You're right, of course, and you're honest. All my sites were built by the same developer over a couple of decades ago, who subsequently disappeared off the face of the earth. Since then I've thrown good money after bad, simply trying to keep them up and running."

"Kennedy told me your businesses are doing really well."

"We're making money. But not as much as we could be."

"Well, if there's anything I can help with, let me know. This is my area of expertise."

"Seriously?" said Len, turning to Kieran with what looked something like hope in his eyes. "You could help with this?"

"Absolutely. Tell you what, why don't you give me the details of all your websites — including any backdoor passwords — and I'll check them out. With Kennedy working, I've got so much time free on the cruise. Then we'll get together one afternoon, you can buy me a cocktail, and I'll give you my recommendations."

"I can't ask you to do that on your holiday."

"You're not. I'm offering. Plus, to be honest, this is the kind of thing I get a kick out of, much more than I do trying to find space to swim in that tiny tub on the boat they call a swimming pool."

"Pete loves to hang around the pool," said Len, grinning. "Says that's where you find all the young hot guys with the ripped bodies."

"Does nothing for me."

"Me neither," said Len, before his curious gaze turned to Kieran. "You wouldn't look out of place, though. Glad to see Kennedy's made a good choice this year — for once. Can I ask you a question?"

"Um, yes, I think."

Len laughed at that.

"Do you work for Kennedy?" asked Len. "As well as the two of you being together."

"What? No. Why would you ask that?"

"It's just, he brought an ex-employee called Ollie on the cruise a couple of times. And I also overheard you talking to Steph about Kennedy's business, and you sounded really well informed. You were talking about the pros and cons of becoming a public-listed company. And some of the steps involved in setting the wheels in motion. Just sounded as though you might already be working for him."

Kieran leant back, enjoying the veiled praise.

"Well, I'm definitely not working for him, but my degree course covered the steps businesses need to take in becoming publicly listed in the UK, so the information is fairly fresh in my head. Although my real interest is in e-commerce. Sorry if I come across as a smart-ass. That wasn't my intention."

"Are you kidding? Kennedy's last squeeze seemed more obsessed with Kylie Jenner and some show called *Riverdale*. So, did Kennedy give you his signature blow job card?" asked Len, his voice lowering, which, considering the noise on the coach was completely unnecessary.

"His what?"

"Black jack. BJ. Did he give you the black jack card, yet?"

Kieran threw himself back in his sat, unable to stop the loud laugh bursting from him. Even though they'd not heard Len's comment, a couple of other passengers turned their heads and grinned at Kieran's reaction. In fairness, Kennedy had told him the card usually held another meaning.

"I take that as a yes. Don't tell me you've used it already."

"No," said Kieran, wiping at his eyes. "No, I haven't used the card."

"You will, though. Kennedy gives mind-boggling blow jobs."

"Oh, yes?" said Kieran, eyeing Len suspiciously. "And just how would you know that?"

"No, no," said Len, grinning. "Not me. God, Kennedy's a nice guy, but he's not my type at all. But let's just say, the boyfriend after Patrick, Ollie, the one he brought on the first two post-Patrick cruises, was not particularly discreet. Demanded a minimum of four cards on the second cruise. And, if you'll excuse the expression, he gave us all a blow-by-blow account, one evening at the bar."

Once again, Kieran burst into laughter.

* * * *

When they pulled up in the temple car park, the sun hung low in the sky, illuminating everything in bright golden sunlight. Ten or so other tourist coaches were already parked there. Most of their busload seemed eager to climb the stairs to the golden Buddha and the panoramic lookout point beyond. Kieran excused himself from his small group, citing a headache caused by mild dehydration, and wandered off to buy a bottle of water—which was a ruse, of course, because he wanted to be alone. Returning to the heart of the temple, he stopped and swigged his water, before taking in the view.

Terracotta-coloured tiles on the pavilions standing either side of the stairs leading up to the Buddha appeared freshly laid, as though they had only recently been constructed. Even the three staircases leading up to the Buddha, two of white ceramic or marble, each bordering another of deep burgundy, with gleaming golden handrails, appeared too clean, too immaculate considering the large number of daily tourists that climbed them. Maybe he was being unfair, had visited too many sombre, musty village churches in England, but the place felt less like a religious temple, and more like a custom-built tourist attraction. Until three monks in orange robes, walking together, nodded at him. Each of them carried a large silver-lidded bowl wrapped in orange.

Okay, so maybe he was wrong.

He decided to perch in the shade of a pavilion by one of the four cross-legged golden Buddhas at the foot of the staircase. From there, he watched the world go by, as the words of the old fortune teller coming back to him.

'You are on an island in Asia standing beneath a giant Buddha. You are waiting to meet your destiny.'

Fleetingly, he considered climbing the steps to the statue, but then realised that everyone heading up to the top via the only staircases had to pass him. Nearby, a Thai guide was talking to a small group of English-speaking tourists.

"In Thai, this called Wat Phra Yai, means Big Buddha temple. This is real working temple, with real Buddhist monk worship here. Buddha statue is twelve metre tall. Here we are on small island named Koh Farn, connected to mainland Koh Samui by causeway. Either side of stairway is half-human, half-serpent cobra called Naga, which lead up to Buddha. Not many year ago, a Dhamma wheel representing the Buddha's teachings to the path of enlightenment was added to the image."

Kieran stared at the group of fifteen or so tourists, four of them girls, all pretty, all with partners. Two of the party were good-looking guys, clearly a pair. Nobody really stood out. Every now and again, small groups or couples moved past him, either to scale the staircase or descend from the top. But there were no lightning bolts, no epiphanies, no sounds of swelling orchestral music. Half an hour passed like a life sentence and, very slowly, very gradually, a sinking feeling overcame him. Until he finally saw the funny side.

What the hell was he doing, he asked himself. Standing there moping, because of a comment made to him as a kid by somebody's grandmother pretending to be a fortune teller? At twenty-nine, he really ought to wise up and learn to let some things go. After finishing off his water, he dragged himself to his feet and decided to find the his friends. Blood-red clouds illuminated the skies now, and, right on cue, Steph appeared in front of him.

"Come on, you," she said, grinning fondly and slipping her arm into his. "Let's get back to the ship. Kennedy's probably missing us, and you most of all."

And, funnily enough, that throwaway remark lifted his spirits and put a smile back on his face.

Chapter Seventeen

Kennedy

On the morning of their ninth day at sea, the day after leaving Hanoi in Vietnam, the weather took a turn for the worse. Torrential rain lashed the deck as the ship skirted a typhoon. Colossal cruise ships such as the Diamond Princess had decent stabilisers, but the constant rolling motion still had a number of passengers holed up in their cabins.

Steph and Leonard went to ground for an entirely different reason. They'd both made a point of sampling street food on each of their excursions ashore. In Hanoi, both had come down with mild cases of food poisoning, according to the ship's doctor, who had prescribed loperamide to help reduce bouts of diarrhoea and oral rehydration sachets to mix with water and keep them hydrated. Apart from that, they were advised to drink plenty of room-temperature water, and get lots of bed rest while staying confined to their cabins.

Kennedy sat at lunch in the half empty restaurant with only Kieran and Laurie. Pete, who suffered acutely from seasickness, had also barricaded himself in his cabin. Eric had stayed to keep him company.

"Are we going to bail?" asked Laurie, who had stepped out for half an hour to grab some food. They had been chatting about Patrick's cocktail party. "I really ought to keep an eye on Steph."

Laurie had been with the group in Hanoi, and would usually have sampled the street fare, but her strict diet meant abstaining—luckily for her. Kieran had declined this particular excursion, preferring to stay onboard and keep Kennedy company.

Kennedy sighed. Not only had they all been invited to the drinks party in the early afternoon—and he felt a duty to make a show—but this was the evening of the captain's table event, where he and Steph were supposed to strut their stuff across the dance floor. Now everything had gone to pot.

"We can still go to Patrick's," said Kieran, leaning into Kennedy. "If you want."

Kennedy turned to him and grinned. Something had crystallised in Kieran since Koh Samui. Kennedy felt the change, but assumed he'd had high expectations of the island and had been disappointed. When Kennedy had questioned him, he'd shrugged off the concern. Whatever the reason, he'd become really relaxed and had stayed close to Kennedy ever since.

"Shame," said Kennedy. "I was looking forward to the dinner and dance. You don't think Steph might feel better by tonight?"

He'd watched the video Kieran had recorded a number of times, memorizing the steps. Now their moment in the spotlight had been snatched away.

"'Doubtful, Kennedy," said Laurie, worry creasing her forehead. "She can barely get out of bed, except for the occasional rush to the loo—"

"I know, I know. Sod's law," he said, before checking his watch. "In which case, one of us ought to make an effort to attend the cocktail party. To make apologies for the others, at the very least. We did get a gentle reminder, after all."

Patrick, who had been pretty much invisible the whole cruise, had sent Joey to Steph and Laurie's cabin the day before they arrived in Ho Chi Minh—the port before Hanoi—to remind them about the get-together.

"Kieran," said Kennedy, his hand on the younger man's shoulder. "Would you mind if I do this on my own? Might give me a chance to get Patrick alone and clear the air."

A brief frown passed across Kieran's face, replaced quickly by a faint smile. But Laurie answered before Kieran could respond.

"Why do you feel you have any air to clear? I don't, and neither does Steph," she said, her quiet anger sounding so much like her partner's. "He's the one that caused the rift. How about you get *him* to do some apologising?"

"Okay, Laurie," said Kennedy, somewhat surprised. Of the two, Laurie usually let Steph take the lead. "Play nicely. I wasn't talking about me apologising for anything—apologising is not something I do. But we need to have a conversation. Besides, my question was for Kieran."

He turned and watched Kieran mull over the words a moment before answering.

"As long as you're sure," he said, with a gentle smile that tugged at Kennedy's heart. "Do what you need to,

Kennedy. But I'm also happy to come with you, to stand by your side in case you need me."

And there it was again. Simple words of support. Nobody in his life offered him that, not even the staff to whom he paid significant wages, not even the partner of nine years who now hated his guts. And until recently, not even his own parents. But really, he needed to get Patrick alone and have the talk. What better opportunity?

"In which case," said Laurie, her obvious annoyance completely out of character, "if it's okay with Kieran, I'll accompany you. Maybe just for half an hour. They know me, so hopefully they won't start anything. But you're not going alone, Kennedy. Fuck that. You're not throwing yourself to those fucking wolves again. I still haven't forgotten that party six months ago. Anyone picks on you today, I'll sit on them."

Kieran laughed aloud. Something in his posture changed too, a slight relaxation of the shoulders.

"Okay. Then let's head there now," said Kennedy, standing to make his point. "I know it's bit early, but I'm with you. I'd prefer to get this over with. But please, can we keep things civil, Laurie?"

"Fine," said Laurie, rising too. One single word, and she sounded anything but fine. "Let me quickly text Steph. Let her know what's happening."

Kennedy felt bad about leaving Kieran. Like a trooper, he nodded and said he'd go back to the cabin to catch up on emails and messages, maybe read a little. Laurie led the way into the elevator and down a couple of floors, until they emerged into a long corridor. Halfway down, they stopped outside the door to Patrick's cabin, which stood open.

Four steps inside the living space of the two-bedroom cabin—a narrow area with a dining table against one wall, a three-seater sofa and a small bar—and Kennedy realised how grateful he felt to have Laurie with him. Looking at her face, he noticed how she'd also tensed up on seeing the cool stares they'd received as they entered. The truth hit home instantly from the expressions on Mike's and Richmond's familiar faces. Neither had expected them to show up. Fortunately, the four other guests were unknown and, apart from a quick once-over, paid them no heed. Patrick and his new partner did not appear to be around. But Richmond and Mike stood together at the bar assessing them like judge and jury. Kennedy approached with Laurie glued to his side, both adopting their game faces.

"You guys are early," said Mike, pleasantly enough.

"Yes, sorry. Thought we'd get here before the masses arrived," said Laurie. "Are you boys enjoying the cruise?"

"So far, so good," said Richmond, the older of the two. Until Kennedy's split with Patrick, Kennedy had always respected Richmond, had found his common sense refreshing and his business observations insightful. "Where are the others?"

"Steph and Leonard have food poisoning—" began Laurie.

"And let me guess," said Mike. "Pete's got a bout of seasickness?"

"Bingo. His dad's taking care of him."

"They do have pills for that kind of thing on the boat," said Richmond.

"He won't take them, Rich," said Mike. "Says they make him nauseous."

As they talked together — pleasantly enough — Kennedy pondered the strangeness of the situation, how these people used to be close friends, used to be in each other's pockets. Now, because of one simple act — him and Patrick splitting — sides had been taken.

Over drinks served by Richmond, they chatted mainly with Mike, reliving old holiday memories and laughing together. Kennedy had just started to relax when Laurie's phone beeped. Her face dropped as soon as she peered down at the display. More than likely, Steph needed her help. After thanking Mike and Richmond, and a quick apologetic and guarded nod to Kennedy, she excused herself. In her absence, Kennedy continued chatting until he peered around the room once more.

"Where's Patrick?" asked Kennedy. "I was hoping to have a chat with him."

Something in Richmond's eyes hardened.

"As I said, you're early. Joey persuaded him to get a massage before the main party. Tension relief. They went together," replied Richmond. "They'll be back any minute. Lay off him though, Kennedy, will you?"

"Rich," said Mike softly, touching his partner's arm. "Let it go."

"What do you mean?" asked Kennedy.

"You know exactly what I mean," said Richmond.

"Look," said Kennedy. "We need to talk, that's all. Just the two of us."

Richmond folded his arms, a grimace twisting his features.

"What you need to do is leave him the fuck alone. Everyone sees what you're doing. Hard not to. Still flaunting your pretty boys on the cruises in front of your friends year after year. How do you think that makes Patrick feel? I'll tell you how. He's now second-guessing himself, about whether you were doing the same thing when you were together—"

Kennedy's anger bristled. Was that really what his old friends—what Patrick—thought of him?

"That's unfair. I never once—"

"Maybe not, but try convincing him of that. You froze him out. How often did you guys have sex the last six months you were together?"

Kennedy glared at Richmond. How dare he call him out in public on something so personal. Had Patrick told all his friends about that last, dreadful year they'd spent together? Peripherally, he noticed the room had gone still and quiet around him.

"That's private—"

"I'll tell you how often. Not once. And now he's fucking torturing himself, because he believes you were getting your kicks elsewhere, because unlike him, you could afford to buy as many tricks as your dick desired. All those times you were away on working weekends, or business trips. What little piece of ass did you have along with you—bought and paid for—to fill your bed?"

Kennedy was too shocked to retaliate. Richmond's voice resonated throughout the cabin. 'Mike appeared uncomfortable, staring at the floor, unable to meet Kennedy's gaze but unwilling to interrupt his partner's onslaught.

"I did nothing of the sort," said Kennedy calmly, regaining some control. "Whoever's spreading those lies needs to check their facts."

"So are you denying that you pay these rent boys to come away with you on holiday?"

"For starters, they're not rent boys. And why they're here is nobody's business—"

"Oh, come on, Kennedy. People talk. Ewan told us all about your arrangement last year. So no doubt this year's plaything is on your payroll. Can you really blame Patrick for hating you? You fucked him up royally."

Everyone's eyes were on them now, boring into him, singling him out. They appeared to relish every accusation coming out of Richmond's mouth, bystanders enjoying a show. By now, Mike had turned away embarrassed.

"I did nothing of the sort—"

"You treated him like a piece of shit when you were together. Did you even know he was seeing a counsellor for depression when you dumped him? No, because you never bothered to ask, never gave a shit, would rather turn a blind eye if it didn't concern you. Even on this trip, he's barely left the cabin, because he's worried about bumping into you parading this year's top model. You are a sad, pathetic excuse of a man, Kennedy Grey."

Kennedy stood there stunned. Richmond's words stung. Did they believe he had purposely hurt Patrick? Because Patrick's exit from their relationship had taken him completely by surprise. Had he not been paying attention? Admittedly, keeping the company afloat had taken up much of his time back then. But why had none of these so-called friends warned him if they could see things falling apart? Until Patrick had walked out of the door, Kennedy had assumed everything was fine. Not perfect, perhaps, but what relationships were? Now Richmond stood there talking to him as though Kennedy were on trial with Richmond's own handpicked jury watching and judging him. Did all his friends feel the same way?

"I don't fucking need this," said Kennedy, slamming his glass down on the bar and heading for the exit. As he ripped the door open wide, Patrick and Joey stood there, about to enter, a look of genuine shock on both their faces.

"Yeah, go on," called Richmond, from somewhere behind. "Run away. It's what you do best."

Kennedy didn't stop, but pushed past them.

Enough of this shit, he thought. *I need a fucking drink.*

Chapter Eighteen

Kieran

Kieran took a hesitant step through the ship's club lounge door — a circular aluminium frame designed like a ship's portal — into the kaleidoscopic room. Mid-afternoon and the Underdeck Club had only a scattering of shadowy figures, most passengers preferring the fun found above deck. Like the aftermath of an all-night party, nobody danced. Few even moved, and those that did, did so in slow motion. Most languished around tall bar tables or lounged against the club's mirrored walls trying to perfect nonchalance or practiced boredom. Like bookends, two silhouettes of similar height stood together, leaning back on their elbows against the long pink-backlit bar, legs crossed at the ankles, staring out at the empty dance floor. Light chill-out music oozed from the speakers, repetitive and hypnotic, ethereal synthesizers with an ever-present and underlying beat. Mirror balls rotated slowly, sending multi-coloured constellations onto every surface. Combined with the gentle rolling motion of the ship, Kieran felt like throwing up.

Even in the gloom, he spotted Kennedy. Sitting hunched forward on the bottom step where three shallow stairs dropped to the frosted vinyl dance floor, he held his head stiffly aloft, elbows on knees, hands pressed together in front of his mouth as though in silent prayer. Kieran could tell by his tense shoulders and the way he glared angrily out across the open space that his mood had not improved. Laurie had texted him about the argument after being tipped-off by Joey, but she'd given him no details. A bottle of Heineken sat beside Kennedy. For a moment he thought he saw him talking to himself, but decided instead that he was chewing the inside of his mouth, a nervous habit Kieran had noticed a couple of times. He caught himself when a sudden wave of compassion mixed with affection flooded him. Kennedy would hate both.

A few single guys stood or sat nearby, but none seemed interested. Or perhaps they also sensed his turmoil. Then again, maybe someone his age needed to make the first move. Kieran had no idea how the whole gay hook-up thing worked. But for a bloke in his early forties, Kennedy was definitely in good shape. Kieran thought about his Uncle Angelo, his father's brother, at forty-nine. Couch potato boozer with bald head, saggy arse, swollen belly and multiple chins. Luckily for Kieran, he had his mother's genes. And Kennedy Grey was an inspiration, an aspiration even.

For a second, Kieran thought about turning around, heading back to the cabin and leaving the man to his pain. Any attempt at sympathy would be snubbed, that much he knew for sure. But whatever had been said in the cabin had taken its toll, and to ignore Kennedy now would be wrong. And after all, he had paid him for his companionship, so companionship he would get—whether he liked it or not. Kieran stopped on the top step to Kennedy's right, waiting until he noticed him.

"What do you want, Kieran?" muttered Kennedy harshly, after quickly glancing around, grimacing and turning back again.

"Thought you might like some company, old man."

"Well, I don't," he said, pushing a hand through his hair while glaring out across the half-empty dance floor. "If I'm lucky I might get laid. And you looming over me will only cramp my style."

Kieran ignored him and perched himself down.

"Style? What style? You don't have any."

"Fuck off, Kieran."

"No. Don't think I will. You never know, I might get lucky myself."

"If it's the blonde behind the bar with the red bow tie you're ogling, then don't waste your time. Belinda's a lipstick lesbian, and you don't have a vagina."

Kieran glanced over at the woman, who was currently wiping a glass and chatting to one of the spectres haunting the bar.

"She doesn't know what she's missing."

"Actually, she does. Before meeting her partner, Janine, she was married to a man for six years. Got two kids."

Kieran mulled that over for a while before responding.

"You ever been with a woman?"

"Of course. Uni days. Even had a girlfriend for six months. Didn't really float my boat. Obviously. Have you ever been with a guy?"

"No!"

Kieran went quiet then, remembering back to his high school days, when he and his mate, Robbie Menden, had jerked each other off in Kieran's bedroom. Admittedly they had been drooling over Robbie's older brother's straight porn mag at the time, but Kieran still remembered the intense orgasm as though it were yesterday. They had purposefully avoided each other after that. But even though it had not been full-blown sex, no way was he going to share that little titbit with Kennedy. Nor the fact that, on the day Kennedy had offered him the job, he had Googled gay sex and started to get a hard-on when one guy had given the other a blow job.

"Then it's you who doesn't know what he's missing. I'm sure any one of these chaps would be up to giving a good-looking bloke like you a good time."

"I'll pass, thanks."

"Suit yourself. I, on the other hand, desperately need a shag."

For some unexplainable reason, that statement sent a quiver of anxiety through Kieran. Maybe because he wondered if Kennedy would still want him around if he managed to shack up with someone.

"What about Simple Simon?"

"Simeon."

"I prefer my version. You do realise he fancies you, don't you?"

"Don't be ridiculous."

"Oh, come on, Kennedy. You're not blind and deaf. The way he can't do enough for you, that loud fake laugh when you make a frankly not very funny wisecrack about something. The way he checks out your ass every chance he can get. And especially the way he looks at me."

"How does he look at you?"

"Daggers. As if he'd like to stab me in the throat with the butter knife, then throw my body over the sea rail. Because he wants to be the one sitting next to you. Why don't you ring for him? I bet he'd be up for a shag."

"Not my type."

"So? Neither am I, as most of your friends have told me repeatedly. Despite me reaching down into the deepest, darkest teachings from the one term of acting classes I took in high school. Honestly, it's beginning to get on my tits, the way they keep casually dropping the fact into every conversation."

When Kieran looked over, Kennedy's shoulders were shaking with laughter.

"Sorry about that. But they know I have a type."

"You don't say. So pardon me for not being an emaciated, dumb blond elf and actually having an informed opinion about things."

Kennedy chuckled softly.

"They're right, though," said Kennedy, gently shaking his head. "God, I really can be shallow at times."

"No argument from me."

"Fuck off."

"You want a drink?" asked Kieran. "I'll put it on the room."

"Cabin. Yeah, go on. If I'm not going to get laid, I might as well get drunk. Get me a Long Island Iced Tea."

"Done."

Kieran returned and sat down next to Kennedy before handing over his drink. When Kennedy saw the two rainbow-colored umbrellas sticking out of his tall glass, he huffed loudly and rolled his eyes, but a corner of his mouth lifted.

"D'you want to talk about it? You and Patrick?"

As soon as the words left Kieran's mouth he regretted them, for instantly dampening Kennedy's improved mood. He glared sidelong at Kieran before shaking his head and exhaling a long sigh. Kieran thought that meant he didn't, but after a few moments Kennedy started talking softly.

"I honestly didn't know he was going to be here. Pete says they booked at the last minute. If I'd known, I probably wouldn't have agreed to come."

"Why?"

"Because it's not worth the aggravation. And if you'd heard Richmond's delightful sermon, you'd know I'm the supervillain in all of this. Used up nine good years of his life. And then I went and ruined everything."

"You cheated on him?"

"Of course not. Unless you call prioritizing work over social life cheating."

"He broke up with you because you worked too hard?"

"In his defence, I did fuck up a lot. Often at the last minute. Dinner dates, birthday parties, Christmases, a number of holidays. But even though it was a nuisance, I assumed he was okay with that, thought he knew I had to work hard to make a success of the business. Which meant we could also afford the luxury house, nice cars, designer clothes and the whole comfortable lifestyle. And the bloody cruises, for Christ's sake."

"I see."

"*He* broke up with *me*, you know? Not the other way round."

"You still have feelings for him?"

Kennedy thought about that for a long moment before responding.

"Yes, but not in the way you think. More like disappointment, really. And sadness, I suppose. He's still bitter at me, otherwise he wouldn't be telling every new partner those unpleasant things. Don't even know what he has to gain. You should have heard what Richmond said about me in their cabin. In front of everyone. Accused me of cheating on him, even when we were together, which is a barefaced lie. And he as good as called you my paid whore."

"Well, I am, really. Without the sex. Shit, maybe we should get married."

Kieran warmed inside when Kennedy laughed aloud. Putting the straw to his lips, he sucked at the cocktail before becoming serious again.

"I should have wised up by now. The same thing happened the last time we all met up. Leonard's birthday party, I think it was. He had some new guy with him then, too. Ben or Bob. Remember this bloke holding court in the kitchen, going on very loudly in front of everyone about how I fuck with people's lives. And how I would probably die alone and single—a sad, lonely old man, with no friends and nobody to take care of me."

"Boo-hoo."

"Exactly. I'd been standing outside, but barged in at that point and told them all that when that particular eventuality comes along, at least I'll be able to afford the best drugs and be able to hire a drop-dead gorgeous gay male nurse to be at my beck and call—"

"Kennedy," Kieran interrupted. "Don't want to pee in your iced tea, but Patrick just walked in."

"Where?" asked Kennedy, sharply, darting his head up and peering around like a frightened ferret.

"Ten o'clock. Side door."

"Shit. Sit in front of me."

"What?"

"Sit in front of me. You're supposed be my bloody boyfriend, remember?"

Rather than sitting in front, Kieran perched himself behind Kennedy, squashed up against the man's back, his knees on either side. For a second, Kennedy froze, before he released an exasperated sigh while shaking his head. Peering over Kennedy's right shoulder, Kieran could see Patrick squinting around the room, trying to get accustomed to the dim lighting. Kieran had no doubt he had come looking for someone, and it wasn't difficult to guess who.

"Quick," Kennedy hissed over his shoulder. "Kiss me."

"What? I am not fucking —"

"Five hundred. I'll give you an extra five hundred pounds. Please!"

"Shit. Turn your face to me, then."

Kennedy turned halfway, while Kieran craned forward and closed the distance between them, crushing their lips together. When Kieran first leaned in, he expected the man's lips to be firm, solid even, certainly not so soft and pliable. Before the thought had a chance to take hold, Kennedy opened his lips and...*whoa*. Moist warmth filled his mouth as their tongues collided, Kieran tasting the sweet cola and sharp bite of spirits in Kennedy's mouth. Part of his brain knew they were faking, but the sudden contact fired up his synapses, tingling his nerve endings, stoking his heartbeat and reaching all the way down to his groin. Within seconds he was no longer pretending, but throwing himself into the kiss, hungry after days of zero physical contact, his body on sexual autopilot. When he tilted his head to take in more of Kennedy's mouth, the man beneath him rumbled with pleasure, the most simple yet carnal of sounds, which set Kieran's blood hammering through his veins and his erection straining against his shorts, nudging Kennedy's back. He barely heard the angry voice growing louder and repeating over and over, the same mantra that kept pace with the blood pounding through his brain — *Ken, Ken, Ken.*

"Ken! For fuck's sake!"

Kennedy pulled his face away and, for a split second, stared aghast at Kieran before slowly turning his attention to the voice.

"I have no idea what game you're trying to play," said Patrick, towering over them, his hands on his hips, "but you're not fooling anyone."

Kieran could see the anger in Patrick's face but barely acknowledged the words coming out of his mouth. Thoughts of the kiss and his reaction to the encounter still shimmered through his slowly calming body, confusing the hell out of him.

"We need to talk. But not in front of that," said Patrick, nodding at Kieran. Finally, his conscious mind and his body began to coalesce, his annoyance sharpening at this man who had just reduced him to something inanimate.

"You want me to stay?" Kieran whispered into Kennedy's ear.

Kennedy said nothing, continuing to stare up at the man.

"No, he wants you gone, you little prick. Go up on deck and play with the other children. Leave the grown-ups to talk grown-up things."

"Kennedy?" asked Kieran, a little louder.

Still no reaction.

"Don't you know when to take a hint, kid? Just get the fuck away and leave us alone, will you?"

"Kennedy!" barked Kieran, angry now, shaking Kennedy's shoulder and startling him out of whatever reverie had taken him.

"Go back to the cabin," said Kennedy, his voice soft and odd. Then over his shoulder, "Please. I'll come and join you soon."

When Kieran peered up, Patrick stood leaning back slightly with his arms folded, a smug grin on his face. Cold anger and embarrassment swept through Kieran as he struggled to his feet. Standing still for a moment, staring at the top of Kennedy's head, he had been about to fire back something caustic at Patrick. But what was the point?

He'd been dismissed.

Instead, he turned around and headed out of the door without a backwards glance.

Enough already.

Chapter Nineteen

Kennedy

The sudden loss of warmth from Kieran's body took Kennedy by surprise. During the kiss — from a supposedly straight man, no less — something strange had happened inside him. A simple truth had come to light, something that had been so obvious, so fundamental, that he had been blind to it all these years.

"We need to talk," came the voice of his ex-lover.

Nine years, to be precise. He had spent nine years of his life with the man in front of him. Pretty much all of his thirties. And in all that time, they had never been in love. Not really, if they were both going to be honest. Maybe they had loved each other once, in a brotherly kind of way. Kennedy had provided a financial security blanket while Patrick had brought domesticity and continuity. But they'd been nothing more than a partnership of convenience.

"Kennedy! Are you listening to me?"

"Yes, Patrick," he replied calmly, peering up at Patrick instead of looking through him. No doubt about it, his ex still looked good — a little heavier of frame perhaps, but still handsome and in good shape. Over Patrick's shoulder, he noticed Joey rush into the bar, but on seeing them together, he moved to one side of the room, a few metres away.

"First of all, what's with snogging the rent boy? Was that show put on just for me?"

"Okay, enough, Patrick. Let's put a few things straight, shall we?"

"Straight? Fine. Let me start. In case you didn't know, your boy's got a girlfriend back in England."

"Yes, I know he *had* a girlfriend. Just like you and I *had* girlfriends back in university."

"You don't get it, do you? Just like the last one, this little cocksucker moron's taking you for a ride —"

"No!" said Kennedy, standing and meeting Patrick's gaze. "You do not get to slag off Kieran! Have a pop at me all you want, but leave Kieran alone. He's been nothing short of heroic for standing by me and putting up with this whole stupid charade. Yes, Richmond told me in no uncertain terms what everyone thinks of me, but Kieran deserves none of it. Only one man on this ship has defended me through all of this, and that's Kieran."

"Yeah, because you're paying him to."

"Not true. I'm paying him to be a companion, not a defender. The lot of you managed to turn Ewan against me last year, and I was paying him, too. But unlike the rest of you evil bastards, Kieran has a good heart. And he's the first person who has ever *got* me. Understands why I do what I do, what I've achieved despite everything and everyone. Someone who sees the things I've accomplished without being jealous or judgmental."

"Like me, you mean?"

"If we're going for honesty, then, yes."

"Fucking unbelievable," Patrick spat out, turning his head away. "Still reinventing history much? You always did put your work before us. Never put any time aside for me. You alone were the one responsible for ruining us."

"No. It takes two, Patrick. I admit I spent a lot of time getting one deal after another off the ground. I was single-handedly trying to salvage my uncle's company from going under. You knew that. But you never gave me any encouragement or support. All you ever did was either whine endlessly or nit-pick everything I did, especially when I got home dog tired. Berating me for where I dropped my jacket, or if I slept the night on the sofa, or what channel I watched on the television. You made life in that house unbearable. And now Richmond tells me you thought I was cheating on you all that time, while I was away at weekends working my ass off. That is not only untrue, but monumentally unfair and, frankly, unforgivable. You know what? The day you stormed out, I felt as though I could finally breathe again."

Patrick stood unspeaking then, but a change occurred in him. His eyes became teary, the revelation having clearly hit home. Kennedy didn't want that. From the start, he had only wanted to clear the air, but not at the expense of hurting Patrick's feelings. When he looked around, he noticed Joey had left.

"It's been five years, Pat. You need to let this go. For both our sakes."

Patrick unfolded his arms and thrust his hands into his pockets.

"Richmond told me you've barely left the cabin the whole cruise," said Kennedy. "Is that true?"

Oddly enough, Patrick smiled at that comment.

"Rich has a tendency to exaggerate. Of course we've left the room for meals. But Joey can be very demanding in the bedroom."

Kennedy's spluttered laughter, which had Patrick chuckling too, finally dissolved any remaining tension between them.

"We're never getting back together, are we?" asked Patrick, as though he already knew the answer.

Kennedy smiled sadly and shook his head very gently.

"Joey's nice, Pat. And he clearly worships you. You two suit each other."

"He's young, and messy. And a bit of a scatterbrain where finances are concerned."

"Which is why he needs someone like you."

* * * *

Kennedy passed only a handful of fellow passengers on his way back to the cabin, everyone else undoubtedly getting dressed up for the captain's dinner that evening. When he reached the double doors, he took a deep breath before swiping his key card. Things had needed to be said—damage limitation—and he had let sleeping dogs lie with Patrick for far too long. Neither of them liked to apologise. Even so, trepidation unsettled his stomach now. He had meant what he'd said to Patrick, about Kieran being a decent guy. But Kennedy had forced that kiss on him and overstepped the boundaries he had set. If Kieran was pissed off at him, he had every right to be.

Inside the room, lights blazed but nobody appeared to be there. When he walked into the bedroom, Kieran's case sat open on top of the bed. Why was he packing? They weren't due in Hong Kong for four days. Had Kennedy succeeded in scaring him away?

"Kieran?" he called out.

No answer.

For the next thirty minutes, after checking with his friends, he searched all the places on the boat Kieran liked to hang out — the coffee shop, the bowling alley, the cinema. Eventually, he headed up onto the rain-glistening deck, where the bad weather had finally cleared, to the relaxing spot along the sea rail with the row of chairs and sun loungers.

"Kieran?"

The familiar figure pressed up against the deck railing made no sign of acknowledgment. Perhaps a slight movement of the head or a stiffening of the body, hard to tell in the dimness of twilight. There was most definitely an exhalation of smoke from a cigarette Kieran had been nursing. Just as Kennedy thought, the damage had been done, maybe too late to salvage anything — but he had to try. Taking a deep breath, he stepped forward and joined the 'Hate Kennedy' party.

Standing there companionably for a while, following Kieran's gaze out to sea, he gathered the right words to say. On the horizon, the last vestiges of the day's light tinted the sky, shimmering an orange and purple mélange across the tips of the waves. A couple of times Kennedy chanced a sidelong look, but Kieran kept his gaze trained on the ocean, taking an occasional puff from the cigarette.

"Beautiful, isn't it?" said Kennedy. "Did you know that twilight has three phases? Civil twilight is what we're seeing now. Starts right after sunset, once the sun's lost from view and drops to around six degrees below the horizon. The second is called nautical twilight, between six and twelve degrees, and the third is astronomical twilight, between twelve and eighteen. On a good day, like today, twilight is accompanied by a spectacular light show."

"So what's dusk?"

"Officially, dusk is the transition from the darkest phase of twilight, just before night kicks in."

"What is it about the human race that we have to categorise something as lovely and natural as sunset?" asked Kieran, still observing the horizon.

"Twilight."

"Sunset. Twilight. What-the-fuck-ever."

"Back before television and the Internet," explained Kennedy, "people had a lot of time to kill. Man had to do something with all those spare hours. Apart from reading, writing and masturbation."

A snort of laughter next to him gave Kennedy a tiny ray of hope.

"What I asked of you earlier, in the club, was wrong. I panicked and I'm— I regret that. What I should have done was to grow some balls and deal with the situation on my own. A few years ago, actually. The way I've had to all my life. If I made you uncomfortable, that was unintentional."

"Are you apologising?"

"I don't apologise, remember? Look, Kieran, we have another four days on the boat. I can't do anything about that. But if you want, I can rearrange your flight so that you can fly back home from Hong Kong. I'll still honour the deal. Make sure you get the full amount plus the additional money for the—umm—extra service I asked you to perform. You've been a trooper— I truly mean that—and you've put up with more shit than anyone else in your place would have done. More than I ever would have. And I respect you for that."

Kennedy fell silent then, hoping that Kieran would say something, anything.

Nothing came.

"And if you don't want to come with me to the captain's table dinner tonight, I'll also understand—"

"Are you fucking kidding me?" said Kieran, turning to him and stubbing out the remains of the cigarette on the sea rail. "What kind of message would that send to the assholes you used to call friends? Fuck that, I'm coming. And I'm bringing my best game."

"O-kay," said Kennedy, a touch apprehensively. As a businessman, Kennedy had learned to deal with a fair amount of bravado in his time. Kieran's fierce tone and somewhat veiled threat made him a little nervous.

"But I'll be getting changed in Steph and Laurie's cabin," continued Kieran. "Even though she's still sick, Steph's insisting on adjusting the length of my dress suit trousers and then pressing them. And Laurie's going to give my hair a quick trim. So I'll be coming with Laurie and I'll see you there."

Kieran's assertive tone appeared to leave no room for negotiation.

"Understood," said Kennedy, disappointment filling his stomach like concrete. Part of his enjoyment over the evenings on the cruise had been in getting dressed for dinner together, assessing each other's choice of evening wear. "And will you be joining us for pre-dinner drinks?"

"Might be a little late, but I'll be there. Okay?"

"Thank you. Are we good, then?"

"We're getting there, Kennedy. We're getting there."

Chapter Twenty

Kieran

While Laurie stood behind him with her scissors clipping away, a wildfire of thoughts and feelings swept through Kieran. After brushing his teeth twice, he could still taste tobacco, something he hated. Steph, who had improved remarkably — colour having returned to her cheeks — plied him with breath mints, which helped. But the anger and confusion unsettled him most of all. All of his friends or family knew that he didn't get annoyed easily. Calm and even-tempered, his mother and teachers had called him. Cold and unemotional had been Jennifer's spin. So why had Kennedy's dismissal lit such an angry fire in his belly?

Jennifer had ejected him from her home and her life and he had accepted without question, had almost welcomed the chance to escape. Kennedy's rejection had ripped a hole in him.

"Are you okay, Kieran?" asked Laurie, once again. Standing in front of him.

"I'm fine, I just…" began Kieran, but he decided not to elaborate. He'd told them both what had happened in the Underdeck Club—an abridged version—and Kennedy's later attempt at an apology.

"Patrick's a prick," said Laurie, snipping decisively at a lock. "Always has been, always will be. Don't take anything he said to heart. He's not worth the effort."

She was right, of course. If he ought to be angry at anyone, that person should be Patrick, not Kennedy. Joey had even turned up at their cabin earlier and explained what had happened after he'd left, how Kennedy had defended him to Patrick. And just like that, his anger had turned to bewilderment.

And the one thing that should have been confusing the hell out of him—the kiss—seemed to be the only thing that made sense. Nothing about the embrace had felt wrong. He'd kissed a man and he'd liked it, he thought, almost humming the words of the song. He'd kissed a number of girls, some passionately, but as far as he could remember, nothing—*nothing*—had compared to that mind-blowing lip lock with Kennedy Grey. *Fuck.* The mere visualization of Kennedy's lips and mouth had his heart speeding up and blood pumping below deck. He'd almost been tempted to text Cole and ask what the hell the fiery embrace might have meant. Then again, did he really want to know?

"What's with you tonight?" said Laurie, stopping and placing her hands on her hips. "One minute you're grimacing like a grizzly, the next you're leering like a leopard."

"Very poetic." Kieran grinned.

"Leave him be, Laurie," said Steph, watching from the ironing board where she was carefully pressing his suit trousers. His white shirt and jacket hung on the wardrobe door, waiting to be worn. "He's had enough drama for one day."

Right then, there came a knock at the cabin door. Laurie turned to look at Steph, who merely shrugged. Being the nearest to the door, Steph went to answer. After a few moments, her tone began to sound irritated, and when she came into the room the anger showed clearly on her face.

"It's Richmond."

"What does that bastard want?" asked Laurie, before Kieran could voice the same thing.

"He wants to talk to Kieran. Privately. I said I'm not letting him in. Do you want me to tell him to piss off, Kieran? I will, if you say so."

Interesting, thought Kieran. *Why does he want to speak to me? And why alone?*

"No, it's fine. Give me a second," he said, getting up, the towel still around his shoulders. "Let me get this out of the way."

Richmond stood in the corridor, looking ill at ease, but brought his attention to Kieran as soon as he appeared.

"Look, I'm not here to make trouble," he said, holding his palms up in front. "I just have one thing to say, and then I'm gone. A lot of us think Kennedy and Patrick belong together, believe they always have done. But ultimately, if that's going to happen, it's between the two of them. I don't know what kind of hold you think you have over Kennedy, but whatever it is, you should know that as soon as this holiday is done, you'll be history. That is not meant to be unkind, nor a reflection on who you are as a person, it's simply a fact. I'm telling you this now in case you think of him as anything more than a holiday fling."

"Do you even like him?" asked Kieran. "Kennedy?"

Whatever response Richmond had been expecting, the one Kieran provided clearly caught him by surprise.

"I used to. When he made my best friend happy."

"Which was rarely, as far as I can tell."

Richmond's gaze hardened. He took a step back and folded his arms, openly assessing Kieran.

"You may not be like the others, but don't be deceived. You're still disposable."

"We'll see," said Kieran, deciding not to rise to the bait. "Thanks for the helpful advice. Hope to see you at dinner."

Richmond frowned and shook his head. Kieran had no idea what the man had expected — maybe a fit of tears or an argument. But after a final glare, he turned and headed back along the corridor.

When Kieran backed into the apartment and closed the door, Steph and Laurie waited frozen where he had left them. Steph broke the silence, by telling him they had overheard snippets of the conversation. After Kieran had provided a summary, punctuated by the girls using words such as 'prick' and 'arsehole' and other suitable expletives, they got back to the business at hand.

"You know, I ought to be paying you two for doing this," he said, sitting back down again. Steph had clambered from her sickbed to iron his clothes, while Laurie had tamed his wild hair and got him looking fresh-faced. Both of them helped him dress in the kind of attire he'd never worn before. Not only that, but being away from Kennedy in their company had been good for him, giving him time to assess himself.

"Maybe I can buy you a meal when we reach Okinawa tomorrow afternoon."

"Ugh," said Steph, placing the iron back in the holder. "Not sure I'll be ready for solids for a few more days."

"Although there might be something else you could help us with—" began Laurie.

"Later, dear," said Steph, cutting her off with a short glance.

"In which case, do me a favour by joining me on the excursion," said Laurie. "They're going to be visiting Shuri Castle—something I've always wanted to see, a UNESCO World Heritage site. The castle has only recently reopened after a fire nearly destroyed the whole place. You can be my companion."

Kieran liked that idea. Kennedy hadn't done any of the excursions, so most probably wouldn't want to step off the boat at Okinawa.

"Of course. But we'd be really doing each other a favour, keeping each other company. I'll still like to buy you both a meal when Steph feels better."

"Then let's save it for Hong Kong," said Laurie, brushing something from his ear. "Maybe you can treat us to dim sum."

"Deal," said Kieran, even though he had no idea what that was. "Are you going to be joining us tonight, Steph?"

"Sorry, doll. Not tonight. Even the thought of seeing food makes me want to barf."

"Plan B, then?"

"Plan B," said Steph, with a smile.

"Right, Mr West. I think you're about ready," said Laurie, after finally raking a comb through his locks before removing the towel from around his shoulders. "Go to the bathroom mirror and take a look."

"Should I shave?" he asked, feeling the slight roughness around his chin. Usually he shaved once every three days, especially when he wasn't working. But he wondered if clean-shaven should be the order of the evening.

"I don't think so," said Steph, and Laurie agreed. "But let's wait until you've showered and tried on the suit before we decide. Go and check your hair first."

Unlike Kennedy's cabin, the girls had a humble living area and their bathroom felt a little cramped, with every surface holding some kind of cosmetic product or device. At first, seeing his hair shorter made him grimace. But then Laurie had left enough stylish twists and tufts to make the cut appear more edgy and fashionable. Maybe he could get used to the new style. Locking the bathroom door and undressing, he climbed into their shower and let the warm waters drench him, cleaning himself with the girls' confusing selection of products.

Once he had dried off, he returned to the main room with a towel wrapped around his waist. Laurie had already changed into her outfit, a stylish lilac pantsuit deftly showing off her weight loss. Earlier on, he'd observed Steph help to apply Laurie's makeup, complete with blended purple eye shadow and deep purple lipstick. Now Steph provided the finishing touches as well as fixing Laurie's hair.

"Don't just stand there ogling. Get dressed," said Laurie, pointing at the wardrobe. "You and I are supposed to be meeting the men for drinks in fifteen minutes."

Kieran set to work, sitting on the edge of their bed, removing the towel and pulling on his underwear and trousers. Next came the wing-tip shirt which, fortunately, was fitted and tucked nicely beneath the waistband. By the time he got to the bow tie and cummerbund, Steph had finished and came over to help. Finally he put on the jacket before squeezing into the tight, shiny black shoes. After brushing something from his shoulder then pinning in place a pink rose buttonhole, Steph got him to back up a few steps so that she and Laurie could survey their handiwork.

"Before you say anything," said Kieran. "Can I just tell how much I love you both for doing this. I wouldn't have known where to start."

Like proud mothers, they smiled and nodded before looking at each other. Steph leaned in and pecked Laurie on the lips, before returning her gaze to him.

"Well? Come on," Kieran said, holding his hands out to the sides. "How do I look?"

"Heavens above," said Steph. She had her arm around Laurie's waist, carefully studying Kieran from head to toe. "What kind of beautiful monster have we created, Mrs Shelley?"

Chapter Twenty-One

Kennedy

Kennedy fiddled with the gold cufflink on his left sleeve and peered nervously towards the large doors to the room. Tonight's event showcased another side of the gay community. Two nights ago, at the White Party, some of these men had been sexy Snow Queens or Marilyn Monroes, complete with platinum wigs and high heels. Others had worn next to nothing — loincloths or Roman togas. Tonight, with most people dressing in either black tie or evening gowns, his mother and father wouldn't have looked out of place. Although on a closer inspection, dotted around the room, some guests had chosen alternatives — white, powder pink, or blue tuxes, and some men had chosen drag, dressing gloriously in stunning gowns. Kennedy would normally have enjoyed the splashes of non-conformity, but his mind remained elsewhere.

Once again, he checked his watch, then brushed at an imaginary dust mark on his sleeve.

"For goodness' sake, Kennedy, will you stop fidgeting—oh, fuckity-fuck," said Pete, gazing over Kennedy's left shoulder, his eyes going wide. Along with the lull in the weather, Pete had emerged from his cabin that evening.

"What?" asked Kennedy, spinning around, but seeing nothing through the crowd.

"Fuck my old boot," said Pete, his mouth hanging open. "Queer One scrubs up good."

And Kennedy spied him—Kieran—with Laurie on his arm, and a sudden pride swelled in his chest like an inflating airbag. Kieran absolutely rocked the dress suit, a perfect fit with a black bow tie and dark red—burgundy—cummerbund. Not only that, but his hair had been trimmed and tamed with gel, and he moved with an easy confidence Kennedy had never noticed before. All heads turned as he passed, some clustering together to dish about this deliciously handsome male specimen.

Prince Charming had arrived at the ball.

Laurie stopped and looked around before whispering something in Kieran's ear. After finishing, she nodded towards Kennedy and Pete before moving off. Kieran strolled over to join them. On his way, he plucked a flute of champagne from a passing waiter, who smiled then turned to give Kieran's departing back a once-over.

"Look at you, Mr Hottie," said Pete, as Kieran arrived. "Licensed to kill."

"You look really good, Kieran," said Kennedy, amazed at how shy he sounded.

"These bloody shoes are killing me," said Kieran, grimacing down at his stylish black patent leather dress shoes.

"Style comes at a price, kid," said Pete, whose own dress suit had seen better days. "Where's Laurie gone?"

"To let the MC know Kennedy and Steph aren't going to be dancing tonight."

"Yes, it's a shame she's not better," said Kennedy. "Still, maybe you and I could take a turn on the floor later? Once the contest is over?"

"We'll see," said Kieran, his expression unreadable.

Even though they'd managed to secure a table bordering the dance floor, their party's depleted size had meant other passengers—complete strangers— joining them at their table. Kieran chose to sit away from Kennedy, between Laurie and a nice-looking older man. Kennedy glanced Kieran's way a couple of times, admiring his newfound confidence. Kieran continued to engage the man beside him in conversation, not once turning in Kennedy's direction.

After a served meal of lobster bisque, with a choice of filet mignon, black cod or vegetarian pasta, followed by a selection of desserts, cheeses and coffee, the first of the dancers took to the floor.

Two large bears, dressed in pink and blue tuxedos, danced the cha-cha. Although light on their feet, they came frighteningly close a couple of times, and at one point he thought they might crash into their table. Kennedy's favourite came in the form of a mountain of a man, completely bald, dressed in a sleeveless, flowing dress in sparkling electric blue, with one arm showcasing an inked sleeve tattoo. The man's lesbian friend, dressed in a bright-red dress suit, looked like a character out of the Dick Tracy movie. They made an unlikely but mesmerizing couple. Energetically performing the Lindy-Hop, the pair had the whole room clapping along to their routine. Once the applause died down, the announcer moved back to the microphone.

"Ladies and gentlemen, a slight change to the programme. Due to one half of the original male-female couple being unwell — a touch of the Saigon squirts, by all accounts — tonight's dance will instead be performed by two gentlemen. Please give a big hand for Kennedy Grey and Kieran West."

Amid the sound of applause, Kennedy looked around, shocked, to find Kieran standing behind his chair, his hand held out, palm upwards.

"Come on, old man," said Kieran, his voice and face stern. "Exactly the same as you practiced with Steph. Every step the same. Let me lead, and you follow. Are we cool?"

Stunned and unable to reply coherently, Kennedy allowed Kieran to take his hand and lead him to the centre of the dance floor. Kieran adopted the same starting position he and Steph had agreed upon. As the music began — the staccato rhythm of *El Tango de Roxanne* — Kieran moved in perfect sync with Kennedy, their eyes glued to each other.

Often, when dancing with Steph, she had been unable to maintain the fierce glare between them, usually dissolving into a fit of giggles. Kieran's eyes never once left his and positively smouldered with sexual innuendo. Each time Kieran crushed their bodies together, at one point bending Kennedy's body backwards while closely hovering over him, he inhaled Kieran's unique body smell mixed with something that smelt bizarrely like Steph, the kind of distinctive perfumed shower gel she used. At the end of the dance, with a final flourish, they ended frozen in place, their hands joined above their heads and their foreheads pressed together. Around the room, the watching crowd erupted into loud cheers and applause. When Kennedy finally relaxed and peered over at their table, he noticed Laurie grinning broadly while fanning her face with her napkin.

The band changed gear into a gentle two-step, allowing everyone to join them on the dancefloor. Kennedy had been about to head back to their table, but Kieran pulled him into the dance. Within seconds the floor filled around them, with a few people — other gay couples — leaning in to congratulate the two of them on their performance. Kennedy shook his head, still stunned.

"That was amazing. How the hell did you memorise those steps?"

"Child's play. Although, of course, the video helped. My cousin and I were West London Under Fifteen Ballroom Champions in our youth. Three years running. Unlike you, though, I loved dancing lessons. Still step out every now and then whenever she's in town."

"Aren't you full of surprises?"

"You have no idea. There's a lot about me you don't know, Mr Grey."

"Clearly. So does this mean I'm forgiven?"

"For what?" asked Kieran, a puzzled expression on his face.

"For everything," said Kennedy. "Forcing the kiss on you. Not standing up for you in front of Patrick when he was being a royal prick. For making you smoke a cigarette."

"According to Joey, you did stand up for me. Only you did so after I'd left."

Kennedy snorted. He'd forgotten Joey had rushed into the bar after Kieran had walked off and would have heard his heated exchange with Patrick.

"And for the record, you didn't force me to kiss you. Bribed, maybe. But nothing was forced on me. Besides, that must be the quickest monkey anyone's ever made."

"Monkey, huh?" said Kennedy, grinning at the cockney money slang. "I meant it, though, you know? I will honour that deal."

"Yeah, but I only really gave you about a hundred and fifty quid's worth. How about the other three-fifty?"

"You get that anyway. For having to put up with my shit."

Kennedy allowed Kieran to twirl him around until he faced the table where Richmond and Mike sat watching, probably murmuring sweet nothings about them both. Patrick and Joey had not joined them.

"Nah," whispered Kieran in his ear, before spinning him back round. "Got a much better idea."

In front of the whole room, Kieran brought their lips together, but before they could connect, Kennedy placed his hands on Kieran's chest, and held him back.

"Kieran, you don't have to do this. People will see us, will see you."

"Uh, that's kind of the point. Plus, I need to test something out. So please indulge me for a minute or two."

Once again Kieran moved forward, and this time Kennedy closed his eyes, felt the full force of Kieran's lips press against his. At first, the kiss was tentative, a brush of lips as though exploring, but then Kieran teased open his lips. Once their tongues collided, Kieran tilted his head, his hands weaving through Kennedy's hair, drawing him forward. When he deepened the kiss, when their tongues began to dance their private tango, Kennedy crushed their bodies tightly together. Eventually they came up for air, and Kennedy's heart filled to see Kieran's startled gaze, as well as his plump lips, moist and reddened, and his dilated pupils.

"My God, Kennedy! I really like kissing you. What does that say about me?"

"That you have good taste."

"Can we head back to the cabin?" asked Kieran, ignoring the quip and instead plucking a playing card from his top pocket. "I've had this jack of spades burning a hole in my pocket for days now. And I think I'm finally ready to trade it in tonight."

"I don't understand. Is that why you're packing?" asked Kennedy, confused. "But you know I can't fly you out until the end of the cruise."

"I wasn't packing. I was trying to find my bloody bow tie. And anyway, that's not what I'm asking. I want to trade this baby in for its original purpose. I want to swap this for one of your world famous, apparently mind-numbing blow jobs. Best in the northern hemisphere, according to my sources."

"Hang on, Kieran. Are you sure? You don't have to do this."

"Fuck that. I'm the one getting the blow job, not you. You think you're man enough?"

After staring at him for a couple of seconds, Kennedy grabbed Kieran by the hand and dragged him off the dance floor back towards their room.

Chapter Twenty-Two

Kieran

"FuckohfuckohfuckohFUCKOHFUCKOH."

Kieran's body had become a massive active volcano, with a devastating eruption only milliseconds away.

Until.

"NOOoooo!"

For the third time, Kennedy had brought Kieran right to the toe-curling edge of what promised to be the best orgasm of his life, caressing Kieran's balls with one hand and drawing that talented mouth and tongue up and down his eager, granite-hard shaft—only to pull his mouth away with a pop seconds before lift-off.

"What the fuck are you doing to me?" Kieran whimpered.

"Giving you your money's worth," said Kennedy, smiling up at Kieran, those cool blue eyes gazing playfully.

"You're not, you're torturing me. I swear, Kennedy," said Kieran, pleading, "if you don't finish me off soon, I'm going to have to take matters into my own hands. Literally."

Just after they'd entered the cabin and Kennedy had switched on the 'do not disturb' sign, as Kieran had kicked off his shoes in the upstairs bedroom, a wave of uncertainty had hit him. But Kennedy had pulled him into a gentle kiss, which had initially calmed him before turning molten, reigniting Kieran's arousal. Grinning hungrily, Kennedy had pushed him back onto the mattress, pulling off Kieran's trousers and underpants completely before obliging with his promised '*deluxe service*'. Lying back on the bed, his knees hanging over the end of the mattress, Kieran had watched in awe and bliss as Kennedy had devoured him. Right now, his head bobbed up and down, mouth sucking hard, combined with his snakelike tongue's caress around his shaft, one hand gripping the base, pumping, gradually building speed.

Kieran's hands clutched handfuls of duvet as his thighs begin to tremble, his head thrown back onto the mattress, a carnal roar issuing from somewhere deep inside. Kennedy finally sent him over the precipice, swallowing Kieran's whole length into his throat as the inevitable orgasm ripped through him. Without removing his mouth, Kennedy took every drop Kieran had to offer, with Kieran moaning loudly and unashamedly, his heart thumping, dark spots flickering across his vision.

Lying there, staring up unseeing, he wondered if he should be freaking out a little right now that another man had just blown him. But he wasn't. In fact, if Kennedy offered to do him again, he'd definitely not only let him, he'd plead with him — well, maybe after resting up a little. Sex had always been a bit like going through the motions with Jennifer. And she had avoided oral sex, usually wanted to get the main deed over and done with as quickly as possible, without too much fuss or foreplay. If this was his initiation to gay sex, then he was fucked. What other incredible delights might be in store?

"Are you okay?" came Kennedy's voice.

Kieran's addled brain tried to find the words.

"Feels as though you turned all the bones in my body to liquid and then sucked them out through my cock."

"Eloquent," said Kennedy, after laughing aloud.

Kieran just about managed to raise his head and stare at the man between his legs.

"Get up here," said Kieran. "Next to me."

Kieran enjoyed ordering Kennedy around, and, oddly enough, every time he did, Kennedy did exactly as he demanded. When Kennedy landed next to him, Kieran pulled him into a kiss, tasting the saltiness of himself on Kennedy's tongue. This time, Kieran took his time and sensed Kennedy doing the same.

"You're turning into a total kiss whore, Mr West," said Kennedy. "So, how was your first ever gay blow job?"

"If I offer to give you back the five hundred, can I get one of those every day for the rest of the trip?"

Kennedy laughed aloud again, that nice rumble Kieran had come to enjoy.

"How about you keep the five hundred, and I'll still give you one of those every day, anyway? So you're staying? For the rest of the trip?"

"Fuck yeah. I always was, but I definitely am now."

Oddly enough, Kennedy let out a deep sigh then, but when Kieran turned his head, he saw him on his back, looking into the air and smiling. But then a sudden thought came to Kieran.

"Shit. What about you? Don't you need to get off, too?"

Once again Kennedy laughed, quieter this time, and placed a hand across his eyes, becoming a little sheepish.

"I already did. Shot a load in my trousers when you came."

"No!"

"I know. Like an over-sexed teenager," he said, before taking his hand away and looking Kieran in the eyes. "But in my defence, watching your expression while you're coming undone is as hot as all hell."

They lay in companionable silence. Kieran almost began to fall asleep, until he became aware of his unorthodox position, draped over the end of the bed. Not to mention still wearing his shirt, bow tie and black socks. Kennedy spoke before he had a chance to break the silence.

"I really need to go and clean up."

"You going to grab a shower?"

"Yeah, I think I'm going to have to. Get some of this gunk off me."

"Want some company?" asked Kieran, feeling unusually bold.

"In the shower?" asked Kennedy, startled, his gaze swinging Kieran's way. "Are you sure?"

"Almost since we boarded, you've been perving at me while I've been in the shower."

"I have not!"

"Sure you have. I'm not complaining. That's why I left the bathroom door wide open. In my book, if you're going to put on a show, you might as well put on a good one."

Kennedy's burst of laughter was followed by him jumping up from the bed and holding out his hand.

"Come on then."

Kieran took his hand and hauled himself to standing.

"But before we do," said Kennedy, reaching for Kieran's bow tie, "we need you to lose a few of these clothes."

Slowly and meticulously, Kennedy unclasped Kieran's bow tie then began unbuttoning his shirt, all the while maintaining eye contact. With the soft but sure touches of his fingers, the sensation intimate and erotic, Kennedy had Kieran's breathing deepening again. In a final flourish, Kennedy lifted the shirt from across Kieran's shoulders and threw the garment onto the carpet. As he knelt to the floor to remove each of Kieran's socks, his nose grazed against Kieran's renewed and straining erection.

When a fully-clothed Kennedy stood and began to unfasten his own shirt, Kieran stopped him with one hand and began to return the favour.

Kieran had seen Kennedy's body a number of times on the holiday—at his parents' house when Kennedy had hauled himself out of and sunned himself around the swimming pool, even on the cruise when he'd left the shower with a towel wrapped around him. But he had never seen him fully naked before and, although he had undressed him the same way—keeping their eyes together—he now rewarded himself by drinking in the perfect proportions and sheer muscular physique of the man, the dusting of dark chest hair trailing down to the substantial erection. Once again he marvelled at being unabashedly aroused by the body of another man.

Thirty minutes washing each other's bodies and one more orgasm each later, they towelled themselves off in the bedroom. Kieran felt so calm and comfortable, with post-orgasmic tiredness overtaking him. As though hearing his thoughts, Kennedy spoke.

"Think I'm ready for bed. How about you?"

"Yeah, I think I am, too."

Kennedy grinned, took the damp towel from him and disappeared into the bathroom. He returned seconds later, butt naked, and headed to his wardrobe.

"Kennedy?"

"Yes?" answered Kennedy, his back to Kieran.

"Can we do away with clothes in bed? I've always preferred sleeping in the buff."

Kennedy brought his hand away from the shelf that held his tees and sweats, and turned his head. A small, devilish smile curled one corner of his mouth.

"Are you sure? You're not worried I might be tempted to take your virginity while you sleep?"

Once again Kieran met the remark face-on, smiling and folding his arms.

"You promised to be the perfect gentleman, remember? And anyway, if that does become an option, I'd rather be awake, if it's all the same to you. Do we have a deal?"

"If it means me having you naked and in bed with me, then yes, we have a deal."

Ten minutes later they lay in bed together, although Kennedy still had his bedside lamp on. Kieran shuffled purposely closer to middle of the bed, turning on his side to talk to Kennedy, who was checking his phone.

"I haven't thanked you yet."

"Thank me?" asked Kennedy, turning quizzically to Kieran. "For what?"

"For choosing me. As your companion. I've seen and experienced so many things I could never even have imagined. And it's all thanks to you."

Something flickered across Kennedy's sight then, and he looked away before shaking his head softly. With a gentle sigh, he put his phone down on the bedside cabinet and turned on his side to face Kieran.

"We dock overnight in Okinawa tomorrow. How do you fancy getting a hotel for the night?"

"Sounds sleazy," said Kieran, grinning. "Count me in. I didn't think you were into doing excursions. You haven't been on a single one yet."

"I'm not, and I won't. But I've got some business to take care off in the evening, so I'm meeting a contact there. A little bar down the backstreets of Naha. Wondered if you'd want to come along. Maybe meet me there."

"I was going to Shuri Castle with Laurie."

"You still can. That's during the day, isn't it? And she'll want to get back to the boat, to see how Steph is doing. Maybe you could come and meet me outside the bar afterwards? Around seven? We can have a drink while I get my business out of the way. After that, we can stroll back to the hotel and have a nice dinner in the restaurant on the top floor. Just you and me. What do you say?"

"Let me think," said Kieran, frowning and tapping a finger in the middle of his lips. "I might have to charge extra for that."

"Oh yes," said Kennedy, playing along. "How much extra?"

"At least one extra special technique blow job from the master. Do you think he can manage that?"

"Do you know, Mr West, I think it's time for the master to teach his student this special technique. See if he's up to the job. How does that grab you?"

Kieran hadn't even considered the notion of reciprocating, the thought of him blowing another man having never crossed his mind. But suddenly the idea of watching Kennedy's face while he brought him to orgasm had his heart racing and his cock growing heavy.

"The student is keen to learn."

Chapter Twenty-Three

Kennedy

Dressed in casual navy cargo pants and a lemon Ralph Lauren polo shirt, Kennedy rested an elbow on the counter as he checked into the five-star hotel in Naha. At his feet he had a small bag containing toiletries, with a change of clothing for him and Kieran, plus a small gift bag. While waiting for the clerk to photocopy his passport, he mulled over his conversation with Steph. What he still couldn't fathom was why Kieran hadn't told him about Richmond warning him off. Why keep that to himself? Although, in all fairness, Richmond hadn't been wrong. Kennedy's usual holiday companions came with a short lease on life. But using the word 'disposable' had not only been brutal, but unnecessary. Kieran didn't deserve that, and if Kennedy saw Richmond again on the cruise, he'd confront him.

At the thought of Kieran's name, Kennedy's mind replayed the events of the morning. He had woken to a warm body aligned against his own, opened his eyes to find Kieran leaning over him and grinning. After a brief 'good morning', Kieran had satisfied his appetite with a deep kiss. Tasting of minty toothpaste, and smelling of orange shower gel, he had obviously been awake for some time, had already showered and done his other ablutions before coming back to bed. Sporting substantial morning wood, Kennedy had felt his lust skyrocket, and he'd rolled a sniggering Kieran onto his back, silencing him by tasting every inch of his body from neck to groin, before swallowing his cock whole again. This time, emboldened by the gasps and moans coming from above, Kennedy had not only sucked on each of his balls, but had then pushed both of Kieran's thighs up and swiped his tongue along his crack.

No sound had come from Kieran, just a sharp intake of breath. Kennedy had looked up then, seen Kieran watching him with wonder, and a fair amount of shock. Kennedy had wondered if he'd gone too far.

'"*Do that again,*'" Kieran had said.

Kennedy had grinned and wasted no time. Not only had he taken his time to prepare Kieran, but he'd probed with his tongue, feeling Kieran's body shiver with each invasion. When he'd finally returned to the task at hand, sucking on Kieran's erection, he'd pushed a fingertip into him, only up to the first joint, to get him used to the invasion. Finally, he'd used Kieran's pre-cum to moisten both of their erections, and, while feeling the muscles tighten around his digit, he'd pulled on their joined arousals — Kieran's introduction to frottage — until they'd both come to a shuddering climax.

* * * *

180

At ten past seven, darkness had already begun to fall, and he spotted the silhouette of a man on the right side of the up-sloping lane, leaning against a wall. As was customary, most of the bar signs had been illuminated in florescent colours, and opposite the man, at the top of the stairs, stood the bar called 036. As Kennedy approached, the tall shadow peeled away from the wall.

Kieran.

Kennedy smiled at the sight.

"Kennedy." Just the sound of Kieran's voice made his heart dance.

"You made it. How long have you been here?"

"Ten minutes max. The sign went on only a few moments ago. What's in the bag?" Kieran nodded to the carrier bag Kennedy had brought with him.

"Presents for Tim and Hiro."

With a quick check along the empty lane, Kennedy stepped towards Kieran and began to pull him in for a kiss, but Kieran stopped him.

"You said we need to be discreet."

"In the bar, yes."

"In the gay bar?"

"Correct. It's a cultural thing. Although they probably wouldn't say anything to us, most locals don't appreciate public displays of affection. It's not homophobic or anything, simply cultural, and something we have to respect. The same thing goes for straight couples."

"But in a *gay* bar?"

"The bars here aren't like England. Most are well-lit and similar to sitting around in someone's living room. Some have karaoke and others have theme nights. A few years ago, I walked into one that had a fundoshi night, kind of like a traditional Japanese jockstrap. All the men sat around completely naked except for these items of underwear. Talking politely to each other, but no touching and definitely no kissing. We walked out pretty much immediately."

"But *no* PDAs?"

"Not that I've seen."

"Then why are you trying to snog me in the street?"

"Because there's nobody watching, dummy."

Kieran laughed, but only long enough for Kennedy to pull him into a kiss. Something had begun to feel incredibly familiar about kissing Kieran, almost like a drug he had become addicted to. Before things got too intense, Kieran pushed them apart when he spotted an elderly Japanese couple in the distance strolling their way. While they stood staring at each other, waiting for the couple to shuffle past, Kennedy's eye was drawn to the bar signs on the building opposite the one housing 036, behind Kieran's head. On the ground floor stood a bar called Gents with what appeared to be a sign for the toilet, except the sign had two men instead of a man and a woman. On the next floor up, the bar announced something in Japanese with a red fluorescent dragon, and, flickering to life at that very moment on the top floor, Giant Buddha Lounge. Tacky, he thought, but at least a name he could decipher. When another person appeared on the lane, Kennedy breathed out a sigh and led them up the steps to their destination—the bar called 036.

Inside the small room, they found only the bar master, and Kennedy's two associates, Tim and Hiro, seated at the counter. He led Kieran over to join them and they were immediately provided with cold towels by the bar master, who introduced himself to Kieran as Kazuki. Kennedy had so much to say, but wanted to let Tim—his English friend and his private investigator who now lived in Tokyo — get some friendly banter out of the way before they got down to business.

"Tim and I went to university together. He was my best mate," said Kennedy, mainly to Kieran, who sat nursing an Asahi beer, whereas Kennedy had opted for the local Awamori with plum soda. "After we graduated, I went into the family business, and Tim decided on a career with the metropolitan police force, before meeting Hiro. They've now set up home in Tokyo. Tim's a highly resourceful private investigator while Hiro does confidential work for me in a research and development capacity. He's a technical wizard and, hopefully, has brought samples of the latest security devices to show me."

Hiro stood up and formally shook hands with Kieran. When he sat back down and nodded a welcome to Kennedy, only those who knew him well would be able to recognise the little tell, the mischievous curl at the edge of his mouth, which meant he had some interesting gadgets to show.

"So anyway," said Kennedy, eager to get down to business, "before we begin, I brought small gifts. A metal remote-controlled model of a London bus for Hiro's nephew. And for you, Tim, a few things from home that you might be missing."

Instead of providing a formal presentation, Kennedy handed over the carrier bag.

Tim rifled through the bag and pulled out Hiro's toy first before his eyes widened as he placed each additional item on the counter.

"Marmite. Branston pickle. Cadbury's cream eggs. Rich tea biscuits. Tetley tea bags. You are a superstar," said Tim, before pushing them to one side. "So, did you read everything I sent you?"

"I did," said Kennedy. "Very interesting. Sounds like Milletto is not only a smart businessman, but a competitive one, who has made a name for himself in the industry. Cold Steel is in good shape because of him. What I don't completely understand is why he wants out. It's not as though he needs the money. And he's clearly good at what he does."

"And what did you make of the information in the private attachment?" asked Tim.

"You mean the fact that Sloan Williamson has a vested interest in the deal going through?"

"Spot on," said Tim. "Milletto stands to make a lot of money from the sale of his company, even though, as you say, he's already nicely off. But from what our inside sources tell us, he plans on putting the proceeds into a trust fund for his only daughter, Mary Jane Milletto. Who also happens to be in line to become the third wife of one —"

"Sloan Williamson."

"Correct. At the moment, Sloan is paying child support to two ex-wives, so doesn't have much money left in the bank each month. But with his future wife's windfall, he'll be able to buy up a substantial amount of shares in Grey Havens whenever you decide to go public. He's probably hoping for a preferential offering for existing employees, too."

"Yeah," said Kennedy. "I got all that. But is Giorgio Milletto aware of any of this?"

"No, I'm pretty sure he's unaware of Sloan's intentions. From the people we spoke to privately, it sounds as though Milletto wasn't particularly pleased about his only daughter agreeing to marry a man almost twice her age, and twice divorced. From what we've overheard, he simply wants to give her a safety net for when things go south."

"When, not *if?"* asked Kennedy, chuckling.

"Milletto's words, apparently, not mine," said Tim.

Kennedy mulled this information over. Karl had voiced his concerns about Cold Steel being overpriced, but Sloan and his finance guy—someone Sloan had cherry-picked—had argued to the contrary. Of course Sloan would want the highest price possible, if he was going to end up with a sizeable handout. What irked Kennedy most was that the money would come from Kennedy's own pocket. Officially the acquisition funds would be drawn from the Grey Havens business account, a business Kennedy owned and had, almost singlehandedly, sweated day and night to build into a market leader.

"So what do I do about Sloan?"

"Saru mo ki kara ochiru," said Kazuki, who had been listening in, and which had both Hiro and Tim laughing aloud.

"What did he say?" asked Kieran.

"It's an old Japanese proverb, which translates as 'even monkeys fall from trees'."

Both Kennedy and Kieran laughed.

"Problem is," said Kennedy, "I don't have time to spare, waiting for this one to fall."

"Maybe you push him out of the tree," said Kieran.

"Or you take the tree away. I've been doing a bit of thinking, and I may have found a solution," said Tim. "I attended a course on problem-solving recently, and they classified all problems into three categories. First, the problem that has already happened and now needs to be fixed. Second, the problem you can foresee that lies ahead. And third, problems you want to prevent from happening in the first place. The way I see things, you are viewing this as the second category, something that lies ahead. But what if you prevent the problem from happening in the first place, take away Sloan's leverage?"

"And how do you suggest I do that?"

"There are a number of ways. You could tell them all you're delaying or postponing the decision to take your privately-owned company to a public limited one. Of course, then you lose out as well."

"Agreed," said Kennedy, but could see Tim had more to say.

"So, as is my wont, I've been going through your private investment portfolio. Did you know you own twenty percent shares in Securiton? They're another domestic security company in the US."

"I didn't. And to be honest, I've never heard of them. They were probably my late uncle's shares, transferred to me when he passed away. How are they performing?"

"Historically, good. Of late, appallingly. Even though they have great potential, they're currently being mismanaged. The point is, after doing a bit of digging, I found out that someone else has a thirty-five percent stake in the company."

"Go on."

"Giorgio Milletto," said Tim, and the grin on his face told Kennedy he had already thought this through. "So imagine if you were to sell him your twenty. He'd have controlling interest—"

"In a business area he's already familiar with and in which he's already performing well."

"Exactly," said Tim. "And if he has any sense, he'll merge the two companies and make a lot of investors very happy. Moreover, he'll need to keep working, need to keep his interest going, after he pulls out of our deal."

"Tim, you're a bloody genius," said Kennedy. Tim's sharp mind together with his vast network of contacts often had Kennedy wondering exactly how far he might go, what dark and dangerous resources he could have at his disposal, if push came to shove.

"You want me to set up a call with Milletto?" asked Tim, pulling him from his thoughts. Kennedy had been wondering about his next move. Perhaps the time had come for him to do the unexpected, to take a few of the players by surprise.

"Yes and no," said Kennedy. "Call him to set up a private meeting in his LA office for next Tuesday. Don't use my name, but make something up and give me a title that'll grab his attention. I'll fly straight from Hong Kong and meet him in their office. This needs to be done face to face. Kieran, are you okay to keep yourself amused in Hong Kong without me for a couple of days? Steph and Laurie will be with you."

"When will you get back?"

"I'll fly straight back on Wednesday, which means arriving Thursday. So I'll probably meet you at the airport for our flight to Bali."

"Are you sure?" asked Kieran. "You'll be shattered."

"I'll be fine. More than fine. I need to rattle a few cages. And we'll have the final eight nights in Bali together."

"So are you going to cancel the meeting in London?" asked Tim. "With Milletto and your management team?"

"Absolutely not. If all goes well, I'm going to see if Giorgio minds flying in and listening to everything they have to say. Before dropping his bombshell. Fuck, I'll even offer to pay for his flight."

"I don't get it," said Kieran. "This Williamson guy sounds like a royal pain in the arse. Surely the simplest solution would be to sack him? Stop him from creating problems in the first place."

"Ah, well. That's an easy one," said Tim. "Sloan may be a pain, but he keeps Kennedy on his toes. And having somebody who desperately wants a piece of the pie once the company goes public can't do any harm. He's going to be working his backside off to make sure what's being offered to the public is in the best possible shape. Am I right, Kennedy?"

"As always."

"Besides," said Tim, grinning wickedly, "there's a whole caseload of dirt on the man, just in case he does go one step too far."

Kennedy laughed and noticed Kieran looking between the two of them.

"You two are dangerous."

"I wouldn't say that, exactly," said Kennedy. "But we're good people to have on your side. Now, Hiro, what new toys have you brought to show me?"

While Kennedy sat at one table with Hiro, listening to him explain some of the features of the new micro security devices he had been working on, Kennedy occasionally peered over and saw Tim and Kieran chatting amiably together and occasionally laughing.

He found it strange watching Kieran interact with his associates, which at one moment filled him with a warm shimmer of fondness, and at another, scared the hell out of him.

What the fuck was he supposed to do with that?

Chapter Twenty-Four

Kieran

Even with the five-star status, the Naha hotel room didn't hold a candle to their luxury cabin on the ship. Besides a significantly smaller bed — probably queen size — the room had simple but stylish furnishings, the one saving grace being the floor-to-ceiling windowed panorama over the whole of night-time Naha. Even the bathroom had a tiny shower cubicle only big enough for one. For their dinner together, Kieran had opted for a plain and quick meal, Italian fare, aching to get Kennedy back to the room.

"I know I already mentioned this over dinner, but what you heard tonight is strictly between us," Kennedy said as they both prepared for bed.

"And as I said already," said Kieran, removing his shirt and heading into the bathroom to shower, "you don't need to worry, Kennedy. You can trust me. I promise."

"Yes, I know. And thank you," came Kennedy's voice.

Dried and with only a towel around his waist, Kieran passed Kennedy as he headed for a shower.

"And are you sure you don't want me to come with you?" he asked. "To LA, I mean? For moral support?"

"It's a turnaround trip. In and out," called Kennedy above the sound of running water. "I'd rather you make the most of your time in Hong Kong. The Mandarin Oriental's already booked and paid for, and it's a beautiful city with some great attractions—the Peak and the Peak Tram, various local markets, Ocean Park, colourful temples, the Big Buddha and, if you really must, Disneyland—"

"They have a giant Buddha in Hong Kong?" called Kieran, his interest piqued.

"They do indeed. On Lantau island. It's next to a Buddhist monastery. You can get a cable car up from a town called Tung Chung near the airport. You should talk to Steph and Laurie. People say it's spectacular."

After his disappointment in Koh Samui, he'd wondered if he should simply give up on his whim. But then, maybe he could go on the premise of simply sight-seeing. Not wanting to make any decision right then, he decided to put the idea to the back of his mind until they reached Hong Kong. Without answering, he clambered naked beneath the covers but sat up with his back against the headboard, his knees pulled into his chest. Even now, here in the room with Kennedy, he was unsure how to broach the next subject. Of course, by now the man knew him well enough to realise something was up.

"What's the matter, Kieran?" said Kennedy, coming back into the room and sitting in just his underwear on

Kieran's side of the bed. "You seem nervous. Is it something I've said or done?"

"No, of course not."

"We don't have to do anything tonight, if you don't want to."

"Are you kidding? Of course I want to. I've been waiting all day—"

Kennedy kissed him tenderly at first, letting the embrace gradually become hungry, and Kieran relaxed. After a few moments, he gently pushed Kennedy's face away.

"All day long, I've been reliving you pushing your tongue into my ass. And every time I do, my ass cheeks clench together and my insides turn to jelly. So as long as you promise to show me what to do and to go slow — and I know I can trust you—I'd like you to fuck me."

Kennedy's eyes went wide, his face still hovering near Kieran's.

"Are you sure?"

"Of course not. But I keep having this vision of you inside me, of your face as you come in me. And I need to know if what I'm imagining is as good as the real thing."

"But I didn't bring any—"

"I did," said Kieran, silently sending his friend Cole a 'thank you'. He reached for the small bag beside the bed, unzipped the top and pulled out the contents. Condoms and lube. "Actually, this was a present from a gay friend. I almost threw it back at him."

"I'm glad you didn't."

"Yeah, me too."

Once Kennedy had shed his briefs and climbed into bed, Kieran wasted no time getting his fill of him. He enjoyed the newfound freedom to touch Kennedy's body, running a hand across the hard planes of his chest, his nipples, trailing down to his genitals, making him gasp and tremble when he cupped his balls and squeezed them. To show Kennedy he meant business, he kissed his body from mouth, throat, chest, all the way down to his groin, and, after a moment's hesitation, took Kennedy's cock into his mouth.

Trying hard not to lose the sensation or the moment, he recalled the things Kennedy had done to him, those small things that had made his body glow. Kennedy clearly enjoyed the attention, because his hands wove into Kieran's hair and he pushed his hips up to meet Kieran's bobbing head.

Not for long, though.

"Stop," gasped Kennedy, pushing Kieran's mouth away. "Full marks for paying attention. But the way we're getting carried away, it's going to be over before it's begun. And I'm thinking maybe it's my turn, that you let me try a little — uh — ass play before deciding on the main event. See how comfortable you are. If it feels too much, then we can put off the deed to another day. How does that sound?"

"I'm in your hands, Kennedy."

Much to Kieran's delight, Kennedy rolled Kieran onto his back and took the lead, sucking the head of his shaft into his mouth, slowly working his already hardened cock with his tongue. After a few moments, Kieran felt a lube-coated finger touch his entrance. At first he froze, but Kennedy worked him with his slow and skilful fingers, moving in a circular motion, allowing him to relax before repeatedly dipping inside. When Kennedy raised his head from Kieran's cock and captured his mouth in a fierce kiss, Kieran barely noticed the digit push all the way inside him. This time when Kennedy returned to sucking him, his finger twisted, working him until he touched a sensitive spot deep inside. A bolt of electricity sizzled through Kieran, and he hiked in a breath before muttering an expletive.

"Ah. The 'on' switch," said Kennedy, after releasing Kieran's cock from his mouth and grinning up at him.

"Fuck. Do that again."

This time Kennedy pushed in a second finger and started to loosen Kieran up while sucking him relentlessly. When both fingers scooped over the spot, Kieran almost blew his load.

"Kennedy," he breathed, barely audible, grabbing Kennedy's hair and pulling his head away.

"I'm here."

"You need to fuck me. Soon."

But instead Kennedy worked another finger and more lube into him until the hot pain, the stretch, had begun to subside. By now, Kieran started to push back onto his fingers, hungry for the sensation. A moan of abandonment burst from Kieran when Kennedy withdrew his talented mouth and fingers simultaneously. But Kennedy appeared over him, and kissed him before bringing Kieran's knees up towards his chest.

"Condom?" asked Kieran.

"Already on. With plenty of lube, too," said Kennedy, smiling and lining himself up with Kieran's body. "I'm pretty good at multitasking. Look, this might feel a little strange and uncomfortable at first, so I'll go easy. If it does, take a deep breath and hold on for ten seconds."

"Two miles," said Kieran softly, feeling Kennedy's cock nudge his entrance.

"How's that?" asked Kennedy, a cute, quizzical furrow between his eyebrows.

"Ten seconds. The time between the lightning and the clap of thunder, which means the storm's two miles away."

Kennedy chuckled. "Whatever works for you. Ready?"

"Give it to me, old man."

Kennedy had been right. Even after he had been loosened up, the first breach of Kennedy's cock past Kieran's anal muscles burned. Kennedy's mouth covered one of Kieran's stiff nipples and he bit firmly, before returning to attack his neck and mouth. The distraction worked, and with each tiny diversion, he pushed a little farther inside.

Kennedy stopped, his eyes hovering over Kieran's.

"I'm in. All the way."

Kieran held his gaze, taking a handful of deep breaths, adjusting to the sensation, before replying. "So what are you waiting for?"

Kennedy chuckled and started pulling out slowly, just a little, before sinking back inside. For what seemed like an eternity he continued, until Kieran almost begged for more. But Kennedy must have read the signs in his face, as he began longer strokes, this time plunging in and hitting Kieran right on target. When Kennedy not only brought their mouths together, but also pinched Kieran's left nipple, Kieran almost fell to pieces. Panting heavily now, he began to reach for his cock, needing to speed his release, only to have Kennedy swat his hand away and begin pumping his shaft in time with his own rhythm. Kieran didn't stand a chance. Already the orgasm had begun to form, causing his toes to scrunch up, and when Kennedy began thrusting harder, erratically, Kieran exploded in Kennedy's hand, spraying semen all the way to their chins, the nerve endings in his body going off like a New Year's firework display. Distantly, he felt Kennedy filling him with warmth in the condom, gradually stilling and collapsing on top of him.

Kieran's body glistened with sweat, vibrating from head to toe, with Kennedy's body covering his, claiming him. They both remained unmoving, Kennedy's head buried in the side of Kieran's neck, both breathing heavily, both unable to speak. Kieran didn't want to move, wanted their bodies to remain glued together forever. Eventually one muffled word escaped Kennedy like a soda bottle opening.

"Fuck."

Slowly and carefully, Kennedy withdrew from Kieran. Even so, Kieran experienced the loss of heat and substance from inside him like an amputation. Kennedy rolled off and lay next to him, both of them staring at the ceiling while Kieran waited for his thoughts and sensations to settle.

"Is it always this intense?" he whispered.

"Not for me. Not in the past, anyway. Maybe this is simply what it's like between you and me."

Kieran thought about that remark for a minute.

"In which case, I am well and truly fucked."

Beside him, Kennedy chuckled.

"I think we can both safely agree to that."

Kieran watched Kennedy stand, remove the condom and head for the bathroom. Still Kieran felt unable to move. Fortunately, Kennedy came back and settled next to him again. Once more they lay in companionable silence, each with their own thoughts.

The soreness in Kieran already began to feel interesting, but something else was on his mind.

"Kennedy."

"Yes?"

"Does this mean I'm gay?"

"If it did — even just a little bit — does that bother you?"

Kieran thought about the question.

"No, not at all. What would bother me immensely would be if we never got to do that again."

Kennedy laughed aloud before rolling on his side and addressing Kieran directly.

"And with such an excellent scholar showing clear promise, the master might even let the student take charge next time."

"Really?" asked Kieran, amazed. He had unfairly assumed Kennedy would always want to be the one in the driving seat.

While they both got comfortable, with Kieran's head resting on Kennedy's shoulder, Kieran recounted the day he had spent visiting historic and not-so-historic sites in Okinawa, making Kennedy laugh — a sound he had begun to love hearing — when recounting their trip to a tourist market where some of the items on display were variously flavoured tins of Spam. When Kieran mentioned something Leonard had said, he noticed Kennedy quietened, waiting for him to finish.

"I forgot to tell you. Leonard phoned me today, just before I met up with you. I should have mentioned the call to you earlier but it slipped my mind. He asked me if I thought you were reliable. Sounds like he's impressed. Something to do with you giving him advice on his websites."

"At lunchtime today. An Okinawa noodle restaurant they took us to, between attractions. Yes, his websites are prehistoric — in both design and functionality — and some don't work on a bunch of the new generation of browsers. So he's naturally losing customers and income. I put him right over a couple of Asahi beers. Could do so much better, even if only by consolidating a few of them and incorporating a reliable online payment gateway. No big deal, really."

"Apparently, it is for him. More importantly, he loves your energy and enthusiasm. Something I can definitely vouch for, especially after tonight."

Kieran peered sidelong at Kennedy and they shared a mutual grin. But Kennedy hadn't finished.

"And he's about to offer you a job. As his head of marketing in their London office. His current person's about to retire and he needs someone with fresh ideas to take the helm. Thinks you have great potential and I agreed. Told him I think he'd be a fucking moron not to offer you the job."

Kieran stared at Kennedy for a moment, his mouth gaping open, unable to speak, before turning his gaze away. He had learned, especially from a professional perspective, to suppress his emotions where potential work was concerned, mainly because of late — apart from this trip to Asia with Kennedy — all news had tended to be bad news. Tears welled in his eyes, something that rarely happened, something Kennedy noticed immediately, because he squeezed his arm around Kieran's shoulders.

"Shit, Kieran. Did I say something wrong? Should I have told him no?"

"No," he replied, swiping at his eyes with the back of his hand. "Fuck, no, Kennedy. Exactly the opposite.

Head of marketing? That's my idea of a dream job. I have no clue what's happening to me right now, everything is so crazy. In a good way. Sorry, what I meant to say is everything is amazing. All thanks to you."

"You undersell yourself, Kieran."

"You know that's not true. Otherwise I wouldn't be here right now."

"Point taken." Kennedy laughed. "Point taken. And for the record, I'm glad it's you that's here."

Me too, thought Kieran. *Even though it's only for the next two weeks.*

Chapter Twenty-Five

Kennedy

Kennedy was awoken from a deep sleep by a loud ping from his phone.

When he'd fallen asleep, he'd been worried about waking to find Kieran—always the early riser—having a panic attack, or a crisis of heart or conscience, or complaining about new and inevitable soreness in parts of his body where this kind of thing had never happened. What he hadn't expected was to find Kieran fast asleep, his warm body and stiff cock pressed up against Kennedy's back, his arm draped around his midriff. Kennedy lay there savouring the moment. Lazily, he reached out a hand and brought the phone to his face, to check the messages on the display.

Steph 10:10: You're not answering your cabin door.

Steph 10:30: Are you onboard? Simeon says he hasn't seen you.

Missed call.

Steph 11:00: Where the fuck are you? The boat leaves at midday.

Panic rippled through him when he checked the time — eleven-ten. He sat up and pulled the covers back, before throwing the phone down.

"Kieran! Shit!" he said, jumping into action and waking a sleep-ruffled Kieran with a shoulder shake. "We've overslept. Get dressed. We have to check out."

"Chill out. I need to use the 'loo," said Kieran, leisurely sitting up on the side of the bed and pushing his hands through his locks. "And grab a shower. And what about breakfast?"

"No time," said Kennedy from the other side of the bed, yanking on his underwear and trousers. "We can do that back on the boat. If we manage to make it."

"What do you mean?" said Kieran.

"The boat leaves port in forty-five minutes."

Finally, the words managed to sink in, and the two of them hurried around the hotel room, trying to avoid bumping into each other, taking turns to use the toilet, dressing hastily and packing the little they had brought before racing down to reception. While Kennedy checked out, he sent Kieran to arrange a taxi with the concierge and explain the need for haste. Fortunately, rows of taxis were lined up outside the hotel, ready for guests, so they were soon on their way.

At eleven-forty-five the port appeared before them with the mammoth Diamond Princess still sitting there against the quay. Kennedy breathed a sigh of relief. With minutes to spare, they both boarded, showing their cruise passes to the crew members before heading to their cabin. All the way from the hotel, they had hardly spoken. Finally, Kennedy asked Kieran what he needed first, shower or food. A trooper to the last, he opted for the latter.

Kennedy rang Simeon to request an all-day breakfast be brought to their cabin. Professional as ever, Simeon responded instantly, but when he pushed the trolley into their cabin, Kennedy could make out a slight change in attitude, the friendliness dialled down a notch or two. Kieran noticed too, because when Simeon served them both coffee — Kennedy his usual espresso, which he downed in one gulp — Kieran winked at him and grinned.

"How was the coffee, darling?" asked Kieran, reaching across the table to take hold of Kennedy's hand. "Would you like Simeon to bring you another?"

"And one espresso's perfect," said Kennedy, attempting to glare at Kieran through his grin. "Thank you, Simeon. You can clear the table now."

"More importantly, how are you feeling?" asked Kennedy, once Simeon had departed.

"Better, now we made the boat in time. What would we have done, if we hadn't?"

"Not a real issue," said Kennedy, with a shrug. "We'd have caught a direct flight to Hong Kong. Just over two hours away. And spent an extra couple of nights in Hong Kong waiting for the ship to arrive."

"My God, you think of everything."

"What I meant earlier was, how do you feel after last night?"

Kieran considered Kennedy's meaning, then got up from his chair and slapped down his napkin. Like a hunter stalking his prey, he came around Kennedy's side of the table and straddled his lap, placing his arms around the back of Kennedy's head.

"If you're asking whether my arse is still sore, then the answer is yes," he said, rubbing his backside into Kennedy's groin before leaning in and pecking Kennedy on the lips and neck. "If you're asking whether I still want to do the same thing again, then the answer is — oh *fuck* yes. But right now, I'm ready for a shower. So hurry up and finish your breakfast. Because my cock isn't going to wash itself."

* * * *

For the next three days and two nights before they reached Hong Kong, Kieran's appetite for sex became voracious, often keeping Kennedy in bed until mid-morning, and dragging him away in the afternoon to try out one new position or another. If Pandora had ever had a brother, then his box had been well and truly opened. The first time Kennedy allowed him to take the lead — something Patrick had never wanted — Kieran took his time, making sure Kennedy felt relaxed, always checking whether Kennedy felt any discomfort. When, midway through the first exchange of roles, he insisted Kennedy roll over and straddle him, ride him at his own pace, the ploy worked perfectly and allowed Kennedy's hands the freedom to explore Kieran's body, helping to bring him home. For the first time in his life, Kennedy found concentrating on work impossible.

Kieran knew exactly which buttons to push. On the final sun-drenched day on deck, as Kennedy joined the girls and they all relaxed on loungers around the bustling swimming pool after lunch, purposefully ignoring Patrick's posse gathered together on the other side of the pool, Kieran turned up. Sporting only gold lamé Aussiebum swimming briefs — *brief* being the optimum word — he rocked the look. Rows of curious heads craned forward while sunglasses were yanked down sweaty noses to get a better view. Tanned now, with his trim muscles and flat stomach, Kieran had developed an easy confidence, which was as sexy as hell. When he sat astride Kennedy and bent down for a deep kiss, all heads turned their way. And when Kieran whispered two words into his ear — *swim or sex* — Kennedy bolted up from the lounger and pulled him away, back towards the cabin.

And when Kieran bottomed? He had become insatiable — what Kennedy's friends would have labelled a power bottom — hungry for everything Kennedy could give him and more. He demanded hard and fast, wrapping his legs tightly around Kennedy's back, pulling him as far inside him as he could and coming with wild abandon, loudly vocal and often hands-free, like an express train hurtling from a tunnel, or a New Zealand geyser bursting hotly from the ground. More than a few times, Kennedy wondered what had happened to mild-mannered Kieran.

All his friends noticed. At meal times — the few moments all the friends spent time together — Kieran took every opportunity to touch Kennedy. Sometimes he would rest an innocent hand on his knee, or lace his fingers with the hand lying next to his, or lean across Kennedy to reach for the salt or pepper, accidentally brushing a hand on his upper thigh, while a thumb stroked the bulge in his trousers. Intended to be discreet — but so bloody obvious, every time Kennedy's friends noticed not only Kieran's smitten reaction, but Kennedy's barely maintained indifference.

All too soon, Hong Kong harbour loomed.

As soon as Kennedy had installed Kieran in the suite of the Mandarin Oriental, he packed his suit and travel case, ready to head to the airport. When they'd checked in, he had organised a taxi to take him directly there. Twice Kieran asked if he wanted him to come, or just to see him off, but Kennedy declined and insisted he wanted to get the trip out of the way. Kieran's sullenness made Kennedy feel unkind, and he almost had a change of heart, but instead pulled him up from the bed into an embrace.

"I need to do this, Kieran."

After a tender kiss, he held Kieran's face in his hands and stared into his eyes.

"Yes, I know you do."

"And I'll be gone two days only, as long as there are no delays."

"I know."

"And then it's just you and me in Bali. For eight nights. To try anything that enters that filthy mind of yours."

Kennedy managed to get a small smile out of Kieran then, which quickly fell away when Kieran's gaze dropped to the small case Kennedy had packed.

"What's the matter, Kieran?"

"It's just—we've been together every day and night for the past eighteen days," said Kieran, trying to make light, but his eyes telling a different story. "And I've begun to think of you as my lucky charm. So forgive me if I'm getting a little nervous about not having you here. What I'm trying to say is, it feels so good when we're together. And I'm going to miss you. Sorry, I'm getting a bit gushy, aren't I?"

"No, you're not. I appreciate the sentiment, Kieran. And I promise I'm coming back soon. Okay?"

"Okay."

"Now will you do something for me?"

"Anything."

"Go and enjoy yourself."

* * * *

While sitting at the boarding gate, Kennedy received a couple of messages on his phone. One from Tim about the meeting — and something unexpected from Reagan.

Reagan: Me and the kids are moving in with our parents for now. Bernie admitted to having an affair. Will let you know more soon.

Kennedy stared out of the airport window to his plane being readied for the flight. Although the news didn't take him by surprise, his sudden reaction did. What saddened him more than he could have imagined with its plain but obvious truth was that he and his sister had failed at relationships. How could he forget the defeated expression on Reagan's face when he'd said goodbye? Never would he forget his own sense of futility when Patrick had walked away. Maybe he should be looking to blame their parents, but most of all, he wanted to protect his own heart. And the reason for this conflict? Kieran had woken something inside him, had made him begin to feel things again. Did he dare take another chance?

As the airline official checked his passport and scanned his ticket, Kennedy kept replaying in his mind the text from his sister. Why the hell would he want to expose his heart again? Stupid. The idea was stupid and dangerous. Besides, he was about to go into battle. Right now he needed no distractions. Heading down the ramp to the plane door, he checked the messages from Tim, to make sure there were going to be no surprises.

Tim: All arranged as planned, everything lined up including transfer documents sent to your special email account. Milletto thinks you are an international investment analyst with particular specialism in his sector. Let me know how things go. Safe travels.

Without looking back, he boarded the plane bound for Los Angeles and strapped himself into his seat.

Chapter Twenty-Six

Kieran

No doubt about it, the suite at the Mandarin Oriental was the nicest, must luxurious hotel room Kieran had ever stayed in. Not that he'd stayed in many. The only drawback? Kennedy was not there to share the king-sized bed with him.

On the first night alone, despite getting text messages from the girls, Kieran hadn't felt like going out, had holed himself up in his room and binge-watched HBO movies over a club sandwich room service meal, while sitting cross-legged on the bed.

His only reminder of Kennedy? After the mix-up with time in Okinawa, Kennedy had noticed Kieran wasn't wearing a watch and had lent him one of his own — nothing expensive or pretentious, just a leather-strapped timepiece his father, Jeff, had given him as a kid. Kieran loved wearing the device, loved smelling the navy leather strap which, every time, reminded him of Kennedy.

The next day the sun shone gloriously, so with Laurie proudly clutching her Hong Kong guidebook, the three of them took the ferry ride to Lantau Island and climbed the steps to the Big Buddha. Strangely, the air of mysticism and spirituality had disappeared for Kieran, as though that particular window of opportunity had passed him by, and he simply enjoyed being in the girls' company and seeing the sights for what they were. After taking individual and group photos at the top, admiring the panoramic views of the territory and climbing back down the tall stairway, they stopped for a vegetarian meal at the Po Lin Monastery before taking a heart-stopping glass-bottomed cable car to the town of Tung Chung. Laurie's guide had promised outlet malls—a guide that had served her well—and the girls had then proceeded to shop frenziedly, as though their lives depended on it. By the time they all reached the hotel late in the afternoon—the girls had also booked into the Mandarin Oriental—everyone felt pooped and ready for an afternoon nap.

Len had invited Kieran, the girls and Pete and his father for a relaxed dinner and drinks in his hotel in Lang Kwai Fong. Stylish and yet still retaining some old Chinese charm, the restaurant served Peking cuisine—Peking duck with paper-thin pastry rolls, finely chopped cucumber and spring onion, and sticky hoisin sauce, huge tiger prawns cooked in a light chilli sauce, broth-like chicken soup, fried noodles, and various stir-fried vegetable dishes. Kieran enthused about everything, having only ever sampled English-style Chinese food—usually as takeaway.

Sitting between Len and Laurie, Kieran conversed genially with them all until Len leaned in to talk to

Kieran. Steph must have sensed something between them, because she diverted their attention to the exploits of Pete and his father, while Len lowered his voice to talk to Kieran.

"My human resources manager emailed me an employment contract for your new job. Give me an email address so I can send it over to you. Ideally, I'd like you to look through it over the next couple of days—I don't want to spoil your holiday, but if you could do this sooner rather than later, I'd be grateful. Let me know if there's anything missing and if you're happy with the package, so we can get you to sign on the dotted line and get you on board as soon as you get back. Are you okay with that?"

"More than okay."

"The starting salary and bonus scheme might seem a little generous, but it's only slightly above market rate for this kind of role, and besides, I am reliably informed by someone not here right now that you will not only work your ass off but are worth every penny."

Kennedy. Even when he was not physically present, he still impacted Kieran's life. He had to look away from Len's gaze for a moment, to level his emotions.

"Send it over to the email address you've already got for me," he said, after a few calming breaths, "and I'll do the honours tonight. Get everything back to you first thing tomorrow."

"Okay, that's impressive. Are you always this efficient?"

"I'll tell you what, Len—and we can make this official if you want and write this into my contract—I guarantee that in six months' time, I will have increased revenues across all of your businesses by between fifteen to twenty percent at the very least. How does that sound?"

"Like I should have hired you a few years ago."

After dinner, Len, Pete and his father opted for the hotel bar, while Kieran and the girls decided to explore the bustling bar scene in Hong Kong. In the balmy evening air, they wandered Wyndham Street, filled with bars and restaurants and people spilling out onto the pavement. Eventually they hit an outdoor escalator and decided to see where the moving staircase would take them. Steph spotted them before anyone else — Richmond, Mike, Patrick and Joey, with another male couple Kieran recognised from the cruise, standing just inside a bar called Staunton's on Staunton Street.

"Should we go and say hello?" asked Laurie, who appeared a little unsure.

"Kieran?" asked Steph, always sensitive to his feelings.

"Honestly, I don't mind," he said, assessing the gathered group. "Looks like Joey might need saving."

"Let's grab a quick drink. And if it gets too much, tonight's time-to-escape word is douchebag. If anyone uses the word douchebag, then it's time for us all to get the hell out of there."

"Since when did we have a time-to-escape word?" asked Kieran.

"Since tonight."

"And why douchebag?" asked Laurie, frowning. "English people don't use that word."

"Exactly."

When they approached the group, Patrick spotted them first and waved them over. After kissing each of the girls, he even shook Kieran's hand and smiled in a way that appeared genuine. Would wonders never cease? Richmond and Mike simply nodded their hellos. Joey's face positively lit up when he saw Kieran and he came straight over to chat. Once Patrick had bought them all drinks—another first—Joey and Kieran excused themselves to move away from the group to a quieter part of the bar. They shared stories about their time in Hong Kong and what they'd each seen. After a while, Joey's face became serious.

"So, listen. I need to fess up. I talked to my sister, Chloe. She's still friends with your ex-girlfriend, Jennifer. They catch up every other week. I hope I didn't drop you in it, but I told her about you being on the cruise with your new boyfriend."

Oh, hell, thought Kieran. *That should go down like a heavily loaded depth charge.*

"What did she say?"

"She said I must have you mixed up with someone else. Until I forwarded a photo of you and Kennedy dancing, and then she went quiet. I have to ask you, Kieran. Are you really gay, or are you putting on a show here? Richmond seems to think you're not the real deal."

Kieran laughed at the question. Three weeks ago, he would have confessed to Joey about the whole thing being a sham. But now? No fucking way was he denying what was so blatantly true.

"I am one hundred percent the real deal. Steph and Laurie were grilling me about the same thing over lunch today. How could I be with Jennifer for so many months and now be with a man, and not be freaking out? I suppose some men might. And I don't have a perfect answer except, objectively, I've always seen the beauty in both forms, male and female. You know, like in the James Bond movies where Halle Berry comes out of the sea in her tangerine bikini. Do I appreciate the sexiness? Hell, yes, I do. And then, when Daniel Craig does the same in his light blue briefs, can I appreciate his sex appeal? Sure I can."

"So you're bi?"

"To be honest, I hate labels. But if I had to label myself right now, I'd say I'm Kennedy Gay."

Joey laughed at that, a nice, infectious laugh that had Kieran grinning.

"Can I ask—and you don't have to answer this—what's he like in bed? Kennedy?"

"You can ask," said Kieran, his voice lowered. "You ever been to Oxford Street at Christmas when they turn on the Christmas lights?"

"Nope."

"One minute the street is normal, dull street lamps and dark pavements. The next—*wham*—above the road, lights of all colours, shapes and sizes, sparkle and shine everywhere, bringing everything to life. That's what sex is like with Kennedy."

"So Kennedy's your Christmas, then?"

"Yep, except he definitely does *not* come just once a year."

Once again Joey laughed aloud, and he clinked his glass with Kieran's bottle of beer.

"Cheers for that. You know, I had a girlfriend in university, too. Felt such a fraud, as though I was cheating on her every time we went out, especially when I checked out another guy. Coming out was such a relief. At medical school nobody gives a flying fuck whether you're into guys, girls or both. It's so liberating."

At that moment, Steph and Laurie appeared in front of them, both looking excited, and Kieran wondered if they were about to use the douchebag word.

"Kieran, we're just going to have a quick browse through that cute little shop opposite. Mike says they're selling these darling Chinese bowls and plates and other pottery items at absolutely bargain prices. Can we leave our drinks with you and Joey for a couple of minutes?"

"Of course you can," said Kieran, laughing.

Kieran and Joey watched them disappear into the small store.

"A few minutes my ass," said Kieran. "Those two can't resist a bargain. Dragged me kicking and screaming around an outlet mall today. Bet you ten quid they'll be gone at least half an hour, and then come back with a couple of shopping bags full of goodies."

In their absence, Kieran and Joey chatted happily together, and with no Kennedy by his side, he was grateful for the distraction, to be able to talk about their own favourite parts of the cruise. From time to time, both of them peered over the heads of the other patrons in the crowded bar to where Richmond was holding court. Patrick wasn't there, and must have excused himself to use the toilet. Richmond's voice rose above the hubbub in the bar, and a few people had begun to move away or give him annoyed stares. Richmond appeared to be addressing his comments to the gay couple they had met on the boat.

"S'like it's become some kind of fucking holiday competition, who can bring the prettiest, dumbest, barely-above-the-age-of-consent sidekick to parade around on a leash with them, like they're showing their pedigree puppies off at Crufts Dog Show."

"Okay, Rich," said Mike, his tone quiet and placating.

Richmond had clearly knocked back a few drinks too many, and both Kieran and Joey could hear every word of the tirade over the sound of other voices in the bar.

"Have you had to put up with that all holiday?" asked Kieran.

Joey huffed out a sigh and shook his head.

"They go way back, him and Patrick. So I try to ignore him most of the time. But honestly, sometimes I'd like to punch the guy's lights out."

"...freeloading off their fucking sugar daddies. Makes me want to puke."

"Okay, dial it down, Rich," came Mike's voice, more urgent this time'.

Joey looked away, but the hurt in his eyes said everything. "I'm not freeloading, you know," he said. "I've paid my way. I do have my own money."

"Why does Mike put up with that jerk?"

"No idea. Maybe Richmond's dick is as big as his mouth."

Both of them chuckled at that quip, until their attention was drawn back across the bar.

"An' you know what sickens me most? Paddy's now playing catch-up, bringing his own fucking useless little piece of shit cocksucker along with him, just so he can rub it in Kennedy's face —"

Kieran put down his bottle of lager, readying to go over and confront Richmond. But before he had a chance, a loud crack followed by a few screams and shouts of consternation, the smashing of glass and something else being overturned, brought the bar to silence. When Kieran turned around, he saw Richmond on the floor with Patrick standing over him, his face red with rage, pointing an accusatory finger at a shocked and bloody-mouthed Richmond.

"If you *ever* refer to Joey that way again, so help me God, I will end you. Joey is a catch, by anyone's standards. And I am not competing with anyone. *I'm* the one who's lucky to have *him*, not the other way around. If you can't deal with that, then you are no longer my friend."

"It's okay, Pat," said Mike, helping a shocked Richmond up from the floor. "He's had a few too many. I'll take him back to the hotel."

But Richmond hadn't finished. While Mike set the small table upright and apologised to the people sitting around, Richmond confronted Patrick.

"I'm on your fucking side, remember?" he said.

"If that's how you're going to behave, I don't want you on my side. Not if you're going to be disrespectful of my friends," said Patrick, about to move away, but then spotting Joey and Kieran standing together in stunned silence. Turning Richmond's body to face their way, Patrick pointed to Kieran across the bar. "And, for the record, do you honestly think Kieran's just a decoration? Did you see him and Kennedy on the dance floor? I have never seen two men so coordinated. Yes, *men*. They are both *men*, Richmond, and I really hope Kennedy realises how lucky he is to have Kieran. Because I sure as hell know how lucky I am to have Joey."

With that, Patrick pushed Richmond towards Mike and turned his attention back to Joey.

"Come on, babe, let me pay up and then we'll get out of here."

While Patrick disappeared into the depths of the bar, and Mike loaded Richmond and himself into a red taxi, a broadly smiling Joey quickly finished his drink.

"Sorry to leave you alone, Kieran, but looks as though I'm going to get lucky tonight."

"You're not sorry at all." Kieran laughed.

"No, I'm not. Patrick's amazing when he's in this kind of mood. So I'm going to make the most of it."

"Hey, we're off to Bali tomorrow, so I probably won't see you before we go. Let's arrange to catch up when we're both back in London."

"You're on. You know, I wasn't really looking forward to Hong Kong, but I wouldn't have missed that little show for the world. Enjoy the rest of your holiday, and safe flight home."

"You too," said Kieran, giving Joey a hug and waving at a departing Patrick, who actually smiled and seemed ready to leave, but then relented and came over.

"Kieran, I owe you an apology. I was rude to you on the cruise and, in hindsight, that was unacceptable. I'm not too proud to admit when I'm wrong, so I hope you'll accept my apology. I think you might be good for Kennedy. I just hope he appreciates you."

"Thank you, Patrick."

Joey and Patrick left in the next red taxi, leaving Kieran standing there, stunned and alone. Straightaway, Kieran wanted to call Kennedy, but had no idea whether he would be able to pick up. More than likely, he was in the air on his way back to Hong Kong. Fortunately, the girls returned from their forage, laden down with bags of goodies.

"We've saved so much money," said Steph, holding up one of the carrier bags.

"I think you mean spent," said Kieran.

"Where is everyone?" asked Laurie, putting her bag down and getting her drink.

"Did we miss anything?" asked Steph, also putting her bags down and peering around.

"Nope," said Kieran, grinning happily. "Apart from watching one serious douchebag go down in flames — metaphorically speaking — you missed nothing at all."

"Okay, Kieran," said Steph, hands on hips. "Hand me my drink. Then spill the beans."

* * * *

In Kieran's mind, Hong Kong airport appeared to have been designed to resemble a giant modern cathedral, with high vaulted ceilings and huge windows showcasing regimented rows of airplanes from all over the world, waiting to be boarded or disembarked, and distant planes taking off and landing. Moving walkways ran through the centre of the main terminal, lined on either side by departure gates and a few last-minute shops or eateries.

Kieran stood at the departure gate, staring over the heads of those around him and shuffling from one foot to the next. Passengers were already boarding and there was still no sign of Kennedy.

"Will you calm down, Kieran," said Steph, for the third time. "He texted that he's on his way."

Nothing could placate Kieran. He'd spent the whole three days wanting Kennedy by his side, and now, finally, the man had arrived back in Hong Kong just as they were about to depart for Bali.

"If he's not here, I'm not getting on the —"

"Here he is now," said Laurie, pointing past Kieran.

Kieran turned and his heart gave a lurch, a grin forming on his face. As Kennedy approached, Kieran could not help noticing the small smile appear on his tired face. Wearing his travel attire — baggy and creased beige chinos and a wrinkled Indian cotton shirt — he still looked good enough to eat. He had only a carry-on bag with him, all he had taken to Los Angeles. Kieran had checked in the rest of their luggage. When Kennedy reached them, he first gave the girls a quick hug then came over to Kieran and hugged him tightly.

"I really missed you," said Kieran.

Kennedy said nothing in return. Maybe he still felt tired, but Kieran wondered if there might be something more to his distance.

Steph hustled them onto the plane, both girls being stopped as they boarded, something beeping on the scanning machine, and both being told that they had been upgraded. All of them would be together in business class. Kieran knew Kennedy had somehow worked his magic. As they marched down the ramp towards the plane door, once again Kieran noticed him focusing ahead, avoiding eye contact. While the girls went ahead, he put his hand on Kennedy's arm and stopped him.

"Are you okay, Kennedy? Did everything go to plan in LA?" asked Kieran.

"No," said Kennedy, a strained expression on his face, one Kieran had not seen before. "Everything did not go to plan. Everything did not go to plan at all. But I'll explain later, once I've had time to rest."

Chapter Twenty-Seven

Kennedy

Once they were airborne, Kennedy accepted a glass of water from a member of the cabin crew and settled back in his seat. After the two long-haul flights with very little rest in between, he felt shattered and looked forward to precious downtime in Bali.

Kieran distracted him with their exploits in Hong Kong, but after he fell silent, clearly waiting to hear about Kennedy's meeting with Milletto, Kennedy suggested he save the tale until they were somewhere less public. Besides, he said, he wanted to get his head down for a few hours. Kieran nodded his agreement. Relieved, Kennedy closed his eyes and thought back on the past thirty-six hours.

During his trip—and despite how much he'd missed having Kieran by his side—he'd decided to dial down their closeness. To do anything different would inevitably hurt Kieran once they returned to their normal lives, and he could not live with himself if that happened. Even without taking into consideration their age difference, Kieran deserved someone fun and reliable, someone who would not eventually disappoint him. Kennedy knew all about the pain of losing someone 'he had come to rely on, and would not let that happen to Kieran. Kennedy eventually let people down — that seemed to be the rule in his life.

Except the business trip had proven the exception to any rule. Yes, he had been taken by surprise during his meeting with Giorgio Milletto. When he'd finally come face to face with a clearly unsurprised Milletto, he'd told himself that someone, somewhere must have leaked his visit. Milletto had sworn to the contrary, that his arrival, however fortuitous, had come out of the blue. Rather than working to his detriment, the information meant there had been no subterfuge when Milletto had turned up in person, to meet him in Cold Steel's tasteful reception area.

"Mister Kennedy Grey. Thank the Lord," Milletto had said, beaming, as Kennedy rose to his feet and matched the man's warm handshake. "This is a pleasant, if slightly unexpected, surprise — you son of a gun. I saw this guy sitting here from the CCTV monitor in my office and thought 'heck, it can't be, can it?' Seems like it is."

Kennedy had laughed, and within a matter of seconds felt comfortable. Something about the man had made him feel they could talk freely. For someone in his late fifties, he gave off a sense of alertness while still being friendly and welcoming — probably a long-cultivated, charismatic charm. Dressed in a stylish light-grey suit and pale-blue open-necked shirt, Milletto had a full head of almost white hair, and his smiling brown eyes behind fashionable silver-framed glasses gave him the air of a scholar.

"I know this is a little unorthodox,'" Kennedy had said, following him along a corridor towards a large conference room, '"but I wanted us to talk off the record, face to face, so to speak. We've only ever conversed by telephone or on video conference. We should have done this long before now, but when you kept changing our meeting — "

"The hell I did. Your end kept changing the goddamn...oh," Milletto had said, his smile slipping. "Sloan. You know, we both need to keep a careful eye on that SOB."

Kennedy had sighed then. They were definitely on the same page. Instead of leading Kennedy to the conference room, Milletto had turned right into another corridor and entered his huge corner office, the semi-circular window arrangement overlooking the whole of downtown Los Angeles. After his smiling personal assistant had brought Kennedy an 'emergency' double espresso, and been put on alert for more, the two of them had opened up. From the word go, Milletto had been an inspiration — funny, insightful, and more importantly, someone Kennedy felt he could trust to do business with.

Of course Milletto knew the score with his future son-in-law, had seen through his plans. And during their six-hour meeting — stopping only for lunch in a trendy restaurant on the top floor of the building — Kennedy had listened to Milletto's counterproposal.

Instead of them running with the acquisition — which in his experience had been like one bigger country invading a smaller one, and rarely without casualties — that instead they join forces, turn the transaction into a merger of two powerhouse companies in the security sector, a meeting of minds and talents.

Once Milletto — "*call me Giorgio*" — had meticulously explained his reasoning, everything had made total sense to Kennedy. Giorgio and his team had even considered a new name, Grey Steel Global. Having expertise in all areas of surveillance, both domestic and corporate markets, on both continents, they would become unstoppable. Once they had opened up in different markets, they could float on both the FTSE and the NASDAQ, and would become one of the top players in the global market. Milletto's eyes had flashed with a mixture of excitement and pride at the idea.

Still struggling with jetlag, Kennedy had sat back and tried to absorb the overwhelming information. Throughout the meeting, he'd kept tapping into his natural business wariness, had tried to look for a catch, to look beyond the words and see if Milletto — Giorgio — might be trying to play him. But everything Giorgio said made complete sense. At some point, he'd need to speak to Tim.

"Why didn't you suggest a merger in the first place, why offer to sell the business?"

Giorgio had sat back in his plush leather chair, grinned sadly and stared out of the window.

"That is exactly the question I'd have asked you, if you'd suggested the same thing. And I think it's only fair you have all the information, if you're going to agree to a partnership."

Giorgio had kept his gaze out to the skyline and shaken his head very slightly.

"A year ago, I had a stroke. Collapsed right here in this office, thank the Lord, because they got to me quickly. Touch and go for a while, but my guys took me to the hospital in record time. We managed to keep it out of the press — didn't want to worry clients — but let me tell you, for me it was a wake-up call. Afterwards, doctors told me to take it easy, hand over the reins of the business. You probably know that anything I make from this business goes to my daughter. I wanted to make sure she'd be well taken care of."

Right then, Giorgio had swung his chair to face Kennedy.

"But you know what else I learned this past year? You can't live your life scared, however much time you have. Sure, I had to learn to let a few things go, but give up? No freaking way. When your boys first put the offer on the table, I thought that'd be a perfect solution. But you know, the more I thought about it, the more I changed my mind. And that's when my wife came up with the idea.

"Unlike my future son-in-law, I've only been married once, and trust me, when you eventually get to meet her, you'll understand why. Kelly-Anne Marie. She's ten years younger, and the only person who ever stood up to me, while standing up for me, if you know what I mean? She's the one told me to go find out more about you and maybe go speak to you privately. See if you might at the very least want someone to stay on as a sleeping partner — not that I'd have done much sleeping. But I could certainly have kept an eye on your managers for you — if you know what I mean? And then it just hit me about three weeks ago. Why don't we go into business together?"

Kennedy had been listening but his jet-lag-addled brain had struggled to take everything on board.

"Look, I ain't going to lie to you, Kennedy. This is going to be a whole helluva lot of work for both of us if we're going to pull it off. Mergers don't come cheap, and many of them crash and burn. But I think we've got a shot. We're complementary — and I don't mean that in the free-of-charge way. Together our businesses are halves of something that could be something great. And, I guess, the clincher for me is I feel as though you're someone I could work alongside. How about you?"

Kennedy had talked about his own idea, about bringing him his shares in Securiton so that maybe he'd consider calling off the acquisition. Milletto's suggestion made far more sense, and the fact that they both had significant shares in Securiton made the deal even sweeter. There would be a lot of things to hammer out, lawyers talking to one another across the pond, probably months of negotiating, but in essence at least, Kennedy approved of the idea wholeheartedly.

"So, should we still hold the meeting in London?" he'd asked.

"Hell, yes," Milletto had said, folding his arms and raising his eyebrows. "Don't go spoiling my fun, now. I want to be there to see faces when we announce the counterproposal. I know you broke your holiday to be here today, but can you be on the call? It'd be better coming from the two of us united."

"I agree," Kennedy had said. He'd easily find a reliable business centre in Bali and teleconference into the meeting. Hell, he wouldn't miss it for the world. "And one way or another, I'll be there."

* * * *

After the four-plus hour flight from Hong Kong to Bali, they had another four-hour drive from the airport in the south to Kennedy's seafront villa in a small town in the north near a place called Pulaki. During the journey, Kennedy told them all as much as he could, about how Giorgio Milletto had known he was sitting in the Cold Steel reception and that not only had they instantly connected, but they had enjoyed a frank exchange of views and ideas about how to progress their businesses. Kennedy mentioned nothing about the merger. Kieran listened quietly, but Kennedy could tell he suspected there was more to the visit, things Kennedy wasn't telling them.

As the sun began to sink over the headland, they arrived at Kennedy's villa. Their driver had called ahead and they were met by villa staff carrying ice-cold glasses of lemon tea. During the year, Kennedy let out the four-bedroom lodgings to friends or close business associates, but he ensured the villa staff maintained the premises, grounds and swimming pool all year round. With the rooms housed on two levels — the ground and the first floor — the villa also had a shaded car parking space beneath the whole structure, which was where the driver parked their car.

On the ground level, they stepped through the front entrance into the spacious living room, then through to the pool and the stunning view overlooking the Bali sea. Shimmering and inviting, the pool ran the length of the villa, surrounded on three sides by the dining room, the kitchen, the lounge, and one of the bedrooms. Three more bedrooms sat on the first floor, overlooking the pool and the sea. Glass sliding doors on each of the internal facing rooms ensured that guests had access to the views. Two features he had always loved were the two-person shaded cabana to one side of the pool, and the outdoor terrace on the first floor, where his guests enjoyed breakfast.

Over the next four days, they relaxed together, although during all but one of those days, Kennedy remained behind when the three went out on excursions. Tim had vetted Giorgio's proposal and given Kennedy the golden thumb — Tim's way of saying that everything came up legitimate. At night, Kennedy and Kieran continued to have sex, Kennedy trying his damnedest to make sure Kieran enjoyed himself. Even so, a couple of times, Kieran asked him if something was wrong. Kennedy sensed a storm brewing.

At midnight on the fourth day, while Kieran slept, Kennedy managed to web conference into the meeting with London and Los Angeles. Giorgio handled the call brilliantly, up-talked the merger then handed over to Kennedy. Although nothing had been signed, they made a point of telling everyone — including Giorgio's staff — that the acquisition was firmly off the table. Kennedy knew he would have to deal with a flood of emails from his staff, but decided to leave them until the morning.

On the morning of the fifth day, Kennedy spotted Kieran talking to Steph on one of the sunbeds beside the swimming pool. After a second, she pointed up to where Kennedy sat at the breakfast table with his laptop open. Kieran looked amazing in shiny scarlet Speedos, a sight Kennedy used to relish but now one that tugged at his heart, as though he had no right to look. Without hesitation, Kieran came towards Kennedy, bounding up two stairs at a time until he stood the other side of the table. Even with his shades on, Kennedy could tell he meant business.

"Kennedy, we need to talk."

Kennedy had been wondering when this conversation would happen. And apparently the time had come. Kieran would want know what was going to happen when they returned, maybe even ask if they could stay close. Ollie had done the same, and everyone knew what a disaster that had been. Not wanting to spoil the rest of the holiday, Kennedy would need to let Kieran down gently, so he sat back in his chair. He had been rehearsing the speech in his head, to make sure he got the words right, to minimise the pain. But before he had a chance to say anything, Kieran spoke first.

"Shut the laptop down and give me ten minutes," said Kieran decisively. "So I can say what I need to say."

Kennedy breathed out a sigh and did as requested.

"I've paid the money I promised into your bank account, by the way," said Kennedy. "With a little extra."

"I—thank you. But that's not what I wanted to talk about."

"Go ahead, then," said Kennedy, his hands clasped together on top of the laptop.

"We go home in three days."

Kennedy remained silent, but nodded.

"I just—I don't want a dark cloud hanging over us as the deadline looms. So let's clear the air right now and that way we can enjoy the next few days the way we've both—at least I hope you have too—enjoyed these past few weeks. Are we agreed?"

Okay, thought Kennedy. *That's not quite what I'd been expecting.*

"Agreed," he replied, cautiously.

"Because I want us to have fun during the few days we have left, and now your business meeting is out of the way. Let's go to the beach or sunbathe together, or swim in the sea or in that amazing pool. Let's have sex in the afternoon, if you want to. And I know you do, the way you're trying so hard not to stare at my cock right now."

Despite himself, Kennedy chuckled and looked away, but when he brought his gaze back, Kieran's face had turned serious again.

"Look, Kennedy, I know things between us probably haven't turned out the way you'd expected, and certainly not how we'd both planned. Believe me, that much I do understand. But a deal's a deal. And when we get on that plane in three days' time, when we set foot back in England and you head off on your way, it ends there. I knew that much coming into this arrangement. I'm not going to gush about how great a time I've had — the things I've seen and done, the new and incredible experiences — because you already know that, you've been with me the whole way. But I am true to my word. So I give you my word of honour — and you certainly know enough about me by now to know that counts for something — that I will not attempt to contact you again, as stated in our agreement, once we're back home. Are we on the same page?"

"We are."

And yet, for the first time in as long as he could remember, Kennedy had no idea which page he was on.

Chapter Twenty-Eight

Kieran

Bali had seen some difficult times since the start of the new millennium. But not even terrorist threats or natural disasters could keep the tourists away. Kieran had to agree with Laurie's description of the small province of Indonesia, that Bali was an island paradise. Lush green paddy fields with a backdrop of verdant mountains contrasted with perfect beaches of white sands and azure sea, lined by tall coconut trees. Hindu pagodas and temples constructed from local stone, now moss-covered and age-worn, blended naturally into the horizon when driving from one location to another, as though they had been grown organically rather than built.

Since their talk, Kieran had given himself over to Bali's magical spell. However much he hadn't felt some of them, his words had worked their charm. Kennedy's guard had dropped and he'd relaxed back into the holiday. They sunbathed in the nearby sandy cove on the morning of their penultimate day, two short flights of steps down from the villa. They'd lain together, the four of them, savouring the cloudless day in companionable silence, until Steph and Laurie cried off because of the intense midday heat.

"Fancy a dip?" asked Kieran, leaning up on one elbow.

Kennedy's body glistened deliciously with coconut sun oil, applied earlier by Kieran. That morning Kennedy was wearing only a pair of stylish shades and tight black-and-gold briefs. At Kieran's words, he turned his head and yawned, stretching out his arms.

"Mmmm. Could do."

"Skinny dip?"

Kennedy sat up, then brought his knees to his hairy chest and raised his sunglasses.

"I think you'll find nude bathing's illegal in Bali."

"Who's going to know? Come on, old man," said Kieran, dropping his scarlet Speedos and standing naked. "Live dangerously for once in your life."

"You think I don't live dangerously?"

"Yep," said Kieran, running into the sea. "Last one in's a sissy."

"Too late for that." Kennedy laughed, stepping out of his briefs and tossing his shades onto the towel.

Within seconds he joined Kieran in the sea, both immersed past waist-height, splashing each other and laughing like school kids. Kieran really enjoyed the rare moments when Kennedy let his guard down, even though he knew that later on things would return to his usual formality. Taking advantage of the situation, Kieran did what he'd been wanting to do all morning and wrapped his arms around Kennedy's neck and his legs around Kennedy's waist. Without asking permission or even checking Kennedy's reaction, he brought their mouths together in a salty kiss, feeling Kennedy's arms tighten around him. For a full five minutes, they remained that way, with Kennedy twirling them slowly around in a circle in the cool waters.

"See," said Kieran, pulling his mouth away. "Nobody's going to know whether we're wearing cozzies or not."

"But they might, if we start having sex in the sea."

"However much the thought of that makes me hard, maybe we should save it for the bedroom."

"I can live with that," said Kennedy, grinning, pushing away from Kieran and swimming a few strokes on his back. "Let's just enjoy the freedom of being in the ocean."

"For one more day, at least."

Kieran hadn't meant the remark to spoil the moment, but Kennedy's smile dissolved. Kieran immediately dived beneath the water and came up next to Kennedy.

"Hey, old man, can I give you a suggestion?" asked Kieran, shaking the water from his hair. "It's a kind of take-it-or-leave-it piece of advice."

"Go on," said Kennedy.

"I understand why you couldn't tell us everything about your meeting in LA, except that you're no longer going for an acquisition. But reading between the lines, it sounds as though you might be considering a merger?"

"No comment."

Kieran laughed and twisted onto his back to match Kennedy.

"Fair enough. But just in case you are, during my master's we looked at contemporary businesses, and one of the specialist areas I studied in depth is successful mergers, identifying the key elements that helped to make them work — particularly where companies are geographically challenged or where there are clear organizational cultural differences. One key differentiator concerns pre-merger integration. Kind of getting to know how each other's business works. One simple but successful way of doing that is to consider swapping one or two key talents for a period of time — pre- and post-merger — for them to gain insights into how the new company operates, to explain how their own company does the same, and then figure out the best way for the two to work together going forward. Of course, you'd also have to consider the needs of the individual. Do you maybe have any key members of staff who might have family connections in LA?"

The slowly spreading smile transforming Kennedy's face was better than the stunning landscape.

"You're dangerous, Kieran West."

"You have no idea."

Shortly afterwards, Kennedy insisted they dry off and put on their swimwear before heading up to the villa for showers. Often, Kieran had been the one to instigate sex between them, but this time Kennedy took control with a sense of urgency. Kieran enjoyed these rare moments, allowed Kennedy take his fill of him. Lying next to each other, both panting, Kieran smiled up at the slowly turning ceiling fan of teak and metal.

He'd noticed Kennedy peering at him quizzically a couple of times of late — when Kieran laughed along with the girls, when he leaned in playfully and pecked

Kennedy on the cheek, or when he jumped up to help the villa staff bring food to the table. Kieran had decided to live by his words, to enjoy the last days of their time together unencumbered by any negative or melancholy emotions.

Because, clearly, something Kennedy hadn't realised or appreciated was how much Kieran had changed. Not only did he feel a newfound confidence in himself, but for the first time in as long as he could remember, he was looking forward to the future.

On the Monday morning after their return, he would be starting a new and exciting job. Not only that, but with the ten thousand pounds — double the amount agreed — sitting in his bank account, he could not only pay his sister, pay off a chunk of his and his brother's studies and get himself a new suit, but have enough to put down a deposit on his own rented place. How could he possibly hate Kennedy for that?

Finally, he had a future — even if that future did not include Kennedy.

On their last night together, they visited a restaurant recommended by the guidebooks, Sunset Spice, a Balinese seafood restaurant built on the beach, overlooking the sea and the sunset. While Kennedy walked barefoot out onto the sand to take a phone call, Kieran marvelled at how healthy he looked with his deep tan, accentuated by his beige chino shorts and short-sleeved white cotton shirt.

"Kieran, we've been meaning to ask. How would you feel about sharing your swimmers with us?" asked Laurie, a little sheepishly.

Kieran's mind had been elsewhere and, with the small bottle of Bintang in his hand, he turned quizzically to them.

"Which ones? The red or the gold?"

Steph choked on her cocktai, then proceeded to cough uncontrollably. Laurie laughed too, and patted Steph on the back.

"Your sperm, Kieran. Steph and I want to start a family and, well, we think you would make the perfect donor. What do you think?"

This time Kieran dropped the bottle he had been holding to his mouth, and only just managed to catch it before the contents spilled all over the tablecloth.

"For heaven's sake, Laurie," said Kieran, aghast, but catching up quickly. "Drop a bombshell, why don't you?"

"Seriously, though," said Steph. "It would be great if you could think this over. We're going to do it anyway—one of the reasons Laurie's been losing weight—and we were set on using a reputable semen bank friends of ours had recommended. Even though they give you information about the history of the donors, you're unlikely to get to meet them. If it's any consolation, we both came up with the idea of asking you."

"What would I need to do? I mean, I'm not sure I'm ready to bring a child into the world."

"To put it bluntly, it's only your sperm we need. Usually donors in the UK don't have any legal obligation to the child or any responsibility in how the child is brought up. They don't need to support the child financially and they're not even named on the birth certificate. But the reason we're asking you is because we'd be more than happy for you to be a part of our child's life, but only if that's what you want."

"Wow, girls. That's a lot to take on board."

"I know. We both do. But will you at least consider it?"

"Of course I will. But why didn't you ask Kennedy? He's your best friend."

"I ran the idea past him months ago. In a subtle, but theoretical way. If you'd seen the look of horror on his face, you'd know why I'd never consider him. Even if it's not strictly his own, I think Kennedy would freak out about the simple notion of knowing there's a kid out there with his genes."

"Funny, I can't think of anything nicer," said Kieran.

Even though he had been looking at Kennedy, he didn't miss the exchange of glances between the girls.

"Don't take too much time to think it over," said Steph. "Clock's ticking, as they say."

Steph reached out her almost empty glass to clink a cheers with the neck of Kieran's bottle.

"Christ! You want me to fill it now?" said Kieran, nodding at the glass, a mischievous smile on his face, which had both girls laughing aloud.

"What did I miss?" came Kennedy's voice.

"Nothing," said Kieran, smiling up at him. "Absolutely nothing."

* * * *

Two hours before their arrival into Heathrow, Kieran awoke to a member of the cabin crew placing a tray of breakfast in front of him, onto a tray table he hadn't set up. When he rubbed his eyes and looked to his right, he found Kennedy smiling at him.

"I know you'd never forgive me if I let you miss breakfast."

"Too right," said Kieran, laughing and raising the seat into a sitting position.

Sex on that last night in Bali had felt more like making love—unhurried, familiar and mutually satisfying. Not a word had passed between them, like a rite of passage, as though they'd both felt this would be the last time. Which, in reality, it probably had been. In the morning, Kieran had refused to feel sad, and had packed his bags while making casual conversation with Kennedy, the girls and the villa staff as they packed his things into the back of their airport transfer van. Even though they all arrived at the airport together, the girls had different flights, so they made their farewells before boarding.

Back in England, Heathrow's organised chaos came as no surprise when the country's busiest airport woke to a new day.

"Kieran, where are you going?" called Kennedy, about to head for the terminal's meeting point.

"To the Tube station," he said, pushing his trolley towards the main doors. On the flight back, he had resolved to make the parting as painless as possible. But he needed to do so quickly.

"Ben's bringing the car round. We can drop you off."

Unless a person knew the real man, they wouldn't know that Kennedy's voice sounded almost pleading.

"No need," said Kieran, plastering a smile on his face, his stomach twisting a little, but his resolve firm. "I've got it from here. Take good care of yourself, Kennedy. And thank you for absolutely everything. You're really special, you know. Don't ever forget that."

With those final parting words, he turned and walked away, unable to look back.

Chapter Twenty-Nine

Kennedy

For the first time in his life, Kennedy felt lost.

Which was odd in itself, because everything concerning the merger had come together beautifully, better than anyone could have dreamed. Erin, Karl and the rest of the management team had been stoked at the idea, and had loudly voiced their approval at their first meeting on his return. In the past, Erin had often questioned why they'd not spread the wings of their expertise into the domestic security market, and now a ready-made, successful company would be joining their ranks not as an acquisition, but as a partnership, with the company's talent working alongside them. Even Sloan had quietly nodded his approval, although Kennedy knew him well enough to recognise the stalwart countenance of a defeated man. Before long, Kennedy would need to have *the* chat with Sloan. The last thing he wanted was to have the man walk and, moreover, Sloan needed to understand *why* he was critical to the merger's success.

With meeting after meeting happening—some at ungodly hours—he'd had little time to think about anything else. And usually work provided an excellent distraction.

Not anymore, though. Things had slowed. Sometimes during meetings, his thoughts would drift back two months, to a certain naked man heading for the shower after a session or two of mutually satisfying sex, or to Kieran's body laid out on the beach, beautiful in mouth-watering scarlet swimming briefs, soaking up the Bali sun. But more than all of those, he missed Kieran's sparkling eyes and incredible smile that lit up in amusement, grinning playfully at something Kennedy had either said or done. And the thought kept hitting him hard, punching a hole through his chest, especially when he arrived home late each night, when he stood for a moment on the threshold of his empty house, knowing he could have had everything.

And all he'd needed to do was ask.

Ask if Kieran would like to be a part of his life. They could have stayed in touch, met up occasionally for drinks and dinner, seen how things went in the real world. But Kennedy had made his cold, plain intentions clear from the outset, something he always did in his business life, and now he felt empty, eviscerated. Mainly because Kieran had honoured the very rules Kennedy had damned himself with. Moreover, would Kennedy be happy having Kieran around occasionally, or did he want something more? Hell, who was he kidding? Could he handle casual with Kieran? The question didn't even need asking. But before he made any personal call to action, would Kieran even be interested?

"What do you want, Kennedy?" came the gentle American-accented female voice next to him, a soft hand landing on his sleeve.

"You know, I have absolutely no idea," came Kennedy's detached voice, from somewhere inside him.

"Me either. Let's get one of each and then we can all share."

When Kennedy raised his eyes, he saw the businesspeople around him, seated at the restaurant table, chatting amiably. Kyle Crystal, the vice president of Cold Steel, sat opposite with his wife, Jerry. Sloan and his fiancée, Mary-Anne, sat next to them with Giorgio sitting to his left. Kelly-Anne Marie Milletto sat next to Kennedy, on his right, her hand almost possessively resting on his sleeve. Only Kennedy had sat unaccompanied with' no significant other to bring. As usual.

Kelly-Anne had been the one speaking to him, mulling over the dessert choices. Kennedy had warmed to her immediately. Probably five or six years older than him, Kelly-Anne Marie had amazing perception. Giorgio had been spot-on with his assessment of his wife.

When Kennedy looked at the young, blond, perfectly sculpted waiter to Mary-Anne's right, the young man's smile and prolonged eye contact with Kennedy could only mean one thing.

"One of each sounds great," said Kennedy, pulling the small, laminated dessert menu up to his face to cover his view. The over-attentiveness of the waiter had begun to rankle. "There're only six of them, after all."

"I'm all for that," said Mary-Anne, grinning at her mother. "Custard apple crumble, apricot layer cake, brandy crème brûlée, New York cheesecake, chocolate brownie with caramel ice cream and English spotted dick—whatever the heck that is. Yuck. Sounds like an STD. Sloan here's not really a dessert person."

"Yes. I'll pass, if that's okay? Until it's time to order coffee."

Kennedy noticed Sloan whisper a few words to his fiancée, peck her on the cheek then stand up from the table. No doubt he was heading outside for a cigarette. With the chill November air and the heavy rain, only an ardent smoker would brave the weather. Maybe now was Kennedy's opportunity.

He decided to wait for desserts to arrive and for everyone to sample the fare before making his move. Once again the young waiter stood to Kennedy's left—in between him and Milletto—to deliver the food, subtly rubbing his thigh up against Kennedy's arm as he placed each dish onto the table.

A year ago Kennedy might have been flattered, might have even taken the young guy up on his advances, but that switch had been flicked off.

Once everyone had sampled the sweets, Giorgio wanted to order coffee, so Kennedy excused himself from the table to go and fetch Sloan. He found his colleague standing under the restaurant canopy, overlooking the car park. When Kennedy moved to stand next to him, Sloan nodded, before continuing to stare out at the heavy rain clattering on the regiment of cars.

"Popular tonight," said Sloan.

For an amused moment, Kennedy realised he and Sloan rarely talked about anything other than work issues.

"Me?" asked Kennedy. "You mean with our colleagues and their other halves?"

Sloan snorted and nodded at something behind Kennedy. When Kennedy turned, he noticed the young waiter who had been flirting with him standing twenty feet away, leaning against a wall beneath a canopy, smoking a cigarette. On noticing them, he raised a hand in greeting. Kennedy waved back.

"You were here first. I think he might be checking you out, not me," said Kennedy.

"If only I were gay, things would be so much easier," said Sloan, puffing a plume of smoke into the night.

Kennedy was not about to let that one go without a comment.

"You think it's easy?" asked Kennedy, folding his arms. "So here's a few home truths. First off, Sloan, with a face and body like yours, you'd have seen a shitload of action. But the all-you-can-eat coming-out buffet soon gets cold and old, and eventually even us gays want to settle down—most of us, anyway. And right then, gay or straight, we're all on the same playing field. But please don't think for one minute that being gay and in a relationship is any easier. You met Patrick. What part of our relationship looked easy to you?"

Sloan laughed. One thing Kennedy liked about him was that he'd never had a problem being around Kennedy and Patrick as a couple. But even Sloan had not been able to refrain from commenting with irritation on Patrick's total lack of interest in their business and their significant successes.

"So," said Sloan, after a moment's contemplation. "I suppose congratulations are in order. You've finally managed to ship off your pain-in-the-ass chief operating officer. Not only to the other side of the world, but to the in-laws, no less. Bravo."

"Is that really how you see this?"

"Is there any other way?"

"Christ, Sloan. Wake up and smell the coffee. You're the one person in my office who keeps me on my toes. Everyone else does what I tell them. You're also one of the few who understands how all the departments drive the business forward, someone who doesn't bury themselves in their own area of specialism. Your future father-in-law needs to see that, needs to witness your drive and ambition first-hand. A year from now, you'll be one of a very short list of people who has gotten beneath the skin of the new, wider company, just as we're ready to go public. And right then, we're going to need someone charismatic to romance investors. I'm not giving you a prison sentence, Sloan, I'm handing you a golden ticket."

"So you're not just getting rid of me?"

"Say the word. I'll keep you here and send Karl instead."

Sloan peered sidelong at Kennedy before turning back and puffing out a trail of smoke.

"No. I'm in for the long haul. Besides, Mary-Anne's looking forward to spending time with her mother, arranging our wedding."

"And the other plus is, you'll be able to fly your kids over to visit, take them to Disneyland and Universal. That should earn you a few brownie points in the absent-dad stakes. And you can do it all without the ex breathing down your neck, or showing up screaming in the office reception."

"Oh God," said Sloan, turning to Kennedy, his expression mortified. "You heard about that?"

"No, I literally *heard* it. My office backs onto reception, remember? Don't worry, Sloan. I've got your back. We all have our crosses to bear. And anyway, seems like you've fallen on your feet with Mary-Anne."

"You know what? She's it for me, Kennedy. Yeah, I know she's a lot younger, but this is the woman I want to spend the rest of my life with. She's probably the first person who actually understands me and will tell me if she thinks I'm being an idiot or can see that I'm in the wrong."

Like mother, like daughter, thought Kennedy, while Sloan continued speaking.

"I know I've acquired something of a reputation, having married twice before. But what people don't know — not really something a man likes to admit to — is that my first wife cheated on me a year into our marriage, and her best friend, who'd been the chief bridesmaid, someone who stood by me through the messy break-up and subsequent divorce, became my second wife. Total disaster. Our two kids were the only good things to come out of the catastrophe. Hindsight is a beautiful thing and only now I see what a mistake I made. A wise soul once told me mistakes fall into three categories. Ones you simply can't fix and have to live with, others you can but only if you really want to, and some you don't want to make right, because the mistake has given you something better."

"Someone recently told me something similar about problems."

Sloan laughed and stubbed out his cigarette.

"Same thing, I suppose. I'm going back inside. You coming?"

"In a minute."

Kennedy needed a moment alone, staring out at the heavy sheets of rain. Maybe someone like Sloan could put problems and mistakes into one pot and call them the same. But they were not. In Kennedy's experience, problems often occurred due to external factors, beyond a person's control, randomly, often unpredictable. Mistakes were different. Mistakes he saw as personal, and really—and here he agreed with Sloan—a person had the choice to decide whether to fix them or not, and whether to show both vulnerability and courage by enlisting the help of others to do so.

And the simple home truth? He'd made a terrible mistake. His dilemma? Could this one be fixed?

After a deep breath, he pulled out his phone and checked the time—eight minutes past ten. Straight afterwards, he scrolled down his list of contacts. After pushing the call option for one, he waited a few seconds before a familiar voice answered.

"Hey, Leonard. Are you up for a drink? I need to run something by you."

Chapter Thirty

Kieran

Ever since Kieran had returned to England and come out to Cole with a confession about his first time with Kennedy, peppered with enough detail to convince his friend of the authenticity — almost two months ago to the day — Cole had been comfortable enough to strut around his apartment in only his Armani underwear. Through an extensively used gym membership, Cole had cultivated a sculpted body and had acquired more than his fair share of admirers, if the number of weekends he returned home in the early hours was anything to go by. And although objectively Kieran appreciated his flatmate's smooth, muscular form, he definitely preferred the carved lines and hairiness of Kennedy's body

"So listen up, Q1," said Cole, thumping his mug of coffee onto the table. Ever since Kieran had mentioned Pete's nickname for him on the cruise — Queer One — Cole had been hooked, calling him either Q1 or plain Q.

"Gay friends of mine are coming over from Tokyo to stay with me at the beginning of December—Jon and Takamori—on their way up to Scotland to spend Christmas with like-minded folk. Apparently a whole bunch of them get together each year and they missed out last year. Staying at some kind of castle owned by friends of theirs. Sounds like a perfect antidote to Christmas. Anyway, can you stay with your sister for a couple of weeks while they're here?"

Kieran lowered the screen of his laptop and forced a smile.

"Of course I can. Sorry, I should've had my own place by now."

"Not your fault, Q. Our female brethren are famous for their fussiness. Besides, it's been nice having you here."

Two days ago, the promise of a flat share with a lesbian couple had fallen through when the two had finally decided they wanted another woman sharing their space, and especially their bathroom and kitchen. Kieran's holiday money from Kennedy hadn't stretched to him being able to put down a deposit to rent his own apartment, although now the second month's salary from Leonard had hit his bank account, he was in a better position. But the whole process took so much time. Now he'd need to call on his sister's goodwill again after finally giving her and her boyfriend back their space.

"I'll call Jules later."

"What are you doing on your laptop? Better be gay porn, or pervy chat rooms, and definitely not study. Our next module isn't due until after Christmas. Shit, don't tell me you're working? On a Saturday morning?"

Cole knew how much he loved his new job. Len had instigated a regular weekly meeting with him — usually in the morning, informally, over cappuccinos and chocolate muffins — to go through his achievements. Much of the technical detail went over Len's head, so Kieran had learnt to show rather than tell — the redesigned antique furniture website, fast and slick, allowing browsers to view the pieces in three dimensions and rotate them on the screen, the site selling listed or character buildings, which now had a handful of three-sixty-degree tours of properties online and direct links to Len's other complementary sites, such as the antique store and the tasteful draper and haberdashery — which included a link to Steph and Laurie's furniture renovation service. He always saved the figures until last, knowing Len's main concern. The most recent spreadsheet showed not only the exponential rise in hits on each of his sites, over four hundred percent, but figures indicated an initial five percentage increase in sales across all sites in the last month alone. And Kieran had only just begun.

"Nah, just browsing media sites. Nothing in particular," he lied.

He had been checking the photograph of Kennedy and Giorgio Milletto again, the one relating to the announcement of their merger. Kennedy had maintained his amazing tan and, with him looking directly into the camera when the shot had been taken, Kieran felt as though Kennedy was staring straight at him. And he knew just what that felt like. Every time, the sight gave his heart a tiny squeeze of regret. Kieran still had Kennedy's number plugged into his phone, and a couple of times he had even been tempted to call.

But each time he'd managed to resist the urge. Kennedy needed to make the next move.

"Q, honey. Not only is it the weekend, it's the end of the month. So not only do we have time, but we also have money. Let's head up to London and do something fabulous. You have any plans for brunch?"

"Heck, don't remind me. I'm meeting my mother up in Waterloo. And coming out to her."

"Oh shit, yes, I'd forgotten. Good luck with that. Even if the weather turns shite, I'm not sitting in watching more episodes of *RuPaul's Drag Race*. So let me know if you need emergency cocktails afterwards. I'll be at The Nipple Clamp in Soho for happy hour from four 'til nine. Gerard, Nob and Lickme are joining."

"Let's see how things go."

"It's just a chill-out bar, Q. No deafeningly loud music, no pungent aroma of poppers, no sweaty bodies wrapped around each other, sliding down the walls — more's the pity. I've learned my lesson. Say you'll come."

Cole had taken Kieran to Pulse, a club beneath Waterloo Bridge. From the moment he'd walked down the steep stairs and through the door, Kieran had disliked the crush and backstage darkness. Two men had stumbled up to him, clearly off their faces on either alcohol or recreational drugs, and both had spoken to him in their usual voices as though he could even hear anything. Even the next morning, his ears had rung with pain. Although he'd never openly complained, Cole knew he hadn't enjoyed the experience.

Cole must have taken Kieran's silence for refusal, because he continued his case.

"Look, darling. Despite the world painting us fabulous people onto one easy-to-point-to billboard, we're different shades of gay. I am flaming pink and you are more of a darker red, like burgundy, more into Daddies—"

"I am not into Daddies."

"With their beer bellies, man boobs, bald heads and hair on their bums."

"Okay, okay. I'll come and join you afterwards. Give you the Mum download."

"Oooh, goss? Priceless. Now we're talking."

* * * *

At midday, Kieran met his mother at the Skyline restaurant in the Royal Festival Hall on the South Bank. Their table for two sat right next to the window, the whole space located above the walkway below, overlooking the Thames and Waterloo Bridge. Every now and again Kieran enjoyed treating his mother to a special meal, even though she would inevitably make a point of commenting on the exorbitant prices. Living in Hove on the south coast, she rarely came into London, so when she did he'd spoil her with lunch and a movie or a trip to the theatre. Unfortunately, this time she needed to get back by six o'clock for dinner at one of her friend's houses.

A few years off sixty, she still looked good—happy and settled. She'd dyed her hair recently, a deep red that covered up the persistent grey. Not really one for makeup—something Kieran admired about his mum—she arrived fresh-faced and red-cheeked, courtesy of the chill weather. Over the past few years she'd had a number of boyfriends, but nothing she'd ever referred to as a relationship.

Over a glass of wine each, they caught each other up on their lives, Kieran enthusing about his new job, much to his mother's delight, but never mentioning his month as a paid travel companion. As far as the rest of the world was concerned, he'd taken the month off to travel the country with his friend, Cole. Nice and general, not too much detail. Besides, he had bigger things to discuss with his mother. Two glasses of wine later and now on desserts, Kieran finally found a pause in the conversation to bring up the topic foremost in his mind.

"Mum, I'm bisexual. Actually, I''m probably leaning more towards being gay."

For a few seconds she stared at him, before smiling and nodding. After a moment, she turned her gaze out to the scene beyond the window.

"I thought you might be. Even in your early twenties you were never really into girls, not like your brother. And, let's face it, you and Jennifer were hardly love's young dream. Even though you told me otherwise, I never saw her making you happy, never saw that spark between you."

"You knew? Why didn't you say anything?"

"Oh, honey. What would I have said? And, more importantly, what would you have said to me? I don't think you even knew yourself. But a mother knows. Of all my children, you were the sensitive one, the worrier, always fretting about me, worrying if we'd be able to make ends meet. Half the time your worrying helped to stop mine, if that makes sense?"

"But how does that make me gay?"

"It doesn't, but—I don't know—I just saw something special in you. Of all my children, you are most like my oldest brother, Peter."

Uncle Peter. Or Gay Uncle Peter, as most of the family had come to refer to him. Kieran liked him and Uncle Gino. Along with his grandparents, they'd helped care for Kieran and his siblings as kids. Both men had been low-key and fun, sharing a tiny bungalow in the country that had a huge garden backing onto a farm.

Did he have the family gay gene? Kieran wondered. *And was that even a thing?*

His mother must have sensed his confusion, because she went on to clarify.

"Don't get me wrong, love. I think you'd have made a brilliant husband for Jennifer. But she'd have been the one ordering you around, getting you to do what she wanted, when she wanted it done. There would've been no give and take. She's that kind of woman. And I know you, dear. Eventually you'd have walked away. So better it happened sooner rather than later, when you'd have had far more to lose. Do you have someone?"

"Sorry?"

"Do you have a boyfriend?"

Kieran blanched. His mother had actually used the word 'boyfriend' with him. As natural as breathing. No drama, no crying, no accusations. For a moment, he felt the sting of tears in his eyes.

"I did. That's where I was in September."

"And what's he like?"

How the heck did he explain Kennedy to his mother?

"He's amazing, Mum. Smart, successful, handsome, funny."

"Sounds like somebody's smitten."

"No, we're not together anymore. Just travelled as companions for the month."

"Then he's not as smart as he thinks. My son is a catch."

Kieran laughed, his mother's approval and the rumble of his own amusement in his chest lightening his mood. After coffee arrived, both of them fell quiet again, until his phone beeped with a message. Even before he'd pulled the phone out, he was pretty sure the sender was Cole. But the display announced something different altogether.

Steph: *Not counting our chicks just yet, but doctor says we're likely going to be a mother.*

Kieran put his phone face down, then grabbed his wine and emptied the glass. After a taking steadying breath, he smiled weakly at his mother.

"Mum. There's something else I need to tell you."

Chapter Thirty-One

Kennedy

In early December, two months after the end of what Kennedy now considered to be the best holiday and the biggest mistake of his life, he found himself marching through an almost empty, unfamiliar office space at seven-thirty on Friday evening, with nobody there except the cleaning staff, most of whom stared at him suspiciously. Not that he cared. This was something he should have done weeks ago. He had been directed to the sixteenth floor and to the reception for Leonard's office space.

Standing still, he stared around himself at the completely empty reception area as a sinking feeling filled him. But then, beyond, in the fishbowl office, he noticed the familiar dark-haired man stand up and walk to the photocopier, prodding buttons on the display.

Kennedy rarely felt unprepared, but this whim was like walking on broken glass. Without hesitation, he marched over and tapped his knuckle on the window of the security door. After peering up, the figure frowned then moved towards the portal.

"Len's not here," said Kieran, after opening the door for him, and before turning back to the machine.

"Oh, okay," said Kennedy, stood awkwardly in the doorway, his back propping the door open, his hands shoved deep in his trouser pockets. "So how—uh— how have you been?"

"Fine. I'm doing fine."

"Okay. And the job's going well?"

Kennedy had never been very good at small talk.

"Loving it. Lots to do, but we're getting there, and I wouldn't have it any other way."

"Good. That's good. Got you working late, I see. So what's with the suitcases?"

Kennedy recognised a large black case up against the wall, the one Kieran had brought with him for the holiday, plus a couple of other, smaller ones. At his remark, Kieran let out a small sigh.

"I've been staying with Cole since I got back. Had a flat-share lined up, but it fell through at the last minute. Anyway, Cole's friends are over from Tokyo, so I'm bunking back with my sister for the week, until I get something permanent sorted."

Kennedy stared at the sad line-up of cases until Kieran broke the silence.

"What do you want, Kennedy? I already told you Len's not here," said Kieran, after lifting the top of the copier, placing another sheet inside and slamming down the lid. The question sounded so harsh and direct that Kennedy faltered for a moment, unable to speak.

"I—I wanted to see you."

"Me? Oh, let me guess. You want your dad's watch back?"

"No, that's not why I'm here at all," said Kennedy, rubbing a hand nervously around his chin. "At least, not unless you come with it."

"Unless...what?"

"You heard me," said Kennedy softly.

"Okay, Kennedy, what's going on?"

This time Kieran stopped his work and folded his arms.

Kennedy came into the room, let the heavy security door slam closed behind him and perched himself on the edge of a desk. For someone so accomplished in his professional life, he felt in unchartered waters here. But he had never been one to back down from getting something that he sorely needed.

"I'm going to say some things to you that I've never said to another living soul."

Kennedy waited to see Kieran's reaction, but he simply leaned back against the copier, his arms still folded.

"I'm listening."

"You'll need to be patient. This is somewhat difficult for me."

"Do I need to sit down?"

"You might want to."

Kieran wheeled over an office chair and sat with the backrest to his chest, his arms draped over and his hands clasped together.

"First off, I need to say I'm sorry. Sorry for not being brave enough to tell you how fond I'd grown of you. Sorry for not keeping in touch after the holiday, although God knows we've been rushed off our feet with the merger, which is all coming along nicely, by the way, with regular updates from Giorgio and Sloan. Yes, I took your advice."

"Good."

"And the second thing is—"

"You mean there's more?"

"Is that as much as I feel this particular word has become bland, overused, and, in this case, is totally inadequate—I mean, for goodness' sake, the Eskimos have fifty words for snow, so why do we only have one—sorry, getting off topic. What I mean is, Kieran, I'm falling in love with you. No, sorry, scrub that. I'm already in love with you. Have been since our tango together on the cruise. Maybe even before that, and now I'm—"

"Stop," said Kieran, softly, which caused Kennedy's voice to break with emotion.

"I'm second-guessing everything, Kieran. Every decision, which is not like me. I'm fucking asking for your opinion in the mirror every morning, asking you as though you're standing there in the bathroom next to me. I can't do this without you. Move in with me, not with your sister. You can have a spare room as long as you want, if that's what you want. Hell, you can stay forever, which is what I'd prefer. But it's your choice. I want you to do what you want."

"What if I tell you I've met somebody?"

Kennedy's heart sank then, all the hope he'd been storing up evaporated, and suddenly he felt a sting in his eyes. And the Greys never shed tears—his father had taught him that. Was he too late? Trying to pull himself together, he stared down at the office carpet.

"Have you?"

"What would you say if I told you I have?"

With an effort of will, Kennedy brought his emotions into check and eventually smiled, still unable to meet Kieran's eyes. Something else his father had taught him was that even in defeat, an Englishman remained gracious, a gentleman above all else.

"I'd say that man—or woman—is the luckiest person alive. I'd tell them they've just hit the jackpot with the most beautiful person in the world. Someone who lights the room up just by walking in and makes the person with him feel like they're blessed. And I'd make sure they tell you so every day you're together—"

Kennedy didn't hear the soft movement from across the room, but suddenly found himself being enveloped by Kieran's arms. While Kennedy wrapped his arms around Kieran's waist, Kieran pulled Kennedy's head down onto his shoulder.

"For fuck's sake, Kennedy. Why couldn't you have told me that before?"

"Because I was scared. Because I was worried I might fuck up and let you down one day. Because I'm a coward and an ass."

"No argument here."

Kennedy chuckled softly, and breathed in Kieran's unique scent, one he'd missed so much. When he pulled his head away and faced Kieran, he saw that his lover's eyes were moist, too.

"Have you really met someone else?"

"Of course not. Cole took me to a couple of clubs— gay and straight. Must say, the music's better in the gay clubs, but it wasn't really my scene. Neither of them were. And, more importantly, nobody looked like you."

"Thank goodness. So will you let me try again, to be your partner, or boyfriend, or whatever you want to call us? And will you come and stay with me? If I ask you nicely? You can have your own room, if you want. Or you can—you know—sleep in mine."

In response, Kieran pressed his lips gently onto Kennedy's. Soft kissing soon became more, something Kennedy had dreamed about every night. Kieran also warmed to the connection, except before things got too heated, he put his hand on Kennedy's chest and pushed him away.

"If I sleep in your bed, where will you sleep?"

Kennedy chuckled and pulled him back, hugged him tightly.

"Heaven knows I've missed you."

"Look, Kennedy. If we're really going to be together, you may want to hear what I want."

"Anything."

"We'll need to be open and honest with each other, especially if we've pissed each other off somehow."

"Okay, I deserve that."

"Not just you, me too."

"Okay."

"We're taking ballroom classes together at least once a fortnight. And you will make the time."

"Agreed."

"And I'm sure you've heard Laurie's more than likely pregnant with her first child and I was the donor. Well, I want us to have kids one day."

"Oh, wow, okay. Wasn't expecting that. How about we start with a dog?"

"Really?"

"Why not? Let's go pick one out at the dog rescue tomorrow."

"I would fucking love that."

"Thought you might. I've cleared my weekend in the hopes you might be free. Now are you ready to leave yet? We can pick up some Thai takeaway on the way. And in the meantime, I can take your bags down to my car if you have things you need to finish up here."

"Nope, I'm done."

Between them, they collected Kieran's bags and headed towards the lift lobby.

"Does Len always expect you to work this late?"

"Len normally kicks everyone out by five-thirty."

"So what's got you working so late tonight?"

Kieran stepped into the lift, pressed the button for the ground floor and turned to Kennedy with a sly smile.

"I was waiting for you."

* * * *

When Kennedy opened the burgundy front door to his house, he saw everything in a new light, nervous about having Kieran there and badly needing his approval. The four-bedroom house had always been nothing more than a space to live and sleep in for Kennedy, and also an investment in case he needed to realise the equity one day. Now, for the first time, he wanted someone to like the place as a home.

"Leave the bags and let me give you the grand tour."

He led Kieran to the living room, and realised for the first time how spartan and functional he had made the room. When Patrick had lived there, at least they'd had some paintings on the walls, to brighten the decor. Patrick had taken them with him. Even though the furnishings were Italian and expensive—three-piece navy sofas in a U-shaped arrangement, dark frosted-glass coffee table and grey silk carpet—everything felt cold and formal.

Kieran said nothing, so Kennedy immediately took him to the place he did most of his work.

"Here's the open kitchen and dining room," said Kennedy, realising he was probably stating the obvious. But this was one space he took pride in, because one whole windowed wall lined the back yard and the houses overlooking the space. He had also bought a large table and fitted the kitchen with a range of expensive appliances—not that many of them ever got used.

"A ten-seater dining table," said Kieran. "Impressive. And your kitchen is spotless. Do either of them ever get used?"

Kennedy snorted and shook his head. Nothing ever got past Kieran.

"Not often. Not anymore. Mrs Dabrowski comes in every morning to do any household chores—cleaning, making the bed, washing, ironing—so everything is always kept looking spick and span. I'm at work most of the time, so don't have a chance to mess things up. There's probably not enough to keep her busy, but I know her family needs the money."

"And she'll have a dog to care for soon, while we're both at work."

"That she will. Shall we get your things upstairs?"

"Look, Kennedy. I'm not going to simply mooch off you. Somehow I need to contribute."

"Of course, but the house is bought and paid for."

"Then I'll pay the bills."

"Contribute, maybe. Fine."

"And I'm cooking for us. At least three or four times a week. Man cannot live by takeaway alone."

"Whatever you say."

"Hang on," said Kieran, peering curiously around. "Where's your Christmas tree?"

"I—I don't usually bother. When it's just me."

'Well, that's going to change, too," said Kieran, folding his arms across his chest. "You know what? We're having the best fuck-off Christmas tree over there by the front window. So the whole world can see. And we're having all our friends over for a fantastic Christmas party."

Kennedy laughed, and already felt a ripple of relief running through him. Life—that was what this house needed, some life. Something Kieran could provide in abundance.

"Whatever you want," said Kennedy, heading towards the stairs. "Let's haul your things upstairs. And, by the way, Leonard's office is on the way to mine. So as long as you don't mind leaving early in the morning—around seven-thirty—I'll give you a lift to work every day. So, here's the upstairs."

Kennedy showed Kieran the three spare bedrooms before trailing him into the master bedroom. After appraising the bed for a moment, Kieran poked his head into the adjoining bathroom before strolling into the room that had been turned into a wardrobe.

"Fuck. Your walk-in wardrobe is almost as big as my sister's apartment. Why is it half-empty?"

"That side used to be Patrick's."

"Oh, I see. Shall I hang my things there?"

"You're going to share this room with me?" asked Kennedy, feeling the smile lighting his face.

"Of course I am, old man."

"In which case, you can put things wherever you like. Before you come and have a shower with me. This is your home now."

Kennedy had been putting his jacket on a hanger, and noticed Kieran quickly turn his head away and bring a hand to his eyes. This time Kennedy stopped him, gently twisted him around and pulled his hand away. Kieran didn't resist. Once again tears filled his eyes.

"What's the matter, love? Did I say something wrong?"

"No, of course you didn't. I'm being soft. But you don't know how long I've waited to hear that single word, one that everyone I know seems to take so much for granted."

"Home?"

"Yes, home."

"Kieran, you *are* home. This is your home now."

Chapter Thirty-Two

Kieran
London, Christmas Day 2016

Kieran savoured being able to wake slowly and naturally without the sound of an alarm urging them to get up for work. Not long after he had moved in, they'd fallen into a comfortable rhythm of work and downtime, the latter held sacrosanct. Now, over a year later, and the all-too-familiar sound of scratching at the bedroom door replaced the now-redundant electronic clock.

Aligned warmly along Kieran's spine, Kennedy was still sleeping, the slow rise of pressure from his chest against Kieran's back, an arm draped protectively around his waist, his hot morning erection lined along the crack of Kieran's backside. Despite efficient central heating, the air in the room held a crisp December coldness and Kennedy's toasty nakedness felt too good an opportunity to waste. But as he began to turn, Kennedy's arm tightened around him, the other squeezing down to line up his erection before reaching around Kieran's body and grabbing lube and a condom from the nightstand.

"May I?" came Kennedy's hot breath in his ear.

Without replying, Kieran waited until the sheath had been rolled on before pushing back onto Kennedy, still loosened up from the previous night but nevertheless experiencing the initial delicious burn as Kennedy entered him. Kennedy followed up with a low grunt, biting Kieran's neck and shoulder while pushing himself all the way inside and beginning the slow, familiar rhythm, which only got better with time.

Since they'd been living together, Kieran had found out a number of things about Kennedy, and one was that he relished morning sex, loved when one of them roused the other from sleep using sex, waking them to the new day like a steam train leaving the station, gradually building speed in their bump and grind, bringing them both to wakefulness with fast breaths and mounting pleasure.

Without losing the momentum, Kieran turned his head so he could take Kennedy's mouth, his orgasm almost upon him. Kennedy came first, ramming hard, filling Kieran with his warmth. Instead of stopping, he kept going, hitting Kieran expertly on his sweet spot until Kieran exploded into Kennedy's hand, sparks and dark spots flashing across his vision.

"Merry Christmas," Kennedy managed to breathe hotly into Kieran's ear.

"You can say that again."

As soon as Kennedy had disposed of the condom, they lay side by side, chests rising and falling as their breaths normalised. Until the soft scratching and whimpering at their bedroom door began again.

Kennedy chuckled, a deep, beautiful sound.

"I wonder who that could be?"

Ed, their good-natured Cockapoo, had been an instant hit with everyone. Kennedy drew the line at letting him sleep in the bedroom with them, maintaining their modicum of privacy. But Kieran knew eventually the charms of their sad-eyed, curly haired ginger rescue pup would wear him down.

"Can I let him in?" asked Kieran. "It is Christmas, after all."

Kennedy gently shook his head and huffed, but a fond smile had settled on his face.

"Go on, then."

Without hesitation, Kieran sprinted naked for the door and yanked on the handle. The fiery ball of dynamite scrambled into the room, running rings around Kieran's ankles before leaping onto the bed and heading straight for Kennedy. When Kieran joined them back in bed, fearless Ed had already started licking Kennedy's face, with Kennedy laughing, helpless to restrain the excited pup.

Kieran took a moment to enjoy the scene—a usually in-control Kennedy allowing himself to be smothered with affection was a sight worth paying for. Something fundamental had changed in his man—he had mellowed. Yes, the hard-ass businessman still appeared, usually in the mornings when they drove to work together, but when Kennedy arrived home, he seemed to throw off that professional mantle and relax into himself. With a supreme effort of will, he'd even made a point of limiting the number of times he checked his phone over the weekends.

Just as Ed calmed down and settled on the quilt, there came a knock at the door.

"Are you boys decent?" came Claire's voice. She had already pushed the door open a crack but didn't enter.

"As decent as we'll ever be," said Kennedy, laughing. "Merry Christmas, Mum. You can come in."

Kennedy's parents had kept their promise and flown over on the twenty-first of December, bringing Reagan, a very subdued Bernie and their three boys to spend Christmas and New Year with them. At first Kennedy had baulked at the idea of the full house, of accommodating seven extra souls. But they'd all been brilliant—Kennedy's three extra bedrooms and spare bathroom helping matters — with the boys fighting over walking Ed to the park every day, and his mother and sister having dinner ready on the table one night when they arrived home after work, leaving Bernie and Jefferson in charge of drinks. Kennedy's house had never seen such an abundance of life.

After a couple of days, Bernie had finally chilled, and one evening, over beers, he and Reagan had told them the story of how they'd decided to give things another go, how Bernie had quit his job in Melbourne in November to make a clean break and had taken a new one in Singapore, so he could spend more time with Reagan and the boys. From what Kennedy told Kieran, Reagan remained quietly optimistic.

"Merry Christmas, Claire," added Kieran, as an impeccably dressed Claire opened their door and stood in the doorway.

"Merry Christmas to you both. Look, I know it's early, but I'm starting breakfast right away. After that, we can open presents, get that out of the way, too. Right now, the boys are still sleeping, but I've no doubt they'll be awake soon and demanding to open them. Then Kieran, Reagan and I have a whole heap of table arrangements, food preparation and cooking to manage for lunch, so I'm going to need you to take your father, Bernie and that little rascal who should not be on your bed down to the local pub. Get you out of the house. I'll set Reagan on putting the boys in front of the television to keep them occupied. What time are our guests arriving?"

"Around one o'clock," answered Kieran.

"Good. In which case, we'll aim to eat at two. What are you laughing at, Kennedy?"

Kieran turned to see Kennedy chuckling beside him.

"Nothing, Sergeant Major Mum," said Kennedy, before turning to Kieran with a sly grin. "My mother, the perennial organiser. Whatever you do, listen very carefully to her instructions in the kitchen and do not — I repeat — do not deviate from the plan in any way. People have died for less."

"Don't you go listening to him, Kieran. He never did a thing he was told growing up —"

"Yes, and look at me now."

"Don't talk back to your mother. Now go get showered and dressed. I need you downstairs in fifteen," said Claire, before stopping and addressing Ed. "And you, young man, come down with me right now. If you want feeding and know what's good for you."

Ed stopped licking himself and froze, staring at Claire, aware he was being addressed, before sitting up, then jumping off the bed and running out past Kennedy's mother.

"See," said Claire. "At least someone does what they're told."

Their bedroom door closed to the pair of them laughing.

* * * *

Kieran answered their doorbell just before one. Dressed in red silk with white furry trimming beneath their warm overcoats — in fancy dress as Santa's little helpers — Laurie and Steph stood there with carrier bags full of goodies, Laurie almost bursting with excitement.

"It's confirmed, Kieran," said Laurie, hugging him, unable to contain her delight. "All going well, we're looking at a July baby."

"And we agreed to tell you, Kieran, but we're keeping things hush-hush at the moment," said Steph, with a loaded glance at Laurie. "Just to be on the safe side. So no big announcements today, isn't that right, Laurie?"

"I know, I know," said Laurie. "But Kennedy will suspect as soon as I refuse a drink."

"Then I'll let him know on the quiet," said Steph, reaching in and hugging Kieran. "In the meantime, something smells absolutely delicious."

Kieran led them through to the open kitchen and dining room. Reagan ran over and hugged the girls, who she'd met before. Claire waved from her sentinel position at the oven.

"Oh wow," said Steph, her mouth dropping open. "This place looks amazing. Looks like somebody gave Kennedy's house a makeover?"

And Kieran had to agree. He peered across the room to find Kennedy by the fridge door pulling out a bottle of champagne, smiling at him and nodding. Every time Kieran entered the room his spirits lifted, seeing their beautiful Christmas tree, sparkling decorations and the tastefully decorated table overseen by Claire. And Kennedy clearly approved.

"Champagne, ladies?" called Kennedy, holding up the bottle.

Before Laurie could answer, Steph jumped in.

"We're both still on our special diets. So no alcohol for us today. But why don't you put some of this sparkling ginger ale we've brought into a couple of champagne glasses and nobody will be any the wiser."

And so the party began. By one-thirty, as the house continued to fill with the delicious aromas of cooking, all their guests had arrived. Claire shooed them all out of the way—including Kieran—into their living room to chat, leaving Claire and Reagan to ready food for the gathering.

And they certainly had a crowd. Figuring how to fit sixteen people around Kennedy's table had been a challenge. But Kennedy had found a couple of folding trestle tables and picnic chairs, and they'd formed a large square so—in true family style—everyone faced into the centre of the table.

Kieran's mum arrived last, together with his sister, Jules, and Curtis, the boyfriend. At first his mum seemed a little nervous and out of place, but after a couple of champagne cocktails she relaxed, chatting to Len, Steph and Laurie as though they were old friends. Even Kieran's brother, Sean, made a short appearance for lunch, although he had to bail at five to visit his latest fling. At one point, Kieran sat back and gazed around the table, at his old and new family and friends, and felt a swell of pride.

Just then, a warm hand landed on his thigh.

"Well done, love."

"Me? Thank your mum and sister, they did most of the cooking."

"You know what I mean. None of this would have happened, had it not been for you."

Kieran smiled, turned to Kennedy and pecked him on the lips.

"We should make this a tradition. Your kitchen suits this kind of occasion brilliantly."

"Whatever you want, Kieran."

During dessert, Ed, who had been confined to the living room, was brought out and, in a display of rebellion, took a fancy to a particular bauble high up on the Christmas tree, managing to jump up and topple the whole thing onto Jefferson, much to the squeals of amusement from Reagan's kids.

After they'd cleared most of the table and set the dishwasher going, Jefferson and Bernie had offered to make coffee or tea for everyone. Soft Christmas tunes played in the living room as everyone made themselves comfortable. During a lull in the various conversations, Steph, sitting the other side of the room, addressed Claire.

"So come on, Claire, I think we're all intrigued. How did you and Jefferson meet?"

"Oh, shush. Nobody wants to know."

After a few encouraging noises, Claire relented.

"Oh, well. If you insist. I know Kennedy's heard this story before, but I met his father at an embassy ball. Dragged along by my mother and father, I didn't want to be there, even though the embassy were supposed to put on something of a spectacle for their guests. I think some lower-ranking member of royalty had arrived for one reason or another. Of course, Jeff's family were well-known, his father being head of the consulate, but

I'd never met any of them. So when this nice young man approached me, asked me if I could waltz — which of course, I could — we took a spin around the floor. Well, by the third dance, I knew. Jefferson was the one for me."

Everyone made pleasant noises at the end of the story, and Kieran gazed over at his own mother, who caught his eye, smiled sadly and shrugged. Not everyone got to have their happy ending.

Once again, small conversations hummed around the room.

"When did you know?" asked Kieran, snuggled into Kennedy.

"Know what?"

"That you wanted me. I mean, when did you really know?"

Kennedy appeared to consider this.

"You know, I think it was on my stroll up the lane in Okinawa, when you were waiting for me. I saw you standing there, grinning at me as I approached and, I don't know, something inside me just clicked. And then, when I got to you, and you gave me a hug outside that Buddha bar — "

"Outside the what?" asked Kieran, turning to face Kennedy.

"That bar. The Giant Buddha lounge, or something like that. The one you were standing beneath when you hugged the life out of me. I only remember because the bar light popped on just as we hugged. What about you?"

But Kieran's mind went back to that evening and later to the night in the hotel, the one branded in Kieran's brain forever, the first time they'd made love. And all this time, he hadn't realised he'd been standing beneath the giant Buddha bar in Okinawa waiting for Kennedy to arrive — waiting for his destiny?

"Hey, Kieran. Are you okay?"

"More than," said Kieran, turning and kissing him on the cheek. "I love you, Kennedy Grey."

"Love you, too. But for the record, I said it first."

Chapter Thirty-Three

Kieran
Singapore, May 2019

Heavy monsoon rains had dissolved the stifling humidity of the May afternoon in Singapore, leaving behind the promise of a clear evening. Droplets fell from the old mango tree in the grounds of Kennedy's parents' place, with garden fragrances of jasmine and sandalwood rising to scent the air. In the eighteen months since Kennedy's parents had visited them for Christmas, their world had transformed.

"Where is he?" asked Kieran, carrying a tray of pungent Indonesian appetisers to the outdoor table, followed closely by Matius, pushing a rattling, clinking drinks trolley laden with bottles of spirits and jugs of soft drinks. Kieran had spent the last hour watching — and occasionally helping — Maya prepare Indonesian dishes in the outside kitchen, mesmerised at the array of natural ingredients and spices going into the wok for each dish.

Laurie and Claire sat watching the last of the rain from beneath a canopy beside the swimming pool. Steph sat a few feet away, next to the back porch doorway, cooled by the air-conditioning from inside the house. Little Polly lay asleep in a crib, with Steph rocking her gently from side to side. Even though Laurie had been the birth mother, their baby had brought out the maternal side of Steph.

"Kennedy? Inside feeding the twins," said Laurie, enjoying a cooling Singapore Sling. Kieran came over and joined them, sitting in the low two-seater rattan sofa. "He's managed to get Link off to sleep, but Clint's got a bit of colic, he thinks."

"Maya will go help now," said Matius, before heading back towards the kitchen.

Lincoln and Clinton had been born four months earlier, courtesy of a surrogate mother. Neither Kieran nor Kennedy had been expecting twins, but both had been as delighted as the other. Kennedy had been the donor, but Kieran had insisted on the names, in keeping with family tradition.

"I can't believe how he is with them. I swear he has the patience of a saint."

Not much in life left Kennedy speechless and in awe, but with the arrival of their twins Kieran had seen a fundamental change in him, in his priorities. Even with Kieran's mother living with them, overjoyed at being a grandmother and only too willing to help, Kieran often drove home at the end of a long day to find Kennedy already there, feeding and burping the boys, or getting them off to sleep. Usually he dismissed the event as 'working from home', but Kieran knew better. If Polly had brought out the maternal in Steph, then the twins had brought out the doting parent in Kennedy.

"Well, he does have a lot of practice, having to live with you and Ed," came Steph's voice from the shade.

"I heard that," said Kieran, joining in Laurie's and Claire's laughter.

"Where's Jeff?" asked Laurie, handing Kieran a chilled glass of white wine and clinking their glasses.

"Doing me a favour," said Kieran, quietly to Laurie. "He's on his way back from the airport right now. Friends are over for a working holiday and having dinner with us before heading to their hotel."

"And tell me again why they're invited to a *family* gathering?" called Steph.

"Bloody hell. Does your wife have super-hearing?" asked Kieran, mugging at Laurie.

"Meet Wonder Woman," said Laurie, giggling.

"You know Jeff," said Claire. "Always finding waifs and strays to bring home."

"Mum!" said Kieran, with mock outrage. "I hardly think the son of the Earl of Stratham is either a waif or a stray. Nor is his partner, Trevor. They were the ones who helped arrange our wedding in Scotland at short notice, as well as the catering, and I didn't hear you complain then."

Everything had fallen into place so quickly almost a year ago, through friends of friends. Cole's pals from Japan, returning in January from their holiday in Scotland, had sown the seeds in Kennedy's mind when they'd met for a drink. And once Kennedy got an idea in his head, there was no stopping him. They'd referred him to their friends who, through family connections, had managed to find a slim window of opportunity to host the wedding for the newly appointed CEO of Grey Steel International and his gay partner. They, in turn, had got in touch with the famous chef Marcus Vine to request his help in catering — something Vine was famous for declining because of a busy career running his international restaurants. But somehow, he'd found the time, and everything had come together beautifully, with Kieran and Kennedy finally getting married on a glorious day in early June with Loch Arkaig, Ben Nevis and the stunning grounds of Mortimer Hall as their backdrop.

"That lovely young man, Rudolph? Why didn't you say so? Stephanie, I know I've said it before, but it was such a shame you and Laurie couldn't be there. So close to Polly's birth and everything. But the whole ceremony was like something out of a Disney movie, with this world-renowned chef actually there, catering the whole event. His partner even helped set up a couple of marquees on the grounds. Did we tell you? Absolutely adorable."

"Yes," said Steph, while Laurie rolled her eyes at Kieran. They'd hated not being there, but Polly had been premature and a difficult pregnancy for Laurie, and they hadn't wanted to take any chances. "We saw the photos, Claire. The official ones, as well as all those posted by guests on Kieran's Facebook wedding page. Even saw a couple of them featured in Attitude mag."

Kieran noticed Kennedy heading out to join them. Forty-five years old and he still looked good enough to eat. As he spotted them and walked into the sunlight, when Kieran saw a flash of gold on his wedding finger, his heart swelled with pride. In the last hour he'd changed his shirt to a loose-fitting, short-sleeved Indian cotton affair in aubergine, opened at the collar to reveal his chest hair. Kieran knew the shirt well, because he owned the damn thing. Seeing Kennedy wearing his clothing, he felt himself getting hard and had to adjust himself, before waving Kennedy over to his seat.

"Thought I might find you here," said Kennedy, squeezing in next to Kieran, taking the glass of wine from him and having a sip. "Leaving the old ones to do all the manual labour."

Before they'd even tied the knot—and probably because he'd warmed to the idea of having his own little Polly—Kennedy had been the one to push for kids through surrogacy. And, as usual, he'd taken to the project like a man with a mission.

"Why are you wearing my shirt? Not that I'm complaining."

"Little Clint puked on mine."

"Ah. How is he?"

"Asleep now. Maya managed to calm him down. She's amazing with them, insisted on watching them, even though I said I'd take the baby monitor. I wonder what it would take to persuade her and Matius back to England—"

"Too late. He's already been snapped up by the new owners," said Claire. "That's why we're all enjoying this place and his wife's cooking, while we still can."

Declaring the Singapore house to be too big for two, Jeff and Claire had found a buyer, a local businessman with a family of six, who would move in at the end of July. If Kieran was going to be totally honest, that was one of the deciding factors for them visiting, especially with the boys being so young. They wanted to see the old place one last time. Kennedy's parents would move into a smaller apartment with clubhouse facilities, still close to their friends, and with room for visiting family or guests. Kennedy told him how Jeff had gifted Matius and his family with a generous payment for their years of service, something Matius had tried—unsuccessfully—to hand back when the new owners asked if Matius and his wife would consider staying on and working for them.

"Have they signed a contract yet?" asked Kennedy.

"Don't even think about it," warned Claire while lifting her glasses into place to check her phone display. "Reagan, Bernie and the boys are almost here."

"And here's Dad," said Kennedy, nodding towards the driveway.

They all watched as Jefferson parked the Toyota. Once the engine had died, he brought his two passengers straight over to where everyone was sitting around the pool. Considering their long flight from England, Rudy and Trevor appeared remarkably awake and alert, even though their loose, rumpled travel clothing told a different story. Rudy's broader build complemented the slighter frame of Trevor, his dark-red hair worn almost militarily short and at odds with Trevor's wild black mop, as though the latter had just woken. Maybe the time shift would hit them later. Kieran remembered only too well his own jet-lag experience the first time arriving in Singapore. Kieran warmed to see them. He had really gotten on well with Trevor, had felt a special bond grow between them on finding out they'd both come from humble origins. After greeting everyone and cooing quietly over a sleeping Polly, they made their way back to one of the rattan sofas.

"So how are you faring?" asked Kieran as the guys settled in their seats.

"Can we get you a drink?" asked Laurie at the same time.

"Funnily enough, Jeff just asked the same thing on the way here," said Rudy. "How we feel. Hadn't really thought about it."

"But we're both great," said Trevor. "If a little disorientated. And I'd love a drink. But I'm not sure if we're ready for an early evening cocktail —"

"Or a morning mug of hot cappuccino," finished Rudy.

"In which case, how about I fix you both an Espresso Martini," said Laurie. "Then you can have a taste of both."

"Perfect."

Over drinks, and while the last of the daylight bled from the sky, Trevor and Rudy brought them up to date with their lives. Although still managing the gym in the south, Rudy was spending more and more time helping to run his family business, Mortimer Whisky, while Trevor was now managing the books of a stable, profitable portfolio of clients. When Trevor stood and asked for the washroom, Jeff offered to show him the way while Rudy continued the conversation.

"We're in a pretty good place. Not sure we're ready for kids, but — and please keep this between us — I'm thinking of proposing to Trevor at Christmas," said Rudy.

"And where are you thinking of doing the deed, assuming he says yes? Scotland?" asked Kieran.

"You know, I think we'd both prefer something small and non-traditional. Someplace with sun and sand. I'm thinking maybe a simple commitment ceremony on a beach in this part of the world. I know Trevor wants to visit Vietnam one day, maybe Halong Bay or Da Nang. But I really love the idea of Bali."

Kieran exchanged a glance with Kennedy, almost certain the idea had popped into his head at the same time. Kennedy smiled and winked at Kieran before addressing their friend.

"Rudy, we still owe you so much for helping with our ceremony at such short notice, so if it helps, I have a four-bedroom villa in Bali that is yours whenever you need it. And apart from the villa, there are plenty of other properties around, if you want to invite a number of guests to attend. There's even a private cove linked to the villa where you could hold the ceremony. Just let me know the dates, so I can alert the staff."

"Seriously?" asked Rudy, his eyes wide.

Kennedy nodded while Kieran laced his fingers into his husband's free hand and squeezed.

"And if you're not sure about Da Nang, Halong Bay or Bali," said Kieran, "how about doing them all? And adding Ho Chi Minh, Singapore and Semarang in Indonesia to the itinerary?"

"Whoa. Trevor's the one who keeps an eye on our finances. But I know our budget's definitely not going to stretch to that," said Rudy.

"Bali will cost you nothing. It'll be my wedding present to you both," said Kennedy, grinning. "Driver pick-up, villa with a pool, all food and drinks in the villa. All you'd need to do is get there and take a little spending money."

"There you are," said Kieran. "Make Bali your last stop."

"Nice idea," said Rudy, gently shaking his head. "But it's the cost of the flights to each of those other destinations and then hotel accommodation that's the killer."

"Could you fly into Hong Kong and fly out of Bali?" asked Kennedy.

Kieran smiled, knowing where Kennedy was going with his question.

"I guess so."

"So what if you could still see all those other places without flying in or staying there?" asked Kennedy, clearly on the same page as Kieran.

"Sorry," said Rudy. "I don't understand."

"What my husband means is, have you considered a cruise?" asked Kieran, smiling at Kennedy. "Because, let me tell you, we both highly recommend them."

"In fact," said Kennedy, "we might even join you."

Rudy laughed aloud.

"Nice idea, but let's keep it between us for now. A lot can happen in a year."

"A year?" said Kieran, smiling and leaning in to kiss Kennedy on the cheek. "A lot can happen in a month."

Want to see more like this?
Here's a taster for you to enjoy!

The Billionaire's Bride
Jambrea Jo Jones

Excerpt

Remington Marlow glared down at the phone on his desk as if it might jump up and bite him. His father was on speaker, spouting nonsense too early in the morning. He needed more coffee for this conversation.

"Damn it, Dad. This is ridiculous." Slamming his hand on the desk, Remington Marlow picked up the handset.

The whole company didn't need to know his business. Jackson Marlow might be his father, but he was out of his ever-loving mind to think Remi was going to just get in line with this cockamamie plan of him settling down. He was very happy his father was at the main office about five minutes away and not down the hall, because he would have done something rash, like throttle him. He hated arguing about his dating habits...again. It wasn't like he was a kid anymore. He'd just had his thirty-sixth birthday.

"No, it isn't," Jackson declared. "I gave up the hope of an heir when I found out you were gay, but there are options out there, Remi."

"Dad—"

"Don't you 'Dad' me. I watch the news and see the kids that need adopting—or you could even go with a surrogate. I'm not saying you need to have kids now, but I won't have you fucking your way through all the men in Fort Wayne."

"I have not fucked my way through all the men." Remi rubbed his temple.

His dad sighed and continued his tirade. "I want you to settle down. Date a man. Get to know him. Fall in love and get married. I want you to have what I did. The years I had with your mother were the best times of my life and I would give anything to have them back."

"I know, Dad. I know. I miss her too," Remi agreed.

"Maybe I did wrong by you, giving you everything you ever wanted, making sure you got a generous monthly stipend until your billions release to you. Well, it stops now. You're going to have to learn to live on your paycheck alone without any other money from me. I'm cutting you off if you don't do something about your life. That's final. You start actively dating someone and I will let your trust release in full on your fortieth birthday and I won't stop your monthly allowance."

"Is this why you put the clause into my trust? I understand payouts, but who makes a person wait until they're forty for the final one?" Remi wanted to throw the phone across the room. He was so frustrated with the conversation. He was almost forty and his dad was still giving him an allowance.

"You're lucky I didn't add in a marriage stipulation from the beginning, Remi." His dad threw more heat on to the fire happening right now in Remi's body.

"I knew you were controlling, but this takes the cake." Remi pinched the bridge of his nose. "You know Mom wanted me to have that money when I turned twenty-one. All of it. No allowance. Full control."

"Yes, but I fought her on it. I wanted you to be more mature, and twenty-one is still too young to have that kind of money. When she died, I knew I'd done the right thing. You were even more self-destructive."

"I'd just lost my mother, but that's beside the point. You do know I'm a grown man, right? Running a multibillion-dollar company?" Remi dropped his face into his hand.

His head pounded. He'd drunk too much at the club the previous night and taken some twink home. Remi couldn't remember his name, but he had a nice tight ass on him. That was worth remembering. His dad voice jolted him out of his hangover memory fuzz.

"I do. I also know you blow money like there's no tomorrow."

"You're making it seem like we're going to run out any day now."

His head hurt, he wasn't even awake yet and now he was thinking about his mom... *Coffee.* God, a cup of coffee would be so good right now, but he hadn't had a chance to grab a cup yet and he couldn't get his secretary Sara Jo to get it when he was on the phone. *Fuck my life.*

"You never know what the future holds, son."

"You're lucky I love you, old man." Remi might be exasperated with his father, but he did love him. He would have to work at talking him out of this stupid idea that he needed to fall in love. Usually it only took a couple weeks to bring him around.

Remi was quite happy with his life. He didn't want to settle down. He didn't want to be someone's sugar daddy. How would he know if a guy wanted him for more than his money? He'd made that mistake before. It had broken his heart when he'd found out that his bank balance was all that his ex had wanted him for.

When the flavor of the week heard his name, they were predictably all over him for a relationship. Fort Wayne wasn't that big and, even in Indianapolis, the Marlow name was known in certain circles. He wasn't a relationship type of guy—not anymore, not after Harry.

"You're lucky that I love you back. I wouldn't be throwing down an ultimatum if I wasn't concerned. And don't think you're going to talk me out of it. As the executor of the living trust your mother and I set up for you, I've already had the lawyers draw up paperwork stating the new terms. There was a clause in the trust."

"Yes, I know. How you talked Mom into letting you set up payout terms as well as allowing you to change it as you saw fit, I'll never know. I'm not happy, Dad." Remi couldn't express that enough.

"I didn't think you would be. But I love you and want you to be happy."

Damn it. Remi didn't want to date. He loved his dad and knew he was coming from a good, if misguided, place. They were getting ready to expand the company. He had enough on his plate with that. He took his work seriously. Sure, he liked to have fun and that took money—more money than he could make pulling a paycheck from the company. The small gift he'd gotten from his grandfather when he'd died wouldn't last forever, and he'd already gotten his allowance for the month. His money in the trust wouldn't release to him in full until he was forty. He only had a few more years, which was probably why his dad was pulling this crap now.

"What if I decide to say 'fuck it all' and live off my paycheck?" Remi sat back in his chair with a slight grin on his face. He could do it. Would it be easy? No, but he was smart enough to figure it out.

"I've seen your bills." Jackson snorted. "I'll give you a week to make your decision. Just remember… You don't get your trust money for four more years, unless I deem you unfit to get it at that time and make you wait even longer."

He'd had his heart ripped out before and he wasn't going to let it happen again. As much as he might want what his father'd had, it wasn't in the cards for him. His father had met his mom when they had still been in high school. Money had never come between them, not like it had with him and Harry. Remi's heart just couldn't take that kind of abuse. He was fine by himself and he needed to convince his father to leave his personal life alone.

"I *am* happy, Dad."

"No, son, you're well fucked. That doesn't always equal happy." Jackson sighed into the phone. "Money can help, but it won't keep you warm at night or coddle you when you're sick."

"A bit crude dad, but sex does make me happy." Well, as happy as he could be.

"No, it means you are satisfied for the moment. I want you fulfilled for a lifetime." His dad's voice was almost a whisper.

"And if I can't find that?" Remi whispered back.

"I want you to at least try. Is that really too much to ask?"

"Yes, it is. You might think you know my life, but you don't. And I don't have time for this. I'm in the middle of negotiations to take over the steel company. You know having a place to pull our metal from could cut cost in the fabrication end of the company. It's a big deal and searching for a guy to date isn't going to be that easy." Remi blew out a breath. He was getting upset again.

"The steel company isn't going anywhere. The deal is almost done. If you can take the time to go find a fuck-buddy, you can find the time to date. I want to see you at least try. I don't want you to end up like me, an old man who lost his love and will die alone. You're almost forty and I'm not getting any younger. If you have kids, I'd like to still be able to be a good grandpa."

"Fuck." Remi rubbed his chest. His dad wasn't pulling any punches.

"Yeah, I got deep on you. After your mom passed, I was a wreck. She was my soul mate. I'm lonely. I don't want you to hit sixty and still be looking for one-night stands. I want you to have someone to come home to, who will love you as much as your mother loved me."

"Emotional blackmail." Remi laughed. If he didn't, he might cry. Thinking about his mom made him emotional. Thinking about her with little sleep and no coffee? It was going to kill him.

"I'll do what I have to."

His father had to be grinning on the other end of the line. Remi could hear it in his voice.

"Dad…" Remi sighed in frustration.

"Remi…"

"Fine. Whatever." He understood where his dad was coming from and it sucked. Remi hated that his father was alone. He tried to see him as much as he could, because it really was only the two of them against the world, but he knew he was no replacement for his mother.

"All right. We still on for dinner later tonight?" His dad sounded hopeful.

"Yes, I'll bring the wine." Remi wasn't going to stop seeing his dad, no matter what.

Jackson cleared his throat. "Love you, son."

"Love you too, Dad." He hung up the phone and sat back in his chair. The headache he'd been fighting all morning was growing stronger. He closed his eyes, rubbing his temple.

What the hell am I going to do?

He didn't want to have his heart broken again, but he also wanted to give his father what he wanted. Shit. He was going to have to date and show his dad that he was serious. He could live without the money. This ultimatum was about more than money. But where the fuck was he going to find someone suitable to date? He was happy being a playboy. Sure, he really didn't get out as much as he had in the past. He was settling down in his life, just not in the way his dad wanted him to.

Remi would have to think about it later. The first thing he needed was coffee before he went over his notes. He pushed his chair back and waved at Sara Jo as he passed.

Remi loved running the fabrication shop. It was all his. He'd built it up to where it was. They had been losing potential profit because they needed to pay other shops around town to do their steel work. And now he was going to expand his division even more, so they wouldn't have to spend so much on the metal they were working with. Usually his dad would take care of adding on to the company, but the fab shop was his baby and he'd had the idea to add on when one of the steel suppliers was having a cash flow issue. His company took in small walk-in projects, big company projects, work for the construction end of the company and unique things. They were now the go-to shop in town.

The coffee was in the breakroom located in the middle of the building so the detailers — the ones who drew up the blueprints and made sure a steel structure would stand on its own—could get to it just as easily as he could. He at least knew everyone's names, even if he didn't see or talk to each of them every day. He trusted his staff to get the job done.

Sara Jo was in the middle of planning a cookout for the company, one of her duties as his admin. It was something Remi liked to do to show appreciation for all the hard work everyone did. It had been a rough couple months with hot jobs and overtime. The shop was crazy when the local General Motors plant shut down so they could get in and do some repairs and put in additional ducts. There was always so much to do for shut down work. The railroad needed steel or a local school needed handrail before they opened the doors for students. Being a metal-job shop meant they got all kinds of projects. Someone had walked in just the other day and wanted a custom fire pit. Those kind of jobs were fun, but they had to work them in on days when they also were juggling big jobs such as building a tower for the high school, so the band instructor could see the full field or the football coach would watch the players, or getting steel over to the college that the construction division needed to fix the roof.

They all needed a break. If they didn't get it, safety could become an issue. If Sara Jo hadn't been in the middle of working on the cookout, he might have asked her to get his coffee, but he tried not to ask her for menial favors too often. His legs weren't broken and he could serve himself. He only sometimes asked in a coffee emergency, like now.

Remi retrieved some of the much-needed brew, headed back to his desk and shut the door. He had a couple of deadlines he was working on and wanted to get the drawings together for the people he had a meeting with for one of his pet projects, to update the abandoned upstairs of the historic Embassy Theater building. Closing himself in with work would keep his mind off his personal problems.

After what seemed like only a few minutes but was probably longer, there was the knock on his door that pulled him out of his concentration.

"Come in," Remi called.

Sara Jo ducked around the door. "Hey, bossman, do you have a minute to talk to Elros Carter?"

Remi tossed down his pencil. "Yeah, sure, I have a few minutes." He rubbed his eyes. The headache from the morning was gone, but his eyes were tired from pouring over the theater-project drawings. He knew the name, Elros Carter, but couldn't put a face to it.

"Want me to refill your cup?" Sara Jo smiled at him.

He looked at his coffee mug and thought about it for a second, "No, I'm good. I think I've had enough for today."

"All right. Remember… Your meeting is at one-thirty." She gave him a small smile.

"I thought it was at one?" Remi looked over his calendar.

"It was, but it was moved back because Mr. Johnson had a conflict." She tsked at him, like he should have remembered.

"All right, I guess I have more than a few minutes for Mr. Carter. Send him in." Remi waved her off.

Sara Jo nodded then opened the door, admitting a tall black-haired guy with the darkest brown eyes Remi had ever seen. *Man, he's tall.* He had to be at least six foot three and had a lean body. The type of guy he'd usually go for.

Hot damn.

Now he put the face with the name. He must really be tired. He knew who Elros was. Remi employed ten detailers, and he knew all their names. When Elros had been hired, Remi had made sure to work with one of the other detailers to keep himself out of trouble.

He didn't date people who worked for him. There was a reason for that. It was called a lawsuit, and he wanted nothing to do with one of those. But a plan started to form. He knew it was a bad idea, but it could get his father off his back. And, really, he wouldn't be breaking his dating rule, not if it the whole thing was made up.

A fake boyfriend? That, he could do.

PUBLISHING

Sign up for our newsletter and find out about all our romance book releases, eBook sales and promotions, sneak peeks and FREE romance books!

About the Author

Brian Lancaster is an author of gay romantic fiction in multiple genres, including contemporary romance, paranormal, fantasy, crime, mystery, and anything else that tickles his muse's fancy. Born in the sleepy South of England where most of his stories are set, he moved to Southeast Asia in 1998, where he now shares a home with his husband and two of the laziest cats on the planet.

Brian loves to hear from readers. You can find his contact information, website details and author profile page at https://www.pride-publishing.com